THE END
OF EMERALD
WOODS

ALSO BY DAVID J. WALKER

WILD ONION, LTD., MYSTERIES
A Ticket to Die For
A Beer at a Bawdy House

MALACHY FOLEY MYSTERIES
Fixed in His Folly
Half the Truth
Applaud the Hollow Ghost

THE END
OF EMERALD
WOODS

David J. Walker

ST. MARTIN'S MINOTAUR ⚌ NEW YORK

www.minotaurbooks.com

Library of Congress Cataloging-in-Publication Data

Walker, David J., date
    The end of Emerald Woods / David J. Walker.—1st ed.
        p. cm.
    ISBN 0-312-25215-3 (hc.)
    1. Private investigators—Illinois—Chicago—Fiction.   2. Real estate development—Corrupt practices—Fiction.   3. Married people—Fiction.   4. Chicago (Ill.)—Fiction.   I. Title.

PS3573.A4253313 E53 2000
813'.54—dc21

00-031734

First Edition: December 2000

10 9 8 7 6 5 4 3 2 1

To Ellen

Chi-ca-go (*shi-kaw-go*) n., a city in northeast Illinois, on the shore of Lake Michigan; the name is said to be derived from the Native American *chicah goo*, literally "stink root" or, perhaps more elegantly, "wild onion."

ONE

Eudora Ragsdale was twenty-four years old, and except for that business of the twins and their daddy, she had never once done anything dishonest. That's why she was so nervous now and had hardly slept all night.

She was the treasurer of the Committee to Rescue Emerald Woods, and their meeting last night didn't go well, especially for her. First she had to tell them that her plan to talk to the son of the real estate developer who wanted to build the mall, and ask him to talk to his father for them, didn't work out. Everyone was disappointed, but a lot of them rolled their eyes as if to say who was *she,* anyway, grew up in the projects and now talking about personally knowing the son of a millionaire businessman like that Mr. Hurley. Then the very next thing was they'd read her treasurer's report, which showed the money from their fundraiser being already in the bank. She'd just sat there, not wanting to admit it wasn't in there yet. So the report wasn't true.

CREW's carnival was the Sunday before last, and when it was over they counted the money. Not half what they hoped for, but, with the rain and all, they could easily have *lost* money. She reminded them how well everybody worked together and how it was a great first effort. So they stuffed the cash into a fat brown envelope. Their mood was high again, but it was late and they were all dog tired, so she said she'd run the money right to the bank herself and stick it in the night slot. But the twins got to fussing in the car—which they never did unless they were coming down with something—so she drove straight home. Then she meant to make the deposit the following Tuesday, the same day she mailed in her report. But she hadn't made it to the bank that night, or all the rest of last week, because she was working and the girls both got the flu, one right after the other.

The twins were with Mama Dee this week, and now it was already Thursday and tomorrow she was to pick them up and drive to Midway Airport and go to Disney World in Florida. She had the plane tickets already. So she definitely had to get CREW's money to the bank today. Probably no one would notice it got there late.

She called in sick, then gulped down her coffee and corn-flakes . . . which she wished right away she hadn't done. Cold cereal like that always upset her stomach when she ate too fast, even when the milk wasn't turning sour, like it was today. Lord, there was so much to do. She hadn't even started packing. She grabbed her jacket and opened the freezer compartment to get out the money. She'd go straight to the bank and get *that* load off her—

It was gone! The envelope, with the money. She'd hidden it way in the back, and now it wasn't there.

Frantic, she pulled everything out. Fish patties, ice cream, generic frozen peas and corn, leftovers she didn't remember, and some she couldn't even identify. But that's all. No fat brown envelope wrapped in freezer paper with cash inside. No two thousand one hundred twelve dollars and fifty cents, to be exact. Gone.

She sat on a kitchen chair to slow down her breath. Her stomach was churning. No one had been in the house but her and the kids. No sign of a break-in. Problem was, though, after she

2

moved down here to Miracle City and rented this little house, she got careless. It was only sixty or seventy miles south of Chicago, but it seemed like a different world, and she didn't always lock both doors and check all the windows. When had it happened? She couldn't remember any specific time she'd looked in the freezer for a week. She must have, of course, but she wouldn't have paid attention to whether the money was in the back.

She should call the police . . . but it was Chief Frawley she'd have to talk to. Damn. He was white and the mayor was black, and if they weren't exactly friends, they were sure working together with the village board to push through the shopping mall and pave Emerald Woods over with concrete. She'd been long and loud in her criticism. That damn Frawley'd be very happy to announce that CREW's treasurer was *claiming* that someone had stolen the group's cash. People'd be saying they knew they should have picked a white person to take care of the money.

The theft was her fault, for sure, and with that false treasurer's report she might even end up in jail. No way could she replace what was stolen, either, not right away. Her bank account was empty and her credit card maxed out on plane tickets and clothes and stuff for Florida. No one she knew had that kind of cash available. Damn. Nothing to do but call the police. She sighed, stood up, and stared at the phone on the counter beside the sink, not wanting to pick it up.

And then it rang.

She jumped a foot. Did someone already find out about the report? Her hand shook as she reached for the phone. Then something—she didn't know what—made her stop. Let the machine answer the call.

She stood in the sunlit kitchen, shivering and clutching her jacket close around her. The chill she felt, though, was more like from inside her. Four rings, then her voice, then the beep. She held her breath.

"I know you're home, Eudora Ragsdale." A white man's voice,

tight and mean and nasal. Not a voice she'd ever heard before, yet somehow strangely familiar. "You got a problem, y'know that?" the man said. "A problem with your . . . cold cash." He giggled, apparently at his own joke. "Maybe I can give you some advice."

Sour milk and cornflakes rose up in her throat and she swallowed hard, working to get control of her nerves. She picked up the phone.

"So," he said, "you *are* there. Did y'know already about your prob—"

"Not me," she said, forcing her voice to stay low and strong. "You're the one's got a problem."

"Say, hold on." Less cocky now, already. "What're—"

"And you know *why* you got a problem?" The firm sound of her own voice made her feel stronger. "You know *why?*"

"Why?" The man actually *asked,* and she was all over him now.

" 'Cause you came inside my home, fool. And I'm gonna find out who you *are,*" which she probably never would, "and when I catch you I will tie you down and slice your goddamn private parts off with a razor and set them out for the crows and raccoons."

"Huh? My private—"

She hung up the phone, and the dam inside her burst then, and she leaned down low over the kitchen sink . . . and threw up.

TWO

Dugan stood looking out his office window. He had an insurance adjuster named Tony Bosco on the speakerphone. They'd been negotiating three personal injury cases at once, when a sudden outburst of sirens and blasting air horns had come up from the street far below. Now he was pressing his forehead against the glass to try to see what was happening—even though a view of the street from that window was impossible, and always would be. The same for the sky.

"Hey, Dugan!" It was Bosco. "You been listening?"

"Of course. On Brawner you want the rest of the hospital records, which I sent three days ago. On Macklin you came up to forty-five thousand, and my answer is fifty-five's still my bottom line. On Zukowski you won't offer your insured's policy limit even though my guy suffered horrible injuries, and my answer is I'll refer the case to Al Fanzone for trial, and you and I both know somewhere down the line you'll pay the limit, but in the meantime your goddamn greedy bloodsucking company'll make interest on the money while Zukowski wonders where his next mortgage payment's coming from."

"Amazing," Bosco said, obviously unfazed by Dugan's comments. "I'd have sworn you weren't paying attention."

ACKNOWLEDGMENTS

This is a work of fiction, and the persons, places, and organizations it depicts are imaginary or are used fictitiously. Needless to say, however, without them this story wouldn't have gotten far.

And it wouldn't have gotten far, either, without help from lots of actual persons to whom I am deeply grateful. These include Steven Marcotte, a police sergeant in a small town that is not Miracle City; David Case, a police sergeant in a large city who helped me with some weapons issues; the Red Herrings, a writers group from heaven; Judy Duhl, a mystery-book dealer from Winnetka; Kelley Ragland, my editor; and last but not least (a cliché the Herrings would gag over), Jane Jordan Browne, my agent.

"I'm a lawyer. We don't *have* to pay attention. We already know everything." Still facing the window, Dugan stared at the building across the street, where other men and women—in offices just like his—picked up phones, walked around, handed each other boring pieces of paper. "So? What about Macklin?"

"Fifty-five it is," Bosco said. "I'll put the paperwork in the mail. Nice talkin' to you." The click of the disconnect came over the speaker. The man was probably already into his next—

"Hi there, big guy."

He spun around. It was Kirsten. She stood in the doorway with her fists cocked on her hips like a model, holding her raincoat open to show off a cute little red dress. The dress was new, he thought, and snug enough to reveal plenty of what it claimed to be covering. "Damn," he said. "My pulse just shot up to a hundred and twenty."

"Sorry to sneak in and scare you to death." She smiled and didn't look at all sorry.

"It's not your sneaking in. It's you . . . or that dress or something."

"Oh, *that* pulse." She was close to him now and gave him a quick kiss on the lips. "Why don't I tear the dress off and hop up on your desk?"

"Sounds like a plan to me." He pointed out the window toward the building across the street. "But what will the neighbors think?"

"They'll think I'm trying to make partner," she said. She sat down in his desk chair and did a three-hundred-sixty-degree swivel. "And speaking of partners, where's Larry Candle?"

"Hey, will you stop saying that? Larry's my employee, not my part—"

"Ooh, a little defensive, are we? Anyway, he said he was going to meet me here."

"Really." He stared at her, but didn't ask why she'd worn that dress to keep an appointment with Larry. "Half an hour ago he said he had an emergency and to apologize for him if anyone came to see him. He didn't say the 'anyone' might be you."

"Shoot. That means he's broke. He told me he'd . . ." She stood up and walked around to the client's side of the desk. "Sooo, husband of mine," smiling a little too sweetly, "how you fixed for cash?"

He reached for his wallet. "I might have a hun—"

"Actually, I was thinking of a little more than that."

"Uh-huh. How much more?"

"Let's see." She took a small notebook from her coat pocket and flipped through it. "Ummm . . ." She put her finger on the page and looked up. "How about two thousand one hundred twelve dollars and fifty cents?"

Forty-five minutes later they'd gotten the cash from Dugan's bank account and were in Kirsten's car, a Camry, headed away from downtown Chicago, southbound on the Dan Ryan Expressway. "I'm not even sure just where Miracle City is," he said.

"I wasn't, either," she said. "Turns out it's south and east of Kankakee, near the Indiana border. Population maybe twelve, fifteen hundred. Larry said it's like a little rundown southern town, like in Alabama or something. About seventy-five percent black."

"Think Larry's ever been in a little rundown southern town?"

"Seems unlikely, doesn't it? Maybe he saw one in a movie. Anyway, he says he went to Miracle City once. He had a client who moved down there, and—"

"The client was this woman you're dragging me down to see? Eudora Ragsdale?"

"I'm not *dragging* you," she said. "You're much too strong-willed to be dragged anywhere, darling. But a little while ago I stood in your doorway and overheard you settle a case for fifty-five thousand dollars. That'll bring a pretty nice fee for just three minutes of work, and I thought you should celebrate by taking the afternoon off."

"A nice fee?" He shook his head. "I took that case on just a twenty percent contingent basis, instead of the usual one-third, much to Larry's distress. But hell, the client couldn't work for a month after the accident and has three kids, one of them handi-capped. Twenty percent's about eleven thousand. Larry brought the case in, so he gets half the fee. I'll spare you the details, but be-tween us we probably spent fifty hours working up the case, and with my sixty-five hundred I have to pay office overhead and—"

"Okay, okay. I get it." She patted his knee. "But it's *fifty*-five."

"What?"

"Half of eleven thousand is fifty-five hundred. You said sixty—"

"That was a test," he said, "to see if you were paying attention."

"I'm a private investigator," she said, and by her tone he knew exactly what was coming next. "We don't *have* to pay attention. We already know everything."

They were on I-57 now. There'd been rain that morning, but now it was a perfect mid-April afternoon, and she probably knew how happy he was to get out of the office, which he wasn't about to admit. "Funny," he said after a while, "how *all* your clients seem to be coming by way of Larry Candle."

"Not really, darling. But recently, all the interesting ones have."

"Uh-huh." *Darling* was a word she seemed to slip into un-consciously, whenever she was dragging him into something *in-teresting,* which meant some sort of mess he'd regret being part of. "We're to meet her at the bank?" he asked.

"Right. It's just off the expressway, on the outskirts of Kan-kakee. She'll make the deposit—it has to be in cash—and then we'll follow her to her place in Miracle City and talk things over.

Larry told me he knows her well, and she's as honest as can be. He said he'd give me the money to loan her if he could get his hands on it right away."

"That's what he said, huh?"

"Don't worry. I'll get it from him," she said. "With interest."

Eudora Ragsdale had been waiting at the bank, and they made the deposit and followed her home. The house was a small one-story frame, in need of paint, at one end of a short block. There were similar small houses across the street, but on Eudora's side the house next to hers was boarded up, and next to that was a vacant lot. Eudora parked in her driveway and they pulled in behind her. Her yard was nicely kept but needed mowing. There was no garage.

Inside, Kirsten and Eudora went to make coffee. Dugan followed them but quickly realized there wasn't room in the tiny kitchen for him, too, so he sat at a table with four plastic place mats in a dining alcove between the kitchen and a small living room. The place was clean, and about as neat as you'd expect for a home with two kids and a single, working mom. Two tall bookcases flanked the TV in the living room, both jammed with books top to bottom.

Kirsten came in with the coffee pot and three unmatched mugs, and Eudora behind her with about twelve Oreo cookies on a glass plate. Dugan hadn't had lunch and was ready to eat them all.

Eudora set the cookies on the table. "Sorry I haven't got anything more to offer you." She was obviously embarrassed. "I really didn't—"

"What a beautiful plate!" Kirsten said. She slid the cookies onto the table, near Dugan, and held the plate up toward the window to look through it. "Look, Dugan! It's crystal, and it's very old." Dugan ate a cookie while she showed him the intricate

9

design—flowers or something—etched into the plate. "It's a lovely piece, Eudora," Kirsten said.

"Why, thank you." Eudora smiled, and Dugan was certain she blushed under her smooth tan complexion. She certainly was a pretty woman, attractive enough to be a model or something. "It belonged to Mama Dee's mama." She paused, then added, "Mama Dee's my . . . well, she's always been a grandmother to me."

Dugan ate another Oreo, and when Eudora went to the kitchen for milk for the coffee, Kirsten whispered, "You stick to the cookies and let me do the talking."

"Sounds like a great deal," he said. "I promise."

"Pardon?" Eudora said, setting a carton of 2-percent milk on the table.

"He was saying you've been through a great deal, and . . . well . . . why don't you tell me what happened?" The two women sat down across from each other. "Larry Candle told me what he knew, which wasn't much."

"Oh, I'm so grateful to Mr. Candle. I didn't know who else to turn to. A few years ago he helped me set up trust accounts for Jessica and Jeralyn—my twins. They're with Mama Dee now, and . . . Anyway, I called Mr. Candle this morning and he said right off he'd loan me the money to make up what was stolen and that I should call you and . . . and I did. I guess Mr. Candle gave you the money to—"

"No way. All Larry did was . . . oops." Dugan grabbed another Oreo from the table and shut up.

"Mr. Candle's quite busy," Kirsten said, "but he'll reimburse me for the money."

"The thing is . . ." Eudora busied herself putting the remaining cookies back on the plate, then looked up again at Kirsten. "The thing is, Mr. Candle told me you were an investigator and you'd help me. So I called you. But I don't know what I was thinking about. I mean, I don't have the kind of money you must charge. And he didn't say anything about there being, you know, two people."

"You mean Dugan?" Kirsten said. "I don't charge extra for him. He just sort of . . . helps out, sometimes." He glared at her, but she didn't seem to notice. "Besides, Larry mentioned some money in bank accounts you might be able to use."

"Those are trust accounts for the twins. I can't withdraw any money from them without the judge's permission, and then it has to be for the kids' special needs. Not even for their food and clothes and stuff. The judge says their ordinary support's my responsibility." She swirled coffee around in her mug. "Mr. Candle said maybe I could say the twins hired you, so the money to pay you could be from them."

"Sounds like Larry," Dugan said. "He—"

"Please," Kirsten said, "don't interrupt."

"I just mean Larry has a very creative mind. I can hear him now: 'Your honor, these two five-year-olds had to hire a private in—' "

"Why don't we just let Eudora explain everything from the beginning," Kirsten said. "I can't really discuss my fee until I know what the case is about."

Once she got started, Eudora apparently didn't want to skip a thing. She told them how she didn't want her girls raised in a public housing project like she was, so she worked two jobs and saved up and finally moved to Miracle City and rented this house. She told about this developer named Hurley who wanted to build a mall that would eat up almost two hundred acres of what was called Emerald Woods, about CREW and its fundraising carnival and her not getting to the bank with the money, and—worst of all—her not admitting her report was untrue. She told them about her breakfast and how she went to get the money that morning and the envelope was gone, and about Chief

11

Frawley and the mayor and the village board, and why she couldn't call the police. She related what the man said on the phone, and what she said she'd do to him.

"You really said that?" Dugan asked.

"Yes, and then I hung up and I was so scared I . . . well, I threw up in the sink. And after I cleaned up, I called Mr. Candle."

"And Larry called me," Kirsten said. "And now the money's deposited, and for now you're out of the—"

A screech of brakes came from out front, then another, and immediately the slamming of several car doors. Dugan got to the living room window first. He looked out, pulled down the shade, then ran to the front door and made sure it was locked. He turned and faced the two women. "Two squad cars, Miracle City PD," he said.

Kirsten disappeared into the kitchen and returned at once. "Back door's locked." The front doorknob was turned from the outside, then the door shook, and only then did the knocking start.

"This Chief Frawley, Eudora," Dugan said. "He a heavyset guy?"

"Not heavyset," she answered. "Uh-uh. Man's fat as a damn hog." Her voice had a surprising new tone to it. "And that fool break my door down, or mess up my house, he gonna regret it, that's for sure."

Dugan watched as her appearance changed. She was leaning slightly forward, facing the door, and her eyes were hard—mean looking, in fact. She'd even gotten a baseball bat from somewhere, for God's sake, and was waving it around. Amazing. If she'd tossed her cornflakes over a phone call, then he knew she was afraid now, too. But there wasn't even a hint of fear showing.

Pounding started at the back door then, even louder than the front.

He looked at Kirsten. "You got a plan . . . boss?"

"You take care of that," she said, pointing toward the kitchen, "before they break it down. I'll stay here with Eudora. But, before you go . . . um . . ." She nodded toward Eudora.

"Of course," he said.

He snatched the bat from a surprised Eudora's grasp and went to answer the back door.

THREE

The pounding from the kitchen stopped, and although Kirsten didn't hear Dugan open the back door, she did hear it slam shut, then some muffled shouting, then nothing. Dugan didn't return right away, so she figured he'd gone out the door and gotten it closed again behind him. They probably took him around to the front. Meanwhile, she convinced Eudora to sit on the sofa and let her handle the cops.

The knocking on the front door had stopped, too, but now it started up again. "I'm coming," Kirsten called, with a lilt in her voice, as though expecting welcome guests. "Who is it, please?" No response, other than more knocking.

She'd been a Chicago cop and knew you were supposed to announce that you were the police. It might even be a constitutional issue, she couldn't recall, but she was sure no police department directed its officers to just keep banging away on a door without identifying themselves.

"Who is it, please?" she called again.

"It's the police!" Finally. "Open the door."

Eudora stood up. "That you, Chief Frawley?" she called.

"You know damn well it is. Open up."

Kirsten unlocked and opened the door.

"Okay, Eudor—" He stared at Kirsten and took a slight step backward. He was in uniform, just under six feet, and Eudora's assessment was accurate: "heavyset" didn't cover it. He was grossly overweight. His face was flushed, and he had about thirteen strands of light-colored hair combed from one side to the other over his round head. He looked surprised, but not stupid. "Who are you, ma'am?" he asked.

She gave him one of her cards. "I'm a guest in Ms. Ragsdale's home."

"Oh, this is good," he said, studying her card. " 'Wild Onion, Limited . . . confidential inquiries . . . personal security services.' This is a good one."

"Glad you like it. I can give you the name of my marketing consul—"

"You and Eudor—that is, Ms. Ragsdale . . . can both sit down on the sofa." He stepped inside the living room and another officer, about Frawley's height, but half his age and half his weight, came in after him. "We're gonna search your house, Ms. Ragsdale," Frawley said.

"Not without a search warrant," Kirsten said.

The younger cop pointed a finger at her face. "You stay out of this," he said. "It's not your premises."

"You got that right." Eudora stepped forward. "This here's my premises. And unless you got a warrant you can both haul your . . . you can leave at once."

"Oh, I got me a warrant, all right." Frawley pulled a folded sheet of paper from his hip pocket. "Right here."

He held it out toward Eudora, but Kirsten intercepted it. "Ms. Ragsdale's lawyer," she said, "will have to check this for validity before you can search."

"Lawyer? I don't see any lawyer."

"Well, I have one," Eudora said. "His name's Larry Candle."

"Fine. Call him on the phone. Meanwhile, I'm gonna execute on this warrant."

"Wait," Kirsten said. "Mr. Candle's . . . associate . . . is here. Outside. At least I think he is. He answered the back door and your men may have taken him into custody . . . for which I'm sure there'll be a lawsuit, by the way."

Frawley turned and called out the door. "Hey, Drake! That guy a lawyer?"

"Yes, sir," a man's voice called back. "I checked his ID."

"Well, where the hell is he? Bring him in here."

"Too late," the voice said. "You said to get him outta—"

"Forget it." Frawley shook his head and turned back to Eudora. "My geniuses have taken your lawyer away already. Anyway, there's no law says a lawyer has to approve a search warrant before it can be executed. On top of that," smiling now at Eudora, "you, Ms. Ragsdale, are under arrest. You have a right to an attorney and . . . and since you got one I'll skip the rest of it and you just shut up and sit down." He turned to the young cop. "Well, Galboa, what're you waiting for? Search this dump."

Galboa swaggered off through the dining alcove and into the kitchen.

"What crime did I commit?" Eudora asked. "That money—"

"Quiet, Eudora," Kirsten said. "Mind telling us what charge, Chief?"

"She just told you. 'That money.'" He poked his finger at Eudora. "You took cash about ten days ago, two thousand and change, said you'd put it in the bank. Just last night you claimed you deposited it a week ago, but this morning the bank said there's been no deposit. Doesn't take a genius to figure out what happened. Felony theft of—"

"Look here, Chief!" Galboa was back. "At the bottom of a garbage bag in the kitchen." Held high in front of him, clasped between his thumb and forefinger, was a large brown envelope, mottled with damp splotches. "Nothing inside, but there's writing on it. Says, 'Two thou—'"

" 'Two thousand one hundred twelve dollars and fifty cents.' "
Frawley said.

"You got it, Chief," Galboa said. "Hit it right on the head."
He had that arrogant, but not very bright, look of a guy who
loved being a cop—but shouldn't be.

"Actually," Kirsten said, "there are some facts you should
know."

"Oh, I got all the *facts* I need." Frawley swept his arm toward
the door. "Let's all go for a ride."

"What?" Kirsten asked. "Me, too?"

"Yes, ma'am. I'm not saying you're under arrest, like Ms.
Ragsdale. Not yet, anyway. But . . . I suppose you're licensed by
the state?"

"Yes."

"Well, then I'm sure you wanna cooperate fully with this investigation."

"I'm sure I do," she said. "And I'm sure I'll follow you in my
own car."

FOUR

At eleven o'clock the next morning, Friday, Kirsten took a cab to the Loop, checked on the mail at her own office, and then walked to Dugan's. She'd tried to call Eudora but got her answering machine. Probably gone to work.

Dugan had gotten Eudora released yesterday afternoon on an "I-bond"—no cash needed. The state's attorney, a slick-haired little snit named Wankel, wouldn't drop the felony theft charge, though, not even after the bank verified that the proper amount of cash had just been deposited that day into CREW's account.

Wankel explained that the police, based on a tip, asked one of CREW's officers to check with the bank, and it was learned that no deposit was made. He said he'd interviewed someone who helped count the money from CREW's fund-raiser and learned that the cash placed in the brown envelope had included mostly smaller bills. Then he'd found out that the actual cash deposited in the bank was mostly hundreds. "So what?" Kirsten had objected. "The cash deposited came from Dugan's money, but what difference does that make?"

The difference, Wankel had told the judge at the bond hearing, was that therefore the deposit was merely restitution. He said it might be relevant as mitigation, but it didn't prove there was no theft to begin with. Even the judge had to shake his head at that one before he granted the I-bond and set a date for a status hearing on the case.

Now, at Dugan's suite, Kirsten stopped outside Larry Candle's office and listened to Dugan complain to Larry, just as he'd complained to her at breakfast, and over and over before that. "Are they crazy, or what?" he was saying. He'd been a state's attorney himself for a few years, before his dad died and Dugan took over his law practice. "I mean, even if the woman took the goddamn money, which any fool knows she didn't, it was only two thousand bucks, and it's been returned. So why charge her with a felony, for God's sake? I mean—"

"Hello again," she said, and stepped into the office.

Dugan looked her way. "Oh, hi," he said, then turned back to Larry. "What jury's gonna convict?"

Dugan had told her more than once that Larry was a better lawyer than he'd expected when he hired him, but she still found it tough to take the little round man seriously. Now, sitting there in a swivel chair, his plump face rising not that far above the top of the the massive desk in his tiny office, he looked even more like a cartoon character than usual.

He had a head full of curly black hair, which must have been permed and was probably dyed, and he broke into a happy grin when he saw her. "Hey, Keerzie," he said, half standing, then dropping back into his chair. "Good to see ya, kid. Siddown. Take a load off your pumps."

"Good morning, Larry." The way the man talked, among other things, irritated the hell out of her. She knew she was overreacting. He wasn't that bad a guy, actually, for someone who'd long ago established a reputation as a fast-talking, ambulance-chasing hustler. "Nice to see you, too," she said. But she didn't sit down.

"I was just telling Larry," Dugan said, "about how that creep Wankel—"

19

"I know," Kirsten said.

"Actually, he's told me twice already." Larry was bouncing the end of his pen on the palm of his left hand. "Trouble with your better half here," he grinned at Kirsten but pointed the pen at Dugan, "is he thinks he's sophisticated, but he never quite *gets* it. He still thinks things are on the up and up. Which I'm not saying they shouldn't *oughta* be. But they aren't, y'know, and good ol' Doogie pal keeps gettin' surprised—every time he bumps his schnahzzola up against—"

There was a buzz from Larry's phone, and a woman's voice came over the intercom. "Dugan, you still in there?" It was Mollie, the office secretary. "New client on line two. Guy got rearended by a truck. Bad injuries. Defendants Acme Trucking and Monsanto, among others."

"I'll take it in my office," Dugan called, and hurried out of the room. Mollie obviously knew which details about a new case would light a fire under him.

Kirsten turned to go, too. "So long, Larry," she said.

"Hey, Keerzie, siddown, kid."

She turned back. "Why?"

"It's about Eudora Ragsdale. C'mon, siddown a minute."

She sat, although she generally tried to avoid conversations with Larry.

"Want some java?" he asked.

"No thanks." She wondered if he was the only person left on earth who called coffee "java," and why she cared if he was.

"What'd you think of Eudora?" he asked.

"Well, she has a surprisingly high opinion of you," she said. Larry smiled and actually looked embarrassed, which seemed out of character for him. "She thinks it was soooo generous of you to lend her the money to put in the bank." His smile dimmed. "I told her you're reimbursing Dugan for the two thousand."

"Of course. Sure. That's what I wanted to tell you."

"Right," she said.

"It's just that . . . right now I'm a little short, cashwise."

She shook her head, mystified. "My God, Larry. What is it with you? Riverboats? Cocaine? Exotic women?"

"Don't I wish." No trace of a smile now. "It's my ex-wife and the lousy fucking over I got . . . sorry . . . the bad deal I got from that damn divorce judge. Plus, there's my daughter." His face brightened. "I guess I spoil her . . . a little."

"But you make good money, don't you? I mean, Dugan has lots of clients, and—"

"Oh, he gets plenty of business, all right," he said. "Although, y'know, there's something about how Dugan . . . well . . ."

"Yes?" She figured he'd found out that Dugan still got some of his cases by paying police officers for referrals, a practice he'd inherited from his dad, and one the ethical rules didn't allow. "Come on, Larry, spit it out."

"It's just that Dugan could make a lot more money, y'know, if he'd just . . . Like when he refers cases to other lawyers for trial, he oughta take a bigger share of the fee. And with clients, he's constantly cutting his fees or refunding money. He's a sucker for a sob story. The guy's just too . . . y'know . . ."

"Generous?"

"I guess that's it." Larry shrugged. "I get a straight salary, plus a percentage on cases I personally bring in, so it doesn't hurt me as much as him . . . and you." He drank some coffee, then grinned. "Just thought I'd mention it. Anyway, I love working here. Dugan has all the worries. I just settle cases and pick up my paycheck. Beats tryin' to run my own firm, like I used to."

"Speaking of that, how did you happen to represent Eudora? I thought you just handled injury cases."

"That's pretty much all I ever did, like Dugan. But someone gave her my name, and she came in to see me without an appointment and . . . well . . . I figured what the hell. All I had to do was set up a minor's estate and a bank account for each little girl. I asked a guy I know who does that stuff all the time. He makes a bundle, too." He shook his head. "I didn't charge Eudora anything, though. She's a nice kid, y'know? Although I *was* a little pissed off when she quit paralegal school."

"Really. Why would that bother you?"

"Well, I'm the one talked her into going, so she could get a better job than she had. Fact is, she's real smart and I paid her tuition."

"You what?"

"Yeah, I paid her tuition because—"

"I'm . . . uh . . . late for a meeting," she said, and stood up. "Gotta go."

That was the thing about Larry. It was easier not to talk to him very often. That way you could keep your low opinion about him straight, and it didn't get confused with something decent he'd done.

FIVE

Kirsten knew Larry was dead right on one point. Things aren't always on the up and up. And sticking Eudora with a felony charge, in a case no prosecutor would look twice at, had the smell of a fix.

Nothing she could do about it, though. The Kankakee County state's attorney, like prosecutors everywhere, had wide discretion about when to press charges and when not to. No way she'd ever prove anything illegal about Wankel's giving in to what Frawley wanted. But that didn't mean either one of them was on the square, either, the weasels.

She stopped at Dugan's office, but he couldn't join her for lunch because he had too much to do, including a trip to the hospital to meet with the new client who'd been rear-ended by a truck.

"A badly injured plaintiff and some well-insured defendants," she said. "I guess you want to get out there and get him signed up . . . before the greedy vultures swoop down and grab his case."

He smiled. " 'Before the *other* greedy vultures,' some people would say."

"I guess it's a matter of perception."

"Right. And of who's labeling whom. Anyway, his family says

23

he wants me, and they've been fighting off ambulance chasers since midnight. I need to get out there and get him on paper. Won't be so bad. The guy's conscious, and the doctors say he'll be okay . . . eventually."

"All right. See you tonight." She waved good-bye, and he was on the phone before she turned to leave.

On her way out she stopped to gossip a bit with Mollie and, just as she was leaving, Mollie gave her a strange look.

"What is it?" Kirsten said.

"Forgive me," Mollie said, "but you're not . . . pregnant, are you?"

"Oh God, no!" She had to laugh. Mollie was everyone's mother. Was she secretly hoping for that? "That's one thing I can guarantee you I'm not."

She was still smiling as she rode down on the elevator until it suddenly struck her . . . Mollie must have noticed she'd put on a few pounds. Darn. She'd better skip lunch and go straight to the health club. In the building lobby, though, she stopped first at the newstand for a pack of gum. A tall, thin man in a tan sport coat was studying computer magazines, and he didn't look over even when she dropped her change and it scattered all over the floor.

That meant she still didn't get a look at his face, but she knew damn well it was the same man who'd followed her from her office to Dugan's an hour earlier.

When she left the health club at two o'clock, the man was there again. Not bad, considering she'd left Dugan's building and gone two blocks south on foot, then dashed out into the street and caught a northbound taxi. Competence like that came at a price, so one of her options was to provide a long, dull afternoon—shopping, maybe—which would bore the hell out of him and cost his employer a bundle, with nothing to show for it.

On the other hand, she'd be bored, too. Besides, his still being there was a blow to her professional pride. So maybe a brief, more interesting shopping trip would be better.

It was a short walk from the health club to the Merchandise Mart, a squat, two-square-block monolith just north of the Loop, on the Chicago River at Wells Street. It had recently been sold by the Kennedy family, who'd owned it since the 1930s, and it still claimed to be the world's largest office building, by God, whatever anyone said in Singapore or anywhere else.

Most of the Mart was devoted to wholesale furniture show-rooms and offices. But on the first couple of floors there were lots of restaurants and retail stores. One of those stores was Intimate Hours, a lingerie boutique that covered the spectrum from Laura Ashley–style nightgowns to skimpy, seductive stuff à la Victoria's Secret—with even a demure bit of specialty leather wear tucked away in one corner.

Kirsten had been in there just once before, returning a Valentine's Day present Dugan had thought was a great idea. The staff was all female, of course, as were nearly all of the customers. Any man with nerve enough to go in and browse would stand out among those pastel silks and satins like a linebacker at a tea party.

What she liked best about Intimate Hours that day, though, was that there were no customers in sight, and that a uniformed security guard—about six-three, and built like the Incredible Hulk—stood by a counter near the entrance from the building lobby, flirting with one of the saleswomen. Kirsten strolled in.

It was a narrow shop, but quite deep, and the man in the tan coat would probably come inside, too, not knowing whether there was a second way out, maybe an emergency exit. At the rear of the store a young black woman in a tailored mauve linen jacket was reorganizing a display of designer bras. The woman smiled as Kirsten approached. "May I help you?"

"Well, maybe you can. Except . . ." She fidgeted with the top button of her raincoat. "You see, my ex-boyfriend's been following me all day. He does it all the time, the creep, just to scare me. He's violating a protective order and," she gave her most conspiratorial smile, "I'd love to catch the bastard at it . . . for once."

"Really." The woman clearly believed her. "Aren't these guys sometimes just too . . . Anyway, what were you thinking of?"

"Well, down that hall, are those the dressing rooms?"

"Yes. But they're all locked now, except for one."

"Okay. And past that, is there a rear exit?"

"No, just a storeroom at the end, and it's always locked, too."

"Good. He may come in the store and—"

"Is he tall and needs a haircut?" She was looking past Kirsten's shoulder. "Tan coat?"

"Right."

"He's already in. Over by the camisoles."

"Good." Kirsten didn't turn to look. "I'll go down the hall and you go and . . . Are you with me, for sure?"

"I guess so." The woman nodded. "Yeah, why not? Girl, he even *looks* mean. How'd you ever—"

"All you have to do is walk me to the hallway and watch me. When I'm almost to the other end you go over and tell him something strange just happened. Tell him I took a peek at him and turned and ran down the hall and out the emergency exit."

"I told you, there *is* no exit."

"But he'll run in after me, see? And when he does, you wait until I start yelling, and then you call the security guard. And numbnuts will be caught chasing after me, and the guard will be my witness and I'll get that creep locked up for a week or two."

"Girl, you sure he won't hit you or something?"

"Nah, he's chickenshit. Never beats me," she lowered her eyes, "unless . . . unless nobody's around."

"Damn, girl, you oughta . . . Okay, let's do it."

Kirsten grabbed three bras from the display rack. "Don't call the guard till you hear me holler. That part's important, okay?" The woman nodded and Kirsten went into the hall.

There were dressing rooms on each side, all of them locked except the last one on the left. A few feet farther down, the hall ended at a door that said *Staff Only*. That was locked, too, so she stepped into the unlocked dressing cubicle and pulled the door closed. There were wooden slats in the door, louvered downward so that she could look out and see the floor.

She waited what seemed like a long time, then finally heard someone come into the hallway from the store.

SIX

It was past noon on Friday by the time Eudora had finally gotten her last-minute errands done. Now everything was packed and she was in the car, on her way to Mama Dee's to pick up the girls to go to Disney World. They were going, no matter what.

As she drove, she wondered whether to tell Mama Dee about her being arrested. The woman was smart as a whip, but she never read the newspapers and it must not have been on TV, because Mama Dee would have seen what happened and would have called. When she *did* hear, it would send her blood pressure way up for sure, so she better wait until there was more time to explain. Mama Dee didn't much like surprises—good or bad—and this would be a bad surprise, for sure.

Funny the way surprising things kept happening to Eudora all her life. So many things she never intended—or didn't think were even possible—just seemed to happen.

Like from the time she was ten years old she had made up her mind not to become another pregnant teenager. She lived then with her aunt and two cousins on the third floor of a sixteen-story Chicago Housing Authority building at Forty-second and Lake Park, where just about all the girls—even her cousins—got pregnant, some of them over and over. "But not me," Eudora said, when she was visiting Mama Dee one time. "No way."

"You just keep them knees together, girl," Mama Dee said. "It don't take but one mistake. Plus, you a Ragsdale, and back home folks used to say, 'Them Ragsdale girls, they can come up pregnant just walkin' through a field o' daisies.' " Mama Dee had a lot of sayings like that, which Eudora sort of understood but couldn't always explain.

"No babies for me," Eudora would say. She went to school, and the community center, and the rest of the time stayed inside off the street and read books. She read books a *lot*. Her plan was to graduate high school, and then college, and then get her a job. After that, when she had a bank account—and a husband, too—she'd have herself a baby. Until then, no way. Plus, she didn't talk about it to Mama Dee, but there were ways to be careful, even if you didn't wanna always keep your knees together.

Then, there they were . . . twin baby girls. "Cute as little ladybugs, too," Mama Dee said, when Eudora brought them down for their first visit. She never intended it to happen, but she *had* made it to age twenty by the time they were born, after all.

Another surprise was what happened with Clyborn Settles. She had sure never intended to let Clyborn get away. He agreed with her that he had to be the twins' daddy, and she'd been gonna marry that boy for sure. He said he would, too, and he had a paying job, at Burger King. But Mama Dee didn't like the idea. Mama Dee was Catholic, and she told Eudora to talk to that priest Eudora knew who ran the drama program at the community center where she and Clyborn were in plays together. She did talk to the priest, and it wasn't easy. She told him Clyborn was the father, but she sure didn't ask any advice. He had liked her a lot and was very disappointed and very kind, and that was the last time she ever *did* talk to him. Fact is, the priest was Father Hurley, the one whose own father—now, five years

29

later—wanted to chop down Emerald Woods and build the mall. Talk about surprising things! Not that it did any good. Father Hurley was sick now and couldn't help them.

Anyway, Mama Dee wanted her to wait in marrying Clyborn, at least till after the babies were born—which by then the doctor said were twins—to check out how Cly took to being a daddy and seeing after babies and all. Eudora didn't like it. She wasn't gonna be no single mama with two babies, no way, but she said she'd wait, out of respect for Mama Dee.

Fact of the matter, Cly quit his job and didn't take to being a daddy much at all, except the part about bragging to his useless friends. "These here babies is proof," he'd crow, holding one in each arm. "Walgreen's can't make no rubber strong enough that ol' Cly can't blast through."

It was a shame—him a high school graduate and good in sports and always the star in plays and all—that he didn't know Walgreen's didn't make those things, just sold them, and how it says right on each little package that they don't give "100 percent protection." Of course Eudora hadn't ever read that tiny print before, either, at least not until after she missed her first period.

So Cly disappeared pretty quick, and Eudora loved those twins to death and the big surprise was how glad she was to be rid of that boy. Then one day she entered the twins in a baby photo contest and—another surprise—they won; and they got money and their picture was used in an ad for a bank. Pretty soon they were getting modeling jobs, and a year or so later even a part in a made-for-TV movie. After that Cly showed up again, but Eudora explained how she had talked to a lawyer and the babies' money went directly into bank accounts for them and nobody could touch it.

"Except you," Cly had said.

"Not *even* me." Plus, she told him how he must owe a whole *pile* of child support by then, which wasn't true because she hadn't gone to court against him. Cly dearly wanted to stay and help out, he said, but the next day he went out the door and was gone again, which was fine with her.

She turned and drove down Main Street now, past Miracle City's sorry excuse for a business district. She'd gotten to kinda like this town, dead as it was, even though her moving out of Chicago had been another surprise. She'd never even thought about it. But then Mama Dee told her about this tiny house she could rent, just close enough—but not *overly* close—to what was left of Mama Dee's rundown farm. All the sudden there she was, a working single mama living in a dirt-poor town with two five-year-old girls, each already with her own bank account.

She drove past the grammar school and turned onto the blacktop that went out toward Mama Dee's, when she thought of another reason why she couldn't tell Mama Dee about her being arrested. She'd have to explain she was out on bond, even if she hadn't had to put up any cash money. And Mama Dee, smart as she was, might think right away of something Eudora hadn't even thought about until Kirsten said it.

That had been after court was all over and they were driving her home. "Don't forget, Eudora," Kirsten said, "the judge said you're not allowed to leave the state. You weren't going anywhere, were you?"

"Um . . . no." Damn, she'd been nervous the whole time in court. If the judge said that, she sure missed it. "I mean, I . . ."

"Well, if something comes up—an emergency or something?—you call Dugan. He can ask the judge for permission. You don't want to give them an excuse to revoke your bond and lock you up."

She just shut up. She didn't know if the judge would think Disney World was an emergency. But she'd been saving up for over two years now, and the trip was all paid for and mostly not refundable. The girls would just die of disappointment if they didn't go. Besides, who knew if they'd ever get another chance?

Nope. She better not tell Mama Dee that she might come home from Florida and find out she had to go straight to jail.

SEVEN

Kirsten stood motionless in the tiny dressing room, staring down through the louvered door at the hardwood floor and listening to the footsteps coming quickly down the short hallway. The man had sense enough not to try any dressing room doors, since they might have been occupied. And she guessed that when he found the door at the end of the hall locked, he'd know enough to get out of there in a hurry.

His shoes appeared, then disappeared, and she stepped silently out behind him. By the time he was trying the handle of the storage room door she was right there, the barrel of her gun pressed as hard as she could into his lower back.

"It's a Colt .380," she said. "The Pocketlite model, if you're curious." She eased up on the gun. This guy looked like he'd been around and he might know that jamming a semiautomatic too hard against him would press back the slide and the weapon wouldn't fire. "Back up with me and then go into that dressing room," she said, "very carefully." She eased backward as he did, keeping the gun in light contact with his back and her left hand on his left shoulder, maneuvering him into the cubicle. "And don't turn around."

Once he was inside she backed away from him, with the open

dressing room door still shielding her from the rest of the hallway to her left. There was a mirror on the wall opposite the door, and they studied each other's reflections for a moment. The man's face was narrow and pinched, and his eyes were empty, unreadable. "Now what?" he asked, staring at her in the mirror.

"Now we—"

"Oh, miss!" It was the sales clerk, calling from the end of the hall. "You didn't holler, I know, but should I get the guard anyway? Or call the police?"

"Not yet," Kirsten called back. "We're . . . trying to work things out."

"Well, okay." She sounded unsure. "But I'll be out here in the store."

"Thanks." Kirsten nodded to the man's reflection. "So," she said, "shall we work things out?" He didn't answer. "Okay then, let's see . . . do I go with attempted sexual assault? Or maybe you just opened the door while I was trying on bras and started waving your wang-wang around."

"What is it you want?" He was trying to sound bored, but she thought he was more than a little worried.

"Two things. First, your driver's license."

"Shit." He didn't move.

"It's all up to you," she said.

Finally he reached back and pulled a wallet from his hip pocket, dug out his license, and handed it to her.

"Thank you." She glanced at it, then dropped it into her coat pocket. "Second, who has you following me?"

"Forget it. You think I'm crazy?"

"Whoever it is won't find out from me that you told me. You just go back and report that I shopped all afternoon and then went home."

He sighed. "John Michael Hurley."

"*The* John Michael Hurley?" He didn't answer, and she added, "Why?"

"You said two things. That's three."

"Yes, well, my math skills were never—"

"Besides, I'm just hired help. All I know is you'd be better off not messing with the big boys. Period."

"Right." She'd learned all she was going to learn, and she certainly didn't need more of *that* particular piece of advice. She slipped the gun into her coat pocket and stepped to her right to give him space. "C'mon out and close the door." He did. "Okay," she said, "I'll follow—"

"Hey! You sure you all right?" The clerk was standing in the doorway to the store again; and behind her, the Hulk. "I got worried," she said.

"Everything's fine." Kirsten and the man kept walking, and the woman and the guard backed out of the way. "We worked things out and he's leaving now. Aren't you, Billy?"

"My driver's license," he said. "You—"

"Billy lost his license," she explained, "and I told him if I found it, I'd mail it to him. So . . . good-bye, Billy."

The man walked off, and the Hulk followed him until he was out of the store.

"Thanks again." Kirsten smiled at the saleswoman. "Oh, I left those three bras in the dressing room. They're just not me. They seem terribly . . . insubstantial."

"Uh-huh." The woman stared at her. "You sure everything's all right, girl?"

"Oh, yes. And you've been so sweet. I hope I haven't been a bother." She gave the woman a fifty-dollar bill and walked out of the store and into the lobby of the Merchandise Mart.

There wasn't a tan sport coat in sight.

"The name on his license is William Travis," she said, "and if he's smart, he won't tell the guy who hired him what happened." Kirsten was on her second cup of fat-free yogurt, this one with peaches. "Not even a version that makes him look a little less incompetent."

"You didn't say who it was who hired him." Parker Gillson sat beside her on the concrete bench. He was working on his second burger. It was midafternoon, and they had the plaza outside the Prudential Building pretty much to themselves. The sun was bright and warm, but about ready to drop below the tall buildings along Michigan Avenue, a block to the west. When it did, the breeze off the lake would make it uncomfortably cool. "Anyone I know?"

"John Michael Hurley."

"Jesus. *The* John Michael Hur—"

"Exactly what I asked."

"If I were him, I'd have been lying."

"I don't think he was, though." She handed Park the man's driver's license. "He knows I'll be able to find him again."

He studied the license, then handed it back. "Jesus."

"Stop saying that, Park, will you? It makes you sound worried."

"Why should I be worried? No one's following *me*." He finished his burger and began dipping fries into a pool of ketchup and eating them, three and four at a time. Although he'd lost some of the excess weight she'd noticed a while back, he'd always be a large man, and a big eater. He looked great, though, in his blue blazer and gray slacks. "But why," he went on, "would a millionaire developer and civic leader like Hurley have little ol' you followed?" He stared at her, waiting. He'd been Chicago's best-known African American news reporter, then a falling-down drunk, and now a senior investigator for the office that prosecuted Illinois attorneys for ethical misconduct. He knew more people, and more about what went on in the city, than anyone else she knew. "You working on something?" he asked.

"Not really."

"Oh. Well, I guess Hurley saw you on the El, fell in love on

35

the spot, and wants a background check before he invites you to his château on the Côte d'Azur—or wherever."

"When I hear 'château,' I think mountains," she said. "Or is that 'chalet'? Anyway, along the coast they have . . . oh . . . beach houses, I guess."

"Uh-huh. So, what does 'not really working on something' mean?"

"It means I have only one client right now, and I'd thought the job was about over. She was holding two thousand dollars of somebody else's money and it got stolen and now she's charged with the theft." She paused. "But Dugan's handling that. Nothing much left for me to do."

"Who is she? How did she find you?"

"She's a lovely young black woman named Eudora Ragsdale, who grew up in the projects and has twin daughters and works as an assistant manager in a video store." She paused. "She found me because she's a former client of Larry Candle's and—"

"Enough said. Any time Larry's involved . . ." He grabbed her empty yogurt cups and stuffed them into the bag his burgers and fries came in, squashed the bag into a tight ball, and set it on the bench between them. "So, whose money was it? Who stole it? And, I guess, why?"

"The money belonged to a citizens group that's fighting a proposed mall that'll wipe out a couple hundred acres of a wooded area that was supposed to be set aside for a wildlife preserve. They had a fund-raiser and Eudora's the treasurer and someone took the money before she got it into the bank. I don't know who stole it." She paused. "As for why, I suppose most thieves want money and would rather steal than work."

"Uh-huh. And this woman, is she herself a . . . financially impaired person?"

"Sure, I guess so." Kirsten shook her head. "But she didn't take it."

36

"You can tell she's honest by looking deep into her eyes, right?"

"As a matter of fact, yes." She stared right back at him, until he grinned.

"I'll buy that. So, where do the big bad people want to build their terrible mall?"

"Way out by Kankakee. It's—"

"Ah, yes. A bit south and east of Kankakee," he said, "outside a little town called Miracle City, right?" She nodded, and Park broke into a proud smile. "Why didn't you say so in the first place?" he asked. "Because *that's* why John Michael Hurley . . ."

"Uh-huh. That's what I was afraid of," she said. "I just wondered whether you'd agree. My client told me the man behind the mall is named Hurley."

"And it's not just some little mall. It's supposed to be huge, with an amusement park, hotels, maybe an RV park . . . the works. There's been talk of a major metropolitan airport out that way for years, and Hurley's hoping to cash in on being close to that. He's got big plans. Maybe not quite another Mall of America, but still a substantial blotch on the landscape."

"Jesus."

"Exactly what I said a minute ago, if you recall. Does that mean *you're* afraid?"

"It means *why* the money was stolen is exactly the right question," she said. "What's scary is that you saw that right away. You're a genius."

"Of course." He grinned again. "Or maybe it's just that when I hear the name *Larry Candle* I immediately figure he's gotten you into something more than meets the eye."

"So it's not just a theft; it's about John Michael Hurley getting Eudora out of the way."

"Maybe," he said, "and, then again, to Hurley she must be a pretty small fly in a pretty large pot of ointment. So, who knows?"

"And?" She gave him her sweetest smile.

"And yes, I'll see what I can find out for you." He stood up. "Like, starting with that driver's license? It's nicely done, very professional. But it's about as genuine as Larry Candle's hair color."

EIGHT

B y five-thirty they were belted into their seats and the plane was taking off. Eudora had never flown before, but she wasn't one bit afraid, which meant the twins weren't afraid, either. Already two flight attendants had said her little girls were about the most well-behaved children they had ever seen. Which was probably true, too.

They were five now, and Eudora herself was surprised at how easily the girls were growing up. Oh, they fussed and argued and got on her nerves sometimes, but even when these children got tired, especially out in public, they didn't often get cranky. They usually just fell asleep. That's one reason the photographers and advertising people liked them.

It was Friday, but they hadn't gone to school. Mama Dee had kept them busy all day, and when Eudora got there they were ready to go. Mama Dee had her own suitcase packed, too, and drove her own car and followed Eudora back through town as far as St. Andrew's. She was going with the church ladies on a weekend bus trip to Wisconsin, to a shrine up near Milwaukee called Holy Hill, where sometimes people got cured, they said, but Eudora didn't believe that. The church bus didn't leave until Saturday morning, but Mama Dee was driving three of her lady friends up that afternoon in her car, so they could go to the Friday night dog races near Racine and then meet the others at Holy Hill the next day.

Eudora smiled, remembering how on the way to the airport the twins chattered on and on—and she did, too—about all the things they'd see and do at Disney World.

Now, Jessica was already asleep. She was in the aisle seat, with Eudora in the middle and Jeralyn by the window. Three seats cost a whole lot of money, even at the lowest fare, having to change planes and not getting to Orlando till real late at night. She leaned over Jeralyn, and they looked out the window together as the plane tipped to one side and circled above the city to head for Florida.

"See down there?" Eudora whispered into Jeralyn's ear. "That's where Mama lived when she was your age." She knew Jeralyn couldn't tell where she was pointing, and she herself had a hard time picking things out. But she could see downtown and Soldier Field. Then, farther south, she actually picked out Oakwood Boulevard where it crossed over South Lake Shore Drive. But after that the plane turned again, and all they could see was the lake.

Even before she moved to Miracle City, Eudora had already left the projects and had a job and a little apartment with the twins and her cousin Neezie and her baby on Seventy-first Street. About a year after they moved, she and Neezie had taken the three kids and gone back early one weekend morning and stood on the bridge at Oakwood and the Drive and watched when the city blew up the building they'd grown up in. A sight to see! One minute three tall buildings in a group. Brick buildings. Strong, ugly, mean-looking buildings. Then a huge explosion of dynamite and then all three sort of falling in on themselves, not strong at all, and clouds of dust rising up and blowing everywhere.

Neezie had screamed and laughed and clapped her hands, so

the little ones did, too. Eudora just stood there, though, not moving, until Neezie looked at her and laughed again, and said, "Girl, what you cryin' for?"

"I'm not," she answered, crouching down and covering up the twins' eyes with her hands. "It's just . . . just all that dust and stuff getting into my eyes."

She *had* felt sort of sad, though, which made no sense because she sure never wanted to live in a hellhole like that again. About the only halfway useful thing she ever learned growing up in the projects was how when somebody comes at you, you don't stop to feel scared, you automatically get up in their face with the meanest look and loudest talk you got. Especially if you were light skinned like she was. You didn't learn that by the time you started kindergarten, girl, it was over for you.

Other than that, kids in the projects mostly learned to do drugs and fight, and run when the gunshots started, and drop out of school and end up either in jail or pregnant . . . or both. Or dead, a lot of them.

Of course, she knew city hall didn't blow up those buildings just because they ruined the lives of all the kids who grew up there. Uh-uh. That property was right on the lakefront, and pretty soon there'd be new buildings there—for rich people was her guess, which meant white people. Hard to picture white folks hanging around Forty-second and Lake Park. But Neezie told her it had started already.

Jeralyn was asleep now, too, and Eudora got blankets tucked around both girls and kissed each one on the forehead. Miracle babies, from Miracle City. She really didn't care if they kept getting modeling and acting jobs and making money for themselves. What she really wanted was for them to go to school all the way up through high school, like she did, and then college, too.

She didn't finish college because she had the babies, but later she went to paralegal school for a while. Mr. Candle had given her a brochure about it when he helped her with the trust accounts. By the time the babies got older she had lost the information, so she called him. It was expensive, but he helped her with that, and she'd pay him back when she could. She had to change jobs and drive into the city three days a week, and mostly it was so boring she could hardly stand it.

Then she got started fighting that damn shopping mall they wanted to put outside Miracle City, near Mama Dee's place, which meant bulldozing Emerald Woods and putting it under concrete. Lots of people thought it was a bad idea, and some of them started CREW, and she was involved and did a lot of the work no one else wanted to do. People started listening to her, for some reason, and looking to her for ideas. Pretty soon CREW was drawing more than a hundred people to their rallies, and it started taking up a lot of her time. Plus her job at Video Escape and driving the twins around to photo shoots and auditions and all, so she dropped out of paralegal school.

Then Chief Frawley and the mayor started calling her a troublemaker and "one of those environmental extremists and tree huggers." She didn't trust them, or any of those damn village board members, either. There had to be money in that mall for them, somehow, for sure.

Mama Dee was happy Eudora was part of CREW. Fact is, Mama Dee had donated Emerald Woods to the town not too long after Eudora had finished up high school. It was part of the farm Mama Dee's second husband, Randolph, had inherited from his father, who was white and was over eighty years old when he got shot in a bar fight in Kankakee. Then Randolph died, too, of some kind of brain stroke, and later Mama Dee wasn't able to keep up the taxes on the land. The part she gave away was almost a thousand acres. Some was farmland, but the Emerald Woods part had never been cleared and was mostly oaks and pines, and a creek and a swampy section Eudora called "the fen," from a book she read in high school about England.

Mama Dee's agreement with the town was that the land would always stay a park, like a wildlife sanctuary, but the paperwork wasn't done right or something. Later, with a new mayor and village board, the lawyers had gone to court, and the judge said the property could be sold or leased to developers for a mall. That had broke both their hearts—hers and Mama Dee's.

As a child Eudora had spent many, many hours in Emerald Woods. It had seemed so big then that you could wander on and on and even get lost, which she had done more than once. But she never got scared there. She would sit, all by herself, and watch the squirrels chase around and the birds flit back and forth and yell at each other. If she stopped real still, sometimes she saw deer come and drink at the fen, and frogs would jump out of the way.

She loved Emerald Woods because it was the exact opposite of the projects—quiet and peaceful and calm. She had asked Mama Dee—only once—why she couldn't come down there and live with her. Mama Dee had cried and said she would love that, too, but . . . well . . . she didn't trust her husband Randolph not to mess with Eudora, her being so pretty and him drinking more the older he got. That had scared Eudora. She had still visited a lot but never asked to come and live there again, and by the time Randolph died she was almost through high school and active in the drama program at the community center.

The droning of the plane was putting her to sleep now. She was glad to be working to try to save Emerald Woods, except she never guessed it might cause her to go to jail. Fact is, she was surprised she wasn't more worried about going to jail for leaving the state when she was out on bond. Maybe because she had Kirsten helping her and she just seemed real competent, somehow. And Dugan, too; he was OK.

43

They'd have to be paid, though. She'd talk to Mr. Candle about it. Maybe he'd pay them and she could pay him that back later, too.

Her head kept falling forward and then jerking back up again, and she knew pretty soon she'd be asleep.

NINE

By ten o'clock Saturday morning Dugan was in his office, opening mail. He usually worked six days a week, and Saturday was his favorite. Not that he enjoyed working on the weekend, of course, but fewer phone calls and interruptions meant he could catch up on the paperwork. Not that he enjoyed paperwork, of course, but . . .

"Hey, pal! Wake up." It was Larry Candle, with a mug of coffee in each hand.

"Smells good," Dugan said.

"I know. I finally convinced Mollie to stop buying that cheap shit." He set a mug on Dugan's desk and settled himself into one of the client's chairs. "Hell, spend as much time as we do in this dump and at least you oughta get gourmet java. Right?"

"This dump?"

"Hey, by the way, thanks again for taking care of that Ragsdale girl. I'd have gone myself if I—"

"Woman," Dugan said.

"What?" Larry looked over his shoulder and then back at Dugan, obviously confused. "What woman?"

"The Ragsdale woman. Eudora."

"Right. Hell, I know her first name. I knew her before you did, y'know? Nice girl, too."

"Anyway, it's not over yet."

"I know," Larry said. "I have to reimburse you the two grand you put up. Don't worry, Doogie pal, I'm good for it."

"No problem. I'll just take it out of your paycheck." When he saw the frightened look on Larry's face Dugan stifled a smile. "Besides, that's not what I mean by it's not being over. There's still the criminal charge." Dugan sipped some coffee. "I decided I'd let you handle the trial yourself."

"Hey, hold on." Larry's expression went from fear to panic. "Last time I tried a felony my guy went away for thirty years. At the end of the trial I spent twenty-four hours in the lockup for contempt of court, and the judge and the state's attorney went out for beer and tacos." He shook his head. "You handle it. It's bullshit, anyway, right?"

"Of course, but apparently bullshit with a purpose. Like you say, things aren't always on the up and up."

"Actually, hardly ever," Larry said. "So what's the hook here?"

"Your friend Eudora's a big player in a fight to keep a shopping mall from going up on some wooded land her grandmother donated to Miracle City years ago, for a park."

"Got it." Larry nodded. "And I bet now the town officials and the state's attorney are in some real estate developer's pocket, and trying to get her out of the way, or trash her credibility or something. Jesus . . . these developers. Why is it *lawyers* take all the shit from the public, when—"

"Maybe developers are smarter than lawyers."

"Sneakier, that's what it is. And they got more money to pass around, too."

"Whatever. Anyway, Kirsten thinks whoever's behind it was figuring Eudora would cave in right away, and the state would never really have to try the case."

"Yeah? Then they sure don't know that girl very well."

"Woman."

"What?"

"Anyway, it's a loser for them. I pled her not guilty, asked for a jury, made a trial demand, and moved for expedited discovery—especially lab tests of an envelope the money was in. Now we just—"

"She's damn lucky, that's all I can say. A brilliant ex-prosecutor like you on her side." Larry was on his feet and looking at his watch. "Got a client comin' in. Someone's gotta keep your firm solvent while you do your pro bono thing." He turned toward the door.

"Who says," Dugan paused for just the right effect, "I'm not getting paid?"

"Really?" Larry turned back around. "She gonna try to use the kids' money?"

"No. She says you'll advance my attorney's fees for her, just like—she thinks—you advanced the two thousand. She'll pay you back when she's able."

"Yeah, well, I'd love to, y'know, but like I say, I'm a little short just—"

"Not to worry. I can take my fee out of your checks, too." Dugan raised his mug. "Thanks for the java, Larry pal."

"Jesus." Larry shook his head woefully and was gone.

But Dugan knew Larry's worry wouldn't last long. For one thing, he'd escaped being dragged into a politically charged criminal case way out in Kankakee. More important, once he gave it some thought he'd realize Dugan could never bring himself to hold money out of his checks. So he wouldn't stay mournful very long.

But it was still fun to stick it to him every now and then.

TEN

Kirsten tried Eudora's number at ten o'clock. No answer. Before he'd left for his office, Dugan had asked what was on her agenda and she told him she'd spend Saturday figuring out what to do next. That was true, of course. She'd never lie to him, and he knew that. But no way she'd just sit on her hands while she did her figuring, either . . . and he probably knew that, too.

It was tempting to consider her part of the Eudora Ragsdale matter a closed issue. There'd be no plea bargain in the criminal case, since Eudora absolutely would not plead guilty to anything, no matter how minor. The state might move to dismiss its own charge, given the weak case and the judge's obvious exasperation at its being before him in the first place. If that didn't happen, there'd be a trial, and Dugan could handle that easily.

But it was unlikely to end there. Someone wanted Eudora discredited, probably to remove her as an obstacle to the mall. She was determined to keep up the fight, though, and if one way to get rid of her didn't work, there might be other things tried. That's what bothered Kirsten.

She was to call Parker Gillson at noon to see what he had so far on John Michael Hurley. Meanwhile, she wanted to tell Eudora to be sure to save the answering machine message from the man who called her after the money was stolen. At ten-fifteen, and then again at ten-thirty, she tried Eudora's number. No answer. Might have gone shopping with the twins, or maybe taken them to a modeling job . . . or maybe to her grandmother's.

Eudora had said Mama Dee's name was Dorothy Hardell, so Kirsten tried directory assistance. The number was unlisted.

She tried Eudora again at eleven and let the phone ring ten times. Still no answer. Strange that she didn't at least have her answering machine on. Maybe the tape—or the computer chip or whatever it was—was full. Maybe.

By one o'clock Kirsten was a block from Eudora's house, driving through a steady rain. She'd tried Eudora's number several times from the car. No answer.

The rain was a surprise. The sun had been shining in Chicago, but the farther south she got, the more clouds had appeared. Then, about ten miles out of Kankakee, she drove into a deluge. No wind, no thunder or lightning. Just a sudden torrent, falling straight down from a low gray sky, and it was still pounding on the roof of the Camry when she pulled into Eudora's driveway. She fumbled around under the seats for an umbrella, but the best she could do was the sports section from an old *Chicago Tribune*.

She sat there a moment with the motor running and the air conditioner on, to keep the windows clear. Eudora's car wasn't in sight, and all her shades were pulled down. Finding her at home looked pretty hopeless, but she switched off the ignition and, holding the newspaper over her head, dashed to the front stoop. She knocked. No answer, and the door was locked. She went around and tried the back, with equal luck.

By the time she got back to the Camry the newspaper was soggy and limp, and so was her hair. The car windows were fogged up, so she started the engine and lowered the window beside her. And when she did, there was a shiny black face peering right in at her.

It was a girl, maybe ten years old, stretched up on her tiptoes to straddle the horizontal bar of a boy's bicycle, and at the same time leaning over to look in at Kirsten. The rain had plastered the girl's hair to her head, and her long-sleeved white blouse was soaked through and transparent, clinging to her skinny, curveless body.

"She ain't here," the girl said, with a serious, even solemn, look on her face.

"You mean Ms. Ragsdale?"

"Uh-huh."

"Well, I'll come back in a little while." She put the car in reverse.

"She ain't gonna *be* back here." The girl spoke with certainty, and Kirsten slipped back into park.

"Why do you say that?"

" 'Cause she got in trouble with the police. I was home sick from school and I seen it." The girl shifted her weight from one leg to the other, still straddling the bike. "Seen that fat ol' Chief Frawley and the rest of 'em. Seen you, too, and that man. I could tell you and him Miz Eudora's friends. Miz Eudora an' me friends, too. She real . . . Anyway, she gone now."

"She's probably at her grandmother's. Do you know where she lives?"

"You mean her Mama Dee. Yes, ma'am. I mean no, ma'am." The girl frowned, concentrating, apparently oblivious of the rain streaming down on her. "I mean she ain't *at* her Mama Dee's. I seen her put a whole bunch of suitcases and stuff in her car and after that she drove away." The girl swung her right leg free of the bike and stood beside it, holding the handlebars. "I wonder did she pick the twins up and . . . When peoples get in trouble with the police and go away, they don't *come* back. They gone."

"Um . . . what's your name?"

"Coral. Coral Hancock Stitch."

"You're awfully wet, Coral. You wanna sit in the car while we talk?"

"No, ma'am. I don't get in no cars with peoples."

"Oh. Right. Let's go to your house, then." She gave Coral one of her business cards. "We'll show that to your mother and—"

"Uh-uh. I stay with my cousin and she . . . she's sick. She work all week and she stay out Friday nights and she be sick every Saturday." Coral lowered her head, quickly, as though she'd suddenly spotted something interesting on the toe of her gym shoe. "My mama gone." She brushed a sopping wet sleeve across her face.

"Coral?" When the girl raised her head and looked at her, Kirsten knew the answer, but asked anyway. "Did . . . ah . . . did your mother get in trouble with the police and . . . go away?"

"Yes, ma'am," she said. "When I was five and a half. She say she gonna pick me up at my cousin's, but—"

A car bounced over the curb and into the driveway—far too fast—and skidded to a stop, just nudging the Camry's rear bumper. It was a Miracle City squad car.

"I gotta go," Coral said.

"Wait. Did you say you knew where Mama Dee—"

"Cor-al!" The call came from a house across the street. A woman, in a fluffy pink robe that showed her brown legs from midthigh down to her bare feet, held a screen door open. "COR-AL!" The woman's voice seemed tinged with hysteria—or maybe alcohol. "Coral girl, you get your damn skinny— You come in out the rain, fool!"

"My cousin," Coral said. "Raynelle." She stuffed Kirsten's card into her jeans pocket and swung her leg back over the bicycle. "I gotta go."

"Right. Um . . . we'll talk again, okay? I'm gonna get Ms. Ragsdale out of her trouble, and maybe you can help."

51

Coral smiled then, for the first time, a small smile that went away so fast it might have been a test, to see if she could get away with it. Then she was up on the pedals, struggling to propel her too-big bike through the wet grass of Eudora's yard, headed home to her cousin, with her short pink robe and her every-Saturday sickness.

ELEVEN

Twenty minutes later, Kirsten was on something called Till's Creek Road, trying hard to keep her speed down. The Camry had never seen an unpaved road before, and wasn't used to bouncing and sliding around on wet chunks of gravel.

The cop had been Galboa, the one who'd found the money envelope in Eudora's garbage. He said someone had called in about a stranger parked for a long time in Eudora's driveway, talking to some kid. Kirsten explained that when she got no answer at the door she'd asked a girl on a bike if she knew when Eudora would be back, but the kid hadn't known anything. That seemed to satisfy Galboa and he went on his way, after telling her she should, too.

She'd stopped at a tiny rundown gas station on Miracle City's main street. Inside, two old men in bib overalls were drinking from plastic cups, sharing a fifth of peach-flavored rum and watching a baseball game on a small black-and-white TV. They both had the wasted look of chronic drunks, but one of them reached out and turned the sound down on the TV. "Ms. Hardell's place?" He sat on a tall stool behind the counter, and a lighted cigarette bobbed up and down in the corner of his mouth.

"That's out far as you can go on Till's Creek Road," he said, "just past the end of Emerald Woods."

The other man sat on a white plastic lawn chair, on the customer's side of the counter. He lifted a brown-stained cardboard take-out container from a Chinese restaurant and spit into it. "Y'all keep on through town and take that there hard road," he said. "That's County B." He set the container on the floor beside his chair. "Past the school you go under a railroad viaduct." He was already talking with a full mouth but paused to stuff in more Skoal. "Past that's a gravel road goes off on your . . . shoot, I can't think . . . right or left . . . anyway, that be Till's Creek Road."

"Is there a sign?"

"Yep." That came from the smoker, who served himself a refill from the bottle on the counter and, while his cigarette still bobbed in its place, took a sip from his cup. " 'Cept it's prob'ly lyin' in the weeds."

"That's 'cause there ain't much for kids to do round here at night and on weekends," the other man explained. His left cheek puffed out like a chipmunk's and stayed that way as he lifted his cup and took a long drink. "So they mostly drink liquor and drive around in cars and knock stuff down."

"A goddamn lack of imagination," the smoker added, and turned up the sound of the baseball game.

Sipping anything from a cup without taking a lighted cigarette from your lips must take a little practice, she'd thought; but drinking peach-flavored rum through a mouth crammed with chewing tobacco was just gross.

Their directions had proved accurate, though, and the sign was still standing. Till's Creek Road led away from the blacktopped "hard road" between fields of small green plants growing in amazingly straight lines that disappeared into the distant fog on both sides. Farther along, the road narrowed abruptly and wound into a ragged woods, with trees and brush and occasional

54

open spaces that looked like swampland. The rain was little more than a thin mist now, and she had the air conditioning off and her window open. She kept her headlights on because the sky was as dark as before.

There'd been houses here and there along the hard road, new looking, mostly ranch style. Along Till's Creek Road, though, there'd been not a single house until here, in the woods, where she passed several widely spaced trailer homes. They all seemed abandoned, as gray and depressing as the day itself, sitting in clearings cut out of the woods, surrounded by windowless cars and collapsing sheds, sagging fences and haphazard piles of junk, all half hidden among tall weeds and vines, as nature struggled to cover up what it couldn't yet reclaim.

She hadn't thought to check her odometer and wondered how far she'd come on Till's Creek. There were no other cars and no people. She suddenly noticed how the muscles in her hands were aching and loosened her grip on the steering wheel, reminding herself she was here because she was doing exactly the work she chose to do. Still, somehow, she didn't like the feel of it.

She'd always loved the country, maybe because she experienced it mostly on an occasional weekend at some comfortable bed-and-breakfast, with Dugan. She enjoyed vistas of rivers and rolling hills; loved to hear birds in the morning and crickets at night; savored the smell of freshly cut grass.

But this was different. Here she hated the way her tires kept sliding and bouncing on the rough, wet gravel, even at just twenty miles an hour. She hated this narrow road that one minute dropped off on both sides into deep wet weeds and then dipped down beneath shallow water in the low spots. She didn't like the dark, dripping trees that closed in on both sides, either; or the moldy, sour smell of . . . of whatever it was. And she certainly could have done without those trailer homes and the grim, ugly residue of people who'd long ago abandoned Emerald Woods for something better.

Finally she crossed a little humped-up concrete bridge over a swollen creek, and the road turned sharply to the left and she was out of the woods and back into cleared land. Fifty yards straight ahead was a red-and-white-striped barricade with huge reflectors that shone orange in her headlights. End of the road. On her right, about halfway to the barricade, was a mailbox and a long driveway back to a farmhouse.

The name on the mailbox was *D. Hardell,* and the driveway was nothing but two tire tracks made of tiny white pebbles, with weeds growing up between. But it was a smoother and more comfortable ride than the gravel road. The barbed-wire fences on each side looked old and rusty, and the tall dark weeds in the fields beyond the fences looked like they'd been there for years.

Mama Dee's was a two-story frame house, fifty yards in from the road, with a screened-in porch across the front. It had to be a hundred years old but seemed in good shape, painted white, with curtains in all the windows. A large yard all around the house needed mowing, but there were well-tended little beds of flowers on either side of the steps leading up to the front porch. The driveway widened into a parking area beside the house, and that's where she parked, next to a Chrysler Sebring convertible. It didn't strike her as a grandmother's car, but who's to say? There were no other cars in sight. The rain had stopped entirely, but now the wind was beginning to blow.

Beyond the house a huge barn, with a silo, loomed against the dark, angry sky. Near the barn were separate fenced-in areas and what she assumed were ramps into the barn for livestock—obviously long unused—and a couple of smaller shedlike buildings. Except for the silo, which was stone, all the farm buildings were the same shade of gray weathered wood, and all of them sagged and leaned and looked about ready to collapse, with gaping empty spaces where boards had rotted and fallen off. The fences were just as bad, and the roof of the silo had caved in or been blown away, and some of the uppermost stones had fallen to the ground.

Between the barn and the house was a very small building, much newer, made of metal and shaped like a miniature barn, barely eight feet tall. She'd seen them advertised in the papers, backyard sheds for suburbanites to store lawn mowers and bicycles.

Some slight movement on the ground caught her eye. A brown cat . . . no, two brown cats . . . sat on the ground in front of the shed and stared at her.

Lightning flashed across the horizon—not in a streak, but diffuse, like a far-off photographer's strobe—and there was a low, distant rumble of thunder. She hurried around to the front of the house. The screen door at the top of the steps was unlocked, and inside the porch the door to the house itself was unlocked, too. The bell didn't seem to be working, and she knocked and knocked. No one came, and she went inside.

"Mama Dee?" No answer.

She ran through the whole house, both floors, and even the basement. "Is anyone home?" Not a thorough search, but nobody seemed to be there.

The back door was locked with a turnbolt that could be opened from inside. She left it locked and went out through the front door and around to the backyard again. There was a small back porch, and beside that a wide, slanted set of wooden doors that obviously led to a basement entrance. She went up on the porch to read a note on a file card stuck with a thumbtack on the back door below the window, protected from the rain. It looked brand new and it said: *Arlo—Forgot you might come Sunday to cut grass. Sorry. Come back next week when I'm home. D.* Below that she'd added, *Hope you went to church this morning.* And then one of those smiley faces.

Oh. Gone for the weekend.

So why didn't Kirsten feel any more relaxed? Why didn't the sun come out and the wind die down? Why didn't those damn cats stop watching her from that damn shed?

Maybe cats were like the country, she thought. You think you like them, but then you get real close, and . . .

She marched straight at the metal shed, and at the cats, daring them. They darted away. There was no padlock on the door of the shed and she opened it. It was dark in there, but from the doorway she could tell there were garden tools, flowerpots, metal shelving with bags of potting soil and whatnot, and the kind of lawn mower that you sit down and ride on.

She pushed the door closed. When she turned around the cats were staring at her again, now sitting side by side on the slanted surface of the cellar door. So again she marched straight at them, and again they darted away. Maybe it was a game.

They were double doors, painted gray, with a hasp to lock them shut with a padlock—but no padlock—and a metal handle on the right-hand door. She reached and pulled up on the handle. The door was heavier than she thought it would be, and when it did come up, its momentum carried it all the way over and she was surprised it didn't break right off its hinges when it fell the rest of the way open. The left door wouldn't budge.

A set of crumbling concrete steps led down, and she crouched to get a better look in the dim light. Old, blackened spiderwebs hung everywhere, even draped over the handle of the closed basement door at the bottom of the stairs. She was pretty certain that the door down there hadn't been opened in a long time, and even more certain that the man sprawled facedown on the steps—his head closer to the bottom, the soles of his well-worn shoes facing her—was dead.

TWELVE

S tanding at the top of the steps, Kirsten breathed deeply and closed her eyes . . . but only until she felt something brush against her right calf.

"Hey!" she yelled. "Get out of there, dammit." But then the other cat streaked past, too, and they were both down there now, sniffing around. One of them leaped up on the man's back and started scratching at the collar of his sport coat. She thought she recognized that coat.

Her cell phone was in the Camry. She turned to go for it, then decided that could wait. She wouldn't go so far as to roll the body over and make a mess of the scene, but she wanted to know if this really was the same man who'd followed her into the lingerie store.

She went down the half-dozen steps to a concrete landing. The cat on the man's back stopped scratching and stared at her. She tried the door into the basement. It was locked, so she went back up a few steps and crouched beside the body. The cat hissed into her face. She hissed right back, louder, and the animal jumped from the man's back and joined its partner at the bottom of the steps. She lifted the back edge of the man's sport coat and slipped a wallet from his hip pocket. There was some cash—

maybe a hundred dollars—and a driver's license. Nothing else. The photo on the license was a different photo, but it looked a lot like the same man. The name was different, though. This time it was John Traynor.

There was another long, low roll of thunder, not as far away now, and behind her the farm buildings creaked and moaned in the rising wind. She put the man's wallet back in his pocket. She should go and call 911, but a few more minutes wouldn't make any difference. The man sure wasn't going anywhere, and if she could get a look at his face, she'd know for sure whether it was the same man. She went down the remaining three steps, and the two cats, while hardly seeming to move, slipped backward away from her and deeper into the dark corner under the unopened half of the door above.

The man's face was against the concrete at the bottom of the steps, turned just slightly her way. She got on her knees and leaned low, her own face nearly touching the rough concrete. She didn't want to touch him, or turn his head to see his face, but . . .

Both cats hissed, as though not liking what she was doing.

"Mind your own damn business," she said, reaching to push the man's coat collar away from his face.

But the cats kept hissing, and she looked over at them. Their backs were arched, their tails high and stiff.

"Dammit!" she said. "I'm just—" But they weren't even looking at her. They were looking up, beyond her.

Before she could turn, the heavy door slammed shut above her. She heard metal scraping against metal and then nothing but more thunder.

A gust of wind roared by, and the door lifted slightly—but only slightly—before it caught against something and settled back again. She knew then that someone had closed the hasp and slid something—maybe a padlock—through the staple.

It was very dark, but she knew damn well the cats were staring

60

at her. "Don't you say a word," she warned them. "I know what you're thinking."

By the time Dugan noticed what time it was, Larry Candle was long gone and he was alone in the office. Kirsten didn't like him working past two on Saturday afternoons. Unless she was out doing something herself, she'd show up and drag him away, or at least call. He tried her cell phone and got no answer, so he called home and got only his own voice on the answering machine. He punched out the code to play back any messages.

There was just one. A man's voice—or at least probably a man's—very soft, almost a whisper. "Listen hard. You don't know me, and you never will." It sounded like a call from a phone in a bar or a restaurant, with lots of background talk and laughter. "That girl, if you're smart, you'll stay away from her. Unless she changes her ways, she'll keep on bringing hurt on herself . . . and on people close to her. You don't want to be one of them." There was a pause. "Oh, and . . . don't forget your wife. A man doesn't want to lose his wife on account of some foolish girl."

He played it twice more and was about to play it a fourth time when he realized the message wasn't going to change—and he wasn't going to forget one word of it.

He could call the police. And what would he tell them? Someone called with a warning: "That girl, if you're smart, you'll stay away from her." More likely to trigger a condescending smile and shake of the head than anything else. Then some more advice: "A man doesn't want to lose his wife on account of some foolish girl."

So yes, he could call the police and try to convince them it wasn't advice at all, but a threat. Which police, though? Chief Frawley's bunch?

The "foolish girl" was Eudora Ragsdale, for sure. He tried her number. The phone rang and rang. Funny her answering ma-

61

chine wasn't on. And not funny that he hadn't heard from Kirsten and couldn't reach her.

Kirsten stayed where she was, as still and silent as the cats she couldn't see in the dark. She might have heard the sound of an automobile engine but couldn't be certain, not with the nearly continuous rolling thunder, and the wind and the rain pouring down now on the wooden doors above her.

She was almost certain no car had driven up since she'd been here, although someone might have parked out on the road and walked in. But why? And why close the cellar door on her?

She should have searched the house more carefully. Maybe someone had been here all along, hiding, and that's who'd shut her in. But again, why? Had the same person murdered the man whose body lay beside her? Actually, maybe no one at all murdered him. She'd seen no wound so far. Maybe he fell down the steps and hit his head. At any rate, whoever had closed the door hadn't tried to harm her. Apparently all the person wanted was to get away unseen.

On the other hand, maybe the person planned to come back.

THIRTEEN

I f the sun had been shining, at least a little light might have
leaked in around the edges of the double doors. But there was
no light at all. Kirsten twisted herself around until she was lying
on her back on the rough concrete steps, with her head close to
the top, beside the feet of the body she tried hard not to touch.
With her palms on the underside of the door, she took a deep
breath and got ready to push upward.

Just then one of the cats spoke up. Not a hiss or a purr; more
like a sigh of advice: "That'll never work."

"Shut up," Kirsten said, "unless you have a better idea." She
pushed up against the door but was no more successful than the
wind had been a few moments ago. One door lifted maybe half
an inch, then caught against the locked hasp.

She pushed again, straining her back and her shoulders. She
tried harder, over and over, but it was useless, and she ended up
slapping and pounding on the underside of the door in frustra-
tion.

Finally she relaxed, and as soon as she did there was a sniveling
whine from one of the cats, which she instantly translated as:
"Seeee?"

"I thought I told you . . ." But she knew better. She should keep her mouth shut and not let herself be drawn into a conversation with a couple of smart-ass cats. She didn't even know their names, for God's sake.

By now her eyes must have adjusted as much as they were going to, but she still couldn't see anything beyond a vague difference in shades of darkness. She lay on her back a while longer, then scooted on her rear end down to the bottom and sat up. She found her purse on the lowest step, where she'd left it. The Colt .380 was there, and she felt around some more in the purse and found her key chain and the tiny flashlight attached to it.

Somehow she wasn't surprised when it turned out the flashlight didn't work.

She could hear the cats breathing softly, as though they were both asleep and content to let her figure out what to do. Rain must be leaking in around the edges of the doors because the steps were getting wet. It was getting colder, too, which was probably a good thing. She wasn't sure how long it would take for a dead body to start stinking. This particular body was already bad enough, reeking of cigar smoke and urine and . . . Cigar smoke?

Something to light a cigar with?

Searching a corpse whose head lay at the bottom of these steps would have been bad enough if she'd been able to see what she was doing. She sat beside the dead man and fumbled around until she got her hand into his right-hand jacket pocket. Cookie crumbs, maybe, but nothing else. She reached across his back but couldn't get to his left pocket because the jacket was tucked under him and she still didn't want to disturb things any more than necessary. His back pockets were easy, with the wallet in one and a stiff, crumpled handkerchief in the other.

She tugged at the right lapel of his sport coat. In the inner pocket she found two crushed cigars in cellophane wrappers, but no lighter or matches. She reached under his side and tried to slip her hand up into his front pants pocket, but pulled it out

64

right away. His pants were wet and she figured that wasn't from from the little bit of rain coming in around the edges of the doors.

Damn. She didn't want to roll this guy over. She crouched at the bottom of the steps and moved sideways past the top of his head, feeling her way with her hands. She was moving into the cats' territory and she heard them shifting around deep in the corner. Her back brushed against the locked door into the basement and it occurred to her—for the first time!—that *maybe* she could break it down.

She threw her weight into the door a few times, but all that got her was a sore shoulder. The very fact that she hadn't tried that right away made her mad, though, and she yanked hard on the left side of the dead man's sport coat and it came out from under him and she found a pack of matches, nearly full, in his pocket.

When she lit one, the first things she saw in its wavering light were two pairs of cats' eyes, staring back at her from the corner. The match went out and she lit another one and looked around her little cell. When that match went out she didn't light another.

"We're pretty even, now," she told the cats. "You've got night vision; but I've got a light."

What none of them had, though, was a way out. She had the gun, the same small semiautomatic she'd carried since she was a cop. It had served her well, if not often, but it packed only seven rounds, and she didn't have another clip on her. And even if she had, the possibility that she could shoot through the thick wooden door above her and blast apart the padlock, or whatever was holding the hasp in place, even if she'd had a dozen tries, was pretty slight. The same went for the door that led into the basement. It was made from some substantial wood, and the keyed turnbolt lock and the plate over it—admittedly ancient and rusting—looked to be made of heavy steel.

So it was too soon to start wasting slugs in a panicky attempt to shoot her way out. Besides, Dugan would wonder where she was. He—or someone—would come looking. That's what she hoped. Anyway, she might as well save her bullets until she was really desperate.

She lit another match and found herself a dry spot on the concrete at the bottom of the steps, her back to the wooden door, her pistol in the open purse on her lap.

The match went out and one of the cats emitted a perfectly ordinary *meow*.

"That's right," Kirsten answered, " 'friends.' We may be here awhile."

FOURTEEN

Dugan rented a car and drove way too fast. He'd waited all afternoon, figuring he couldn't get all excited every time Kirsten disappeared for a couple of hours. Now he wished he'd left as soon as he'd heard the threat on the phone. By the time he was passing Kankakee the rain had moved on to the east, over Indiana, while far across the flat land to his right, at the opposite horizon, the sun had just set and the sky was layered in orange and red and grayish blue.

It occurred to him that he hadn't seen a sunset in quite a while. Hell, he hadn't even seen the damn horizon in God knows how long. Except along Lake Michigan, of course, and he never paid attention to that.

By the time he turned the corner onto Eudora's street, it was very dark and that matched his mood perfectly. He drove slowly, with his headlights off so no one would notice him, but not even certain whether that mattered. When he pulled into Eudora's driveway her car wasn't there and no lights shone in her windows. No one answered the door, either. He looked up and down the block. The air smelled fresh and cool and clean after the storm, and somehow that didn't make him feel one bit better. He could hear a basketball bouncing in the distance and some vague shouting but saw no one in either direction. His muscles and joints all ached. He was far too big to be crammed so long behind the wheel of a Dodge Neon, but he'd been in a hurry and took what he could get.

At the back door of the house he knocked first, then tried the knob. No luck. He'd seen the cheap lock on that kitchen door from the inside and knew Kirsten could have had it open in sixty seconds without leaving a trace. He'd never tried that in his life, though, and this was no time to start practicing. Besides, goddammit, he was Eudora's attorney, wasn't he? Empowered to act on her behalf, and in her best interests, and . . . what the hell.

Spreading his arms wide for balance, he lifted his right foot and blasted the bottom of his size twelve into the door, just to the right of the knob.

If he'd used only half the force, he'd still have left the doorjamb in splinters, but the door might not have slammed so hard against the wall behind it, and the glass might not have broken. But he was inside and it didn't take five minutes to make sure that no one was there, and that the reason the answering machine wasn't on was because the machine was gone. That, of course, reminded him that he should have told Eudora to save the phone message she'd gotten when the money was stolen.

The phone was still there, though, on the kitchen counter, and in a cabinet above the counter was a spiral-bound address book. It looked pretty old and was full of erasures, cross-outs, and rewrites, but it had Mama Dee's address and phone number on the back cover. He plugged in the phone and tried the number. No answer.

The address was 101 Till's Creek Road. He'd have to stop at a gas station or something and ask where the hell that was. He closed the back door as well as he could and walked to the car.

It was when he was backing out of the driveway that he saw a skinny kid in a white shirt, standing in the dark near the curb down the block, straddling the horizontal bar of a bike that was too tall for him. The nearest streetlight that was working was in the next block, and when Dugan drove closer and lowered his window he half expected the boy to ride away on the bike—and then he saw that it was a girl, and he *knew* she would.

But she didn't. She stared at him as though studying his face.

"Excuse me," he said. "Do you—"

"Your lights is off," she said.

"I know. I . . . uh . . . I didn't want them to shine in your eyes." She tilted her head to the side, and he didn't think she believed him. "Anyway," he said, "you know how to get to Till's Creek Road?"

"Uh-huh. It's two different ways to get to it." She closed her eyes, then opened them again and pointed. "But in a car you have to go around the corner there and go ahead on through town. Turn this way." She twisted toward her left. "Go past the school and go under that . . . that bridge thing, and then there's one of them roads made of rocks. That's it." She nodded, slowly, just once. This was one serious little girl. "That's Till's Creek Road."

"Does it go, like, north and south or east and west?"

She stared at him, obviously confused. "Till's Creek only go one way." She stood up on the pedals to ride away. "An' Mama Dee, she all the way to the end."

"Hold on," he said. "How did you know . . ." But she was pumping hard, headed in the opposite direction, and he let her go. He was in a bigger hurry than she was.

It was Saturday night and Miracle City's main street looked like a ghost town, except for a couple of taverns that had cars clustered around them. The night sky was overcast, but the girl's directions were clear, and Dugan found Till's Creek Road easily. Then he had to slow down. He seldom drove outside the city or beyond its million sources of light, and he found the narrow gravel road—and bouncing down a tunnel of light surrounded by total darkness—a little unnerving. It got even worse when he entered what seemed like a woods, and he kept wondering what he'd do if a car came at him from the other direction.

There were no other cars, though, and after a while he was suddenly out in the open again, but with a barricade blocking the road up ahead. He slowed almost to a stop, then saw a mailbox that said *D. Hardell*. He turned into the driveway, and when he got closer he saw the farmhouse and two cars parked beside it—one of which looked an awful lot like Kirsten's Camry.

The house was absolutely dark and his first thought was to go slowly, look around a bit. But that idea—in fact, thinking at all—gave way once he got close enough to read Kirsten's license plate. He skidded to a stop on the grass in front of the house and was out of the car and up the front steps in about three seconds.

He pushed through an unlocked door into a dark screened-in porch and was pounding on the front of the house with his fists when he sensed . . . what? The rustle of movement? A breath? He stiffened, would have spun around, but something exploded against the right side of his head.

The flash and the roar of pain were terrifying, but they slowly slipped away from him. Hands were pulling on his shoulders, but that slipped away, too.

The whole world slipped away.

It had gotten very quiet after the rain stopped and the wind died down. So quiet that Kirsten had heard an owl hooting, and softer sounds like rustling grass and creaking wood from the farm buildings. She might have dozed a little. Once she'd heard the phone ring inside Mama Dee's house. It rang for a long time, then stopped. Later there'd been a sort of crash, as though maybe a piece of the barn had fallen off. That must have made the cats nervous because there'd been movement in their corner and soon a stronger odor of urine than there had been.

Maybe half an hour later, she heard a car engine, far away, then coming closer. Finally.

It could be Dugan, looking for her when she didn't come home. He'd see her car, find no one home, and circle the house. He'd call out. Anyone who was a friend would see her car and call out.

She was sure she heard the car pull up near the house and stop. But no one called. No more sound at all. She wanted to scream herself, but the silence was somehow ominous. She crouched at the bottom of the steps, the Colt angled up toward the doors above her. It wasn't someone friendly out there.

She didn't know how long she crouched there. Several minutes, maybe, and she found herself out of breath. Still she waited . . . and no one came. Then, from outside and above her, she heard something. The back door to the house. Someone was opening it. Not Dugan; he'd be calling out. Now footsteps on the little porch.

She had her mouth open, trying to decide whether to cry out, when she heard a slosh of liquid, like water splashing on the porch, and then on the closed cellar doors above her.

But no, not water at all. The odor was unmistakable. Gasoline.

FIFTEEN

What Dugan felt first was the cool floor against the side of his face, but then a terrible ache in his head wiped out that and every other feeling, and the only escape was to drop back into sleep. He turned and twisted to find a comfortable position, but no luck. It was such a hard floor. He pushed up to his hands and knees, finally, and tried to open his eyes. Only one of them opened, the left one, and it told him very little. Just that he was in a room without light. Smelled good, though. Like fruit, or spices or something.

He struggled to his feet, felt around in the dark. It seemed a tiny room, narrow, with no windows and a locked door that felt surprisingly solid when he pushed on it. He could feel that the walls were lined with shelves, the top ones empty and the lower ones full of cans and boxes and jars. Ah. He'd never seen one, couldn't see this one, really; but it was a pantry, of course. Mama Dee's place. This was a farmhouse and it would have a pantry. And that would be right by the kitchen, which would be at the rear of the house. He wondered why a pantry would have a lock, but this one sure did. And he was locked in because . . . because why?

He dropped to his knees again. Wave after wave of pain

washed through his head and standing up made him nauseated. He was dizzy, but he had to sort this out. He had to concentrate. But first, why not lie down again? No. He should call out for help.

So he did call. But the words wouldn't come out very loud, seemed to be muffled by all the containers on the shelves and the smallness of the room—and the pain in his head.

The smell was stronger now, and Kirsten thought gasoline must have leaked in around the doors, just like the rain. The cats were panicked, mewling and hissing, scratching at the concrete, moving up and down the steps in the dark. She pulled a match from the pack and almost lit it, not thinking. Jesus!

Whoever it was hadn't ignited the gasoline. Maybe they were spreading it throughout the house. Then they'd light it.

She went up and pushed against the door above her, over and over, hollering out as she did, but the damn door still wouldn't budge more than the same half inch.

She went back down and crouched at the bottom of the steps, afraid, but not as spooked as the damn cats. Fire was terrifying, but she knew, too, that it was so unpredictable. Maybe she could stay low and it would burn through the wooden doors and she could get out. Maybe.

And then she heard something. Someone was there, right outside, pulling up on the door above her, trying to open it . . . and then giving up. Then metal scraping against metal. Removing whatever was keeping the hasp latched, of course. Kirsten slid the safety off the Colt, but knowing she didn't dare fire in the presence of gas fumes.

The door above her lifted, maybe six inches, then dropped back.

It lifted again, but by that time she was pushing her way up the steps, forcing one of the double doors up with her forearm.

It gave way and swung open to her left, and she stumbled on the top step and tripped and fell forward onto the wet grass. She kept on rolling as she hit, putting distance between herself and the cellar doors, and whoever had unlocked them, aware of the cats rushing past her—happy for them, too.

She was in a crouch, the Colt in two hands out in front of her. It was night, but so much brighter out here than where she'd come from that she could see easily. The door she'd pushed open had flipped over . . . but not quite *all* the way over. Someone was crouching under it, hiding.

"Out from under there, goddammit. Move!" Her cop's voice. "Hands wide and empty, or your—"

"It's jus' me," a thin voice said, and a little girl crawled out from under the door.

"My God!" She lowered the pistol. "Coral, what are you—"

An odd, muffled explosion made them both jump. It seemed to come from the front of the house. And what was that? A man? Calling out to someone? But there was a sort of roaring then, and the sound of wind—even though there was no wind—and a crackling like fire. Kirsten's brain seemed to be working in slow motion, sorting out the different sounds.

"Who is that?" Coral said, her eyes wide with obvious confusion. She turned and went toward the steps to the back door.

"I don't know, but whoever it is set the house on fire. C'mon, Coral, run!"

"No, I mean that *man*. He sayin' your name."

Then Kirsten heard him, too. "Dugan!" she screamed. "For God's sake, Dugan!"

She was past Coral and up the steps. The back door was unlocked. She found a switch and . . . no. Even the light might ignite the gasoline. Through an open doorway across the kitchen she could see down a hall to the front of the house into a room that glowed with a soft, wavering orange light. The fumes were

74

very strong in the kitchen, but maybe they hadn't poured gasoline along the hallway, because the fire hadn't gotten back here yet.

"Get me out of here!" It was Dugan, and she realized he'd been yelling all along. "Dammit, get me—"

"Dugan! It's me. Kirsten!" But where was he? She ran to the open doorway, and heat poured at her from the corridor, as though from a furnace, and then she saw the front room burst into flame. "Dugan! Where are you?"

"Here, here, here!" She heard him pounding. "Here! The door's locked."

She spun around and in the dim light finally picked out a door that shook as Dugan banged on it. She even saw the white porcelain knob turning as he twisted it. She looked around the kitchen. It was too dark, and the key might be anywhere . . . or nowhere. Or maybe in the lock? She heard a hissing sound behind her and turned. Tiny flames were creeping along the baseboard, coming down the hall toward the kitchen.

She ran across to the locked door. No key.

"Your gun!" he yelled. "Shoot the damn lock out!"

"I can't! I'd blow us both away. It's just a pantry door. Come right through it, for chrissake."

She heard him throw himself against the door, but the lock held. "Get out of here!" he screamed. "Save yourself."

"Dammit, Dugan! You break down that door, or else I stay right here and die with you."

"Shit! Get out of my goddamn way!"

She heard him screaming like a crazy man, and then the kitchen exploded into flames, even as the pantry door splintered apart on the hinges side and burst open and he was out. They stumbled and dragged each other for a lifetime through hell and made it outside and fell together down the back porch steps.

She had him in her arms and they rolled over and over together in the thick, wet grass. She smelled that terrible, terrible smell and prayed to God it was only hair and not flesh that was singed. And if it *was* flesh, prayed it was her flesh and not his. And she kept rolling him with her through the cool grass . . . right up to a pair of small gym shoes that poked out from faded wet jeans, where they came to a stop.

She let go of him.

"I guess we're far enough from the fire," he said, "but I kinda like this rolling around together and—"

"Quiet, godammit!" she said, and didn't know why she sounded so angry.

They sat on the ground near the metal storage shed. Coral stood over them, staring down with that same wide-eyed, serious look, an empty plastic bucket hanging from one little brown fist. Kirsten got to her feet. The back of the house was in full flame now, and in its light she suddenly saw the bruising on the side of his face, saw that his right eye was swollen shut, and saw that he was trying to smile.

"Just . . . keep quiet," she said, only in a gentler tone, "and . . . and . . ." And then she couldn't stop herself any longer from crying. Dugan stood, too, and held her close to him until they were both able to breathe normally again.

Coral made a sort of a coughing noise, and Kirsten remembered she was there and pulled away from Dugan to look at her.

"I couldn't find no water," Coral said. She set the bucket down in the grass, carefully, and then stared at the burning house. "Poor Mama Dee. She gonna be real sad."

Kirsten dropped to her knees and wrapped her arms around the child and squeezed her bony little body, rocking from side to side. She rested her cheek against Coral's cheek, and then started to cry all over again.

SIXTEEN

Kirsten's cell phone was missing from the Camry, so they couldn't have called 911 even if she'd wanted to, and she wasn't sure she did. The note on the back door had said Mama Dee was gone for the weekend. If that wasn't true, and if she was in fact somewhere inside the house—something Kirsten refused to believe—she was way past help by this time. And if the fire spread to those falling-down farm buildings, which seemed unlikely with everything well-soaked by the rain, it might do Mama Dee a favor. As for reporting the man on the cellar steps . . . well, Dugan didn't even know about that yet, and she didn't have anything she wanted to tell the police about the man—at least not until she knew more about what the hell was going on.

Dugan's rental car was missing, too, and for some reason he was determined to drive the Camry. He claimed he was fine, not feeling dizzy or sick or anything. Kirsten didn't believe him, but she gave in and said he could drive. She decided he must be embarrassed by her having had to talk him into saving his own life.

Then Coral refused to go with them, insisting she'd ride her bike home by her "shortcut," which included a part of Till's

Creek Road that kept going beyond the barricade, a dirt road she claimed was smooth and easy to ride on, and then an old bike path along a creek. She said she could see in the dark "real good" and had ridden that way "a whole lotta times."

Kirsten took her aside. "Look, Coral, won't your cousin want to know where you've been and . . . and what happened?"

The child stared at her. "She don't hardly ever ask me nothin'," she said. "And I mostly don't tell her nothin'. I don't tell nobody nothin', if I don't want to." She looked down at the ground for a moment, then back up at Kirsten. "Miz Eudora, she my friend, and you helpin' her, and I ain't gonna tell nobody not one thing, not 'less you say so." She crossed her fists over her chest. "And that's a blood oath."

Kirsten gave in again. She watched Coral ride off on her bike until she'd gone around the barricade and disappeared in the darkness, and then she joined Dugan in the Camry. They hadn't even gotten to the end of Mama Dee's long driveway, though, when he skidded to a stop. He opened his door, leaned out of the car, and threw up onto the ground.

"So much for not feeling sick," she said.

"It just sort of snuck up on me." He sat up but didn't close his door. "Um . . . there may be more where that came from."

"I'll drive," she said, and they exchanged places.

Once they were out on Till's Creek Road, she was torn between driving fast to get beyond that narrow road before anyone came from the opposite direction and driving slow so Dugan didn't throw up right there in her car.

"Everything okay?" she asked.

"I'm fine," he said, "but I think we gave up too easily."

"We didn't exactly 'give up,'" she said. "You got ambushed and I got locked—"

"Not that. I mean letting that little girl ride her bike home by herself. It's late and her folks'll be out of their minds worrying about her."

"We couldn't very well kidnap her. Besides, it's not even ten o'clock, and she says she's eleven years old and that's not late for her to be out on a Saturday night."

"She must have parents, and they'll—"

"She's not that lucky. She lives with her cousin, and it's just the two of them and . . . well, the cousin has her own agenda. My sense is that Coral Hancock Stitch—that's her name—is pretty much free to come and go as she pleases."

"Which is what's probably made her so self-reliant and full of initiative," Dugan said.

"Maybe. It's certainly what's made her so lonely. Sometimes I—" She slowed down. "What's that up there?"

"What's what?"

"See? Where the road bends a little?"

Dugan leaned forward as she drove closer, very slowly. "Oh, yeah," he said. "A car, pulled off the road. And behind it a house or some—"

"It's one of those deserted-looking trailer homes. Did you see a car at any of them when you drove by earlier?"

"Hell, I didn't even see any trailer homes. Too dark."

"What kind of car did you rent?"

"A green Dodge Ne— Oh. Can't tell the color, but I'd say that's probably it."

She came to a stop, leaving the headlights on, and slid the Colt from her purse.

"Y'know," Dugan said, "I'm not sure I like you always carrying that—"

"I don't *always* carry it. But you sure wanted me to use it a half hour ago."

"True. But a gun makes a person overconfident. Like now, when the intelligent thing to do is put your foot to the floor and get us the hell outta here."

"I don't think so. I don't think there's anyone here. I think what happened is the guy hid his car here and walked to Mama

Dee's, maybe looking for the person whose body's on the cellar steps. Then, when—"

"What person? What body?"

"I didn't want to mention it in front of Coral. I don't think she saw it, either."

"We better call the cops."

"I don't know. They'll find it, anyway. Maybe we should just call from a pay phone and say we saw what looked like a fire from a distance. I mean, what do we know that could be helpful?"

"But you saw a dead body. Who was he?"

"How do you know it was a 'he'?"

"Wasn't it?"

"Yes. But I have no idea who he really was," she said. "Although he looked like the same man who followed me a couple of—"

"Followed you? You didn't tell me anyone followed you."

"Well, no way I can tell you every little thing that happens every day."

"Right. Only the big stuff, like what to pick up at the store and . . . Anyway, I guess that fits in with that phone message, about Eudora and people around her getting hurt."

"What message? You didn't mention any phone message."

"Well, no way I can tell you every little thing that hap—"

"That's what brought you out to Mama Dee's?"

"It made me . . . concerned. So I went looking for you."

"Maybe whoever closed the cellar door on me recognized me and lured you out to Mama Dee's. Maybe he was waiting the whole time."

"But there was nothing in the message about where you were. What if I never showed up?"

"Maybe he doesn't care. Maybe he's paid by the hour. Maybe he—"

"Wait a minute." He leaned toward her and whispered in a conspiratorial tone. "How do you know it's . . . a *he*?"

She touched the tip of her finger to his nose. "You look so cute, darling," she said, "with all that vomit drying on your chin."

They went to check out the Neon and then, taking their time and moving cautiously in the darkness, finally decided the area was deserted. The trailer home was quite small and locked from the outside with a padlock. The signs seemed to verify Kirsten's theory. Tire tracks led through the tall wet weeds from behind the trailer to the road.

The keys were in the Neon, and it smelled like someone had smoked a cigarette in it since Dugan left it. They talked things over and decided Dugan was well enough to drive by now, with her following him. They went straight home and got there before midnight. They didn't stop at, or call, the police or the fire department. They didn't stop at, or call, Eudora's house.

And they didn't check to make sure Coral got home safely.

SEVENTEEN

Dugan woke up about eleven and thrashed around the bed a while, looking for Kirsten. It was Sunday morning and they always . . . well, she wasn't there. He smelled coffee and stumbled out to the kitchen to drag her back to bed. On the counter beside the coffee maker was a note. She'd gone out for a run and would be back "sometime this afternoon."

Bulging Sunday editions of both the *Trib* and the *Sun-Times* were on the kitchen table, so he sat down with coffee and a couple of thick slices of whole wheat toast and black raspberry jam. He was hungry and some bacon or sausage would have been nice, but there was a noticeable absence of meat in the refrigerator.

He'd taken lots of aspirins and decided not to shave. The swelling around his eye wasn't too bad, but the bruise would be there awhile. He set aside the junk and the ads from both papers and skimmed through what little was left. If anyone had discovered the fire at Mama Dee's yet, it had been too late to make either paper.

By noon, he'd washed the dishes and was wondering if there was any news on TV on Sundays. Cable, maybe.

Ordinarily, a farmhouse burning down—even if the fire was

"of suspicious origin," as they put it—in the middle of nowhere seventy miles outside the city wouldn't have made the Chicagoland cable news channel. Mama Dee's fire did though, obviously because of the "as yet unidentified man" whose body was found at the scene.

No other victims were discovered, and the property owner was unavailable and thought to be out of town on a weekend trip with a church group. There was a map showing where Miracle City was in relation to Kankakee and Chicago, and a reporter from a Kankakee channel—a nice-looking woman, too, Dugan thought—interviewed Chief Frawley and asked about reports that the dead man might himself have set the fire and then died when he fell and hit his head on some concrete steps, and also that maybe the incident was somehow "drug related."

"That's all speculation and rumor at this time," Frawley answered. "All I can say is that the investigation is in the hands of state police and fire investigators, and the Miracle City Police Department is cooperating fully."

Dugan's head still ached a little, so he took two more aspirins with a glass of orange juice. It looked like a beautiful day outside, and he decided to go for a walk and, if he felt okay, work up to a run.

Kirsten had started the day by calling Eudora, confident she'd catch her at home because it was Sunday and not even eight o'clock, but the phone rang and rang without an answer. After that, she'd had no agenda beyond clearing out her head and hoping an idea moved in. She sure didn't want to show her face in Miracle City, not for a couple of days, anyway.

First she'd run about three miles along the lakefront, from Diversey Harbor to Montrose and back, then gone to the health club for a shower and a few easy laps in the pool. Traffic was light and she'd driven to her favorite pistol range, behind a gun shop way up near O'Hare Airport, and squeezed off a hundred rounds or so. During the entire time, she'd hardly spoken a word to anyone and deliberately left the car radio off so she could think.

Not one really constructive thought had shown up by noon, by which time she'd left the gun shop and was heading for home, so she gave up and turned on the radio. It was a talk-and-sports station, and a man on the phone with the ex-jock host of the show was urging people to take the family somewhere that afternoon and "help answer a lot of kids' prayers." She was about to hit the station scanner when the host said "Father Rooney," and she realized the caller was the priest who ran Mother of Mercy Village, a home for children, and he was plugging their annual Spring Festival. She'd read about the event, and the various VIPs expected to be there—athletes, entertainers, big names in business and politics—in the *Weekend* section of Friday's *Tribune*.

She threw the Camry into a U-turn that aggravated the hell out of a whole bunch of Sunday drivers, and headed north. If she'd been praying for an idea, she sure didn't know it, but an answer had just come to her, or at least a suggestion about where to go to stir things up a little, and stirring things up often led to answers.

In half an hour she was being directed by one after another of a cadre of teenagers in yellow T-shirts and blue baseball caps. They waved her through the entrance to Mother of Mercy Village, down an asphalt drive to a huge grassy field, and finally to a parking place on the grass where she was urged to inch forward and nudge the nose of the car in the row facing her. As she stepped out of the Camry, a smiling Hispanic fifteen-year-old handed her a card that said: *Thanks for visiting MOM's kids! You're parked in row 17! Have a great day!*

She stared at the card. Mom? Oh, M-O-M. Got it.

It cost her twenty bucks just to go through the turnstile, but after that it was probably a lot like Eudora's fund-raiser for CREW, and like every other such event she'd ever seen—except far more grandiose. More carnival rides, more strolling jugglers and clowns, more rings and balls and coins to toss at more stakes and holes and jars, more raffles for more cars and cruises, more ponies for kids to ride, more food stands with more types of ethnic foods. Laughter and shouting, kids crying and music blaring; hundreds—maybe thousands—of people happily spending money like crazy for MOM's kids. And everywhere there were men in red shirts walking around, watching with tired-looking eyes. Off-duty cops, working security.

In her wandering she came across two rows of portable toilets, all of them in the shade. This festival was a class act. She also found a rather small elephant that trumpeted every time its handler asked it to—which was way more often than anyone over six years old appreciated. The elephant looked well cared for, she thought, and quite content to haul hysterical little kids around in a circle. There were no animal rights activists in sight.

There were also no clouds in the sky and, with low humidity and a temperature stuck in the low seventies, she decided Father Rooney was as good at twisting God's arm as he was with just about every pro athlete, media star, and political VIP within a two-hundred-mile radius.

More power to him. Mother of Mercy Village handled kids—mostly wards of the court, she thought—from first through twelfth grades. It obviously needed lots of money. But she had no time to stop and spend. She remembered what she'd read in the paper, and she was looking for one particular attraction.

Finally she stopped one of the red shirts. "You know where the Dunk the Big Shot booth is?"

"Yeah, I do. It's . . ." He stopped and stared at her. "Hey, you were that female dick in Area Four a couple years ago, right?"

"Wow! Good memory," she said. "You're . . . Henderson, right? It's more like four years now, and I was only there six months."

"Yeah? Me, I'm *still* fucking there," the cop said, and she forced a smile and kept nodding as he explained how Area 4 was still the same goddamn jungle full of savages and how, no matter how bad you thought things were, they always got worse. She had the impression he could recite all this in his sleep—and probably did. "Maybe I oughta go private myself," he finally said. "Hey, how about we get together and talk about how *you* did it?"

"Sure, call me. I'd like that." She couldn't think of anything she'd like less, actually, but she knew Henderson. He was bright enough, but forever stuck where he was. He'd never call. "So," she said, "Dunk the Big Shot? Hit the target with a ball and some guy drops into a tub of water?"

"It's way the hell down there." He pointed. "Sort of hidden behind the bingo tent. But it's closed right now. They did great with a couple White Sox players, but they left and Sammy Sosa's an hour late, so John Michael Hurley sat up there for a while. But that didn't bring in much. Who knows *him?*"

"I've heard of him."

"Sure, *you* have. Me, too. But your average Jack and Jill Citizen here, they don't even read the papers. Got no idea who's really runnin' their world. Fucking guy must own half the goddamn county, and a whole lot of politicians. Got a finger in every pie—Police Board, Planning Commission, Sanitary District, Forest Preserve Board, whatever. Donates big time to this place, chairs the United Fund . . . But he's no fucking sports hero, y'know? Where's the fun in payin' hard cash to dunk *him?*"

She managed to get away and find the Dunk the Big Shot booth, where people were lining up to dunk Sammy Sosa. The booth itself was fifteen feet high, metal pipes and chain-link fence, all painted bright red and draped with canvas on three sides, with netting across the top to catch wild throws. It was divided into two parts. A man with a hose was topping off a huge tub that took up most of the right side, beneath the perch where the dunkee sat and made fun of the throwers so they'd keep on trying till they hit the little round target. A blue-capped teenage girl was picking baseballs off the ground on the other side, where the target was fixed to the end of a long arm that triggered the collapse of the perch and the dunking of the Big Shot of the moment.

The girl was lining the balls up in flat boxes to be ready for customers. Kirsten stepped close and asked, "Is Mr. Hurley still around?"

"Yes, ma'am. Least, I *think* he be round back by the tent they got for puttin' on dry clothes. Mr. Hurley, he in charge of this booth, and him and Father Brown be back there waitin' on Sammy Sosa."

"Oh, good. Thanks."

"But you can't go back there. Ain't nobody allowed past them ropes there. It's private."

Kirsten smiled and pressed a twenty into the girl's hand. She ducked under the ropes and went around to the back of the booth. At once it seemed strangely silent, the crowd noise muted by the tall dunking booth and the huge canvas-walled bingo pavilion beside it. By a much tinier tent—like a cabana for changing clothes—two uniformed Chicago police officers, both of them close to retirement age, sat on folding chairs. They were ten or twenty miles outside their jurisdiction, but—with Sammy on his way—who's to quibble?

Two gray-haired, suntanned men stood nearby, deep in conversation. She picked the one who was slim, about six-two, and wearing a black suit and Roman collar to be Father Rooney, and the shorter, stocky one in the white trousers and brown golf shirt to be John Michael Hurley.

A third man stood some ten feet off to the side. He was taller than the priest, wider than the millionaire, and way younger than either of them. His skin was dark and deeply tanned; his hair slick and shiny and black, maybe to match his pants and his sunglasses. He wore a sort of gauzy-looking white pullover shirt that accented his bodybuilder's physique. The guy looked to her like an ex-con—and like a loser—and him she picked to be Hurley's muscle.

She slid her hand into the purse that hung from her shoulder. "Excuse me," she called. "Mr. Hurley?"

The two older men's heads turned her way, but it was the thug—surprisingly quick and light on his feet—who moved toward her. "Yeah?" He stopped and stood between her and the other two. "What is it you want, lady?"

"Excuse me," she said, turning his way, "but no one said anything to you, Bozo."

The man stood perfectly still, his lips curled back, baring his teeth in an odd sort of smile. He was staring at her, although she couldn't see his eyes behind the dark shades. No one said anything; no one moved. They were all frozen in a silence that drowned out the sounds of merriment around them. The two police officers studied their shoes. The priest and Hurley both seemed to want to say something, and she suddenly read the looks on their faces. They were afraid . . . and their fear was for *her*.

The younger man leaned toward her, just slightly, then snatched off his sunglasses and flipped them onto the grass. He'd looked mean, but something worse than that was slipping over his face now, even as she watched. Something vicious, slurring the humanity from his features. His eyes narrowed and an animal looked out at her.

She stepped backward, but he moved, too, closing the distance. The two cops stood up, but then—to her dismay—started easing in the opposite direction.

"Tommy! Wait!" Hurley finally spoke. "She didn't mean any—"

"Shut the fuck up! You heard what she said!" He stepped suddenly close to her and his right hand lashed out toward her face.

She leaned and ducked away, or the blow would have lifted her off her feet. Even so, he made contact, and the slap of his huge hand across the side of her head rattled her brain. And that wasn't the end of it. He was way beyond stopping himself. She knew that and stumbled backward, away from him.

He lunged at her and she slid to the side, drawing the .380 from her purse. The safety was on, and as he jerked his left arm around, reaching out to grab her, she swept the automatic up . . . and then down again, hard, smashing the barrel across the back of his hand. The shock of the blow shot a fierce pain up her own arm, all the way to her shoulder, but she held on to the gun.

He went down on one knee, clutching his left hand with his right, staring up at her. She saw his mouth gaped open in pain and rage but couldn't hear his howling because of the roar in her own ears. She faced him, feet planted wide, weapon in two hands, safety off, barrel aimed at his chest. She glanced around, and the cops were nowhere in sight. If this creep came at her again, she'd have to shoot him. Her heart was pounding. Maybe she wished he would come at her, now, and get it over with. Shoot him until he stopped coming.

And then Hurley stepped between them, his back to her. He bent over and wrapped his arms around the thug, holding him, whispering in his ear. She finally felt herself start to breathe again, felt the tightness in her shoulders and neck ease up. She lowered the weapon and slipped it back in her purse—and only then felt someone at her side.

"Please, miss, we should go." It was Father Rooney. "We should all get out of here."

"But I don't—"

"Listen," the priest said.

Rhythmic shouts were coming from the other side of the dunking booth. Actually, a chant. "Sam-MEE! Sam-MEE!" The next big shot, on his way to get dunked for MOM's kids.

Hurley was still holding on to the thug, half hugging him, walking him away from them.

"There's been some terrible mistake." The priest's voice quavered. "I've never seen him . . . We should all just forget about it."

"Not a chance." She took one of her business cards from her purse and handed it to him. "Give this to Hurley. Tell him I want to meet with him. Tomorrow. Wherever he wants. But tell him to keep that slug of a bodyguard he seems so worried about under a rock."

"Bodyguard?"

"Yeah, the animal, the goon. You saw what he did."

"Yes, I saw everything. I saw what he did. But that's not a bodyguard. That's Tommy. That's John Michael's son."

EIGHTEEN

Dugan spent most of the afternoon on the sofa, wishing Kirsten were home, and that's where he still was, watching the news, when she came in with two bags of groceries. She bent down to kiss him on the cheek and then headed for the kitchen to make supper. They usually went out around noon or so on Sunday for a huge brunch. Since he hadn't eaten since breakfast, he was hungry and not about to delay her by asking where she'd been all day.

Mama Dee's fire made two channels, but just barely. It was now being called "a possible arson." The cops had identified the dead man but weren't saying publicly yet who he was. There was no mention of his starting the fire, or of drug deals or anything else new.

He followed the scent of garlic back to the kitchen, where Kirsten was tossing Brie with cooked pasta in a wide shallow bowl. The pasta was *radiatore,* and the box it came in called the pieces "nuggets," but they'd always looked to him like miniature Malibu lights. They had lots of little edges, but you still had to spear them to keep them on your fork. He watched her add olive oil and thought she was being careful not to look at him. There

91

was a mound of chopped tomato on a cutting board on the counter.

"Looks great," he said. "Do the meatballs go in before or after the tomatoes?"

"Why not just set the table and slice the bread?" she said.

"Just asking." Actually, she'd made this particular meatless dish before and he loved it, but he had to keep the pressure on or God knows how far she'd go with this healthy-eating idea. "I missed you this morning. A lot. In fact, all day there's been an aching in my left—"

"In your heart?" she said. "Your left atrium?"

"Yeah, sort of."

"Sorry to disappear like that. I was just so . . . wired. I couldn't sit around and wait for you to wake up. So I went for a run."

"Nice day for a run. I did that myself. Actually a walk, mostly. I was back by, oh, two o'clock."

"I ran about three miles, then had a shower and a swim at the health club. After that I went to the pistol range." She filled two plates and set them on the kitchen table. "And then . . . just some other stuff I had to take care of." She had a strange expression on her face. She looked tired, but more than that. Sad, maybe.

"Oh, 'other stuff.' " He put a basket of sliced French bread on the table, and they both sat down. She'd tell him if she wanted to. He could wait. "You haven't met Mama Dee yet, have you?"

"Not yet," she said. "Why?"

"S'pose she could be running a drug house?"

"What?" Her first forkful of Malibu lights stopped halfway to her mouth.

"Have you seen the TV reports?"

"No. But they can't be saying anything like that."

"Well, they *could* be, I suppose," he said. "But they aren't." Then he told her about the Kankakee reporter's questions to Chief Frawley.

She sat and listened but seemed distracted, detached.

She was obviously as hungry as he was, though, and he realized she probably hadn't eaten all day. They finished the pasta dish, and all the bread, and then all the frozen peach yogurt. When there was nothing left to eat, he stood up. "I'll get the dishes," he said. "You look tired. Why don't you go take a bath?"

"I'm not tired."

"No, of course not. What do *I* know?"

"I mean, yes, I *am* tired." She looked up at him and probably thought she was smiling. He could have told her it wasn't working, but he didn't. "There's something else, though," she said.

"Yes. That 'other stuff' you mentioned." He waited, then finally asked, "What stuff?"

"I met a man today who . . . who brought me down."

"Brought you down?"

"Down to his level. Made me act like him. Or . . . made me *want* to act like him, anyway. I don't feel good about that. I don't *want* to have the desire to hurt someone. Ever." She looked like she might start crying, but didn't. "I don't want to become like . . . like some of these people I deal with."

He went behind her and knelt on the floor, his arms wrapped around the back of the wooden chair and her both, squeezing her toward him. "You never will," he said, whispering the words into her ear. "You can't. It's not there. It's not in you."

"But it happened," she said. "It went away, but it happened. From the minute I saw him I wanted to hurt him. I could see he was a loser and was fragile, and I called him a clown because . . . because he was so stupid and obnoxious, and I didn't like him. He hadn't done anything at all, but I wanted to show him something. Prove something. I could have done it differently. And then . . . then he did just what I knew he would do. Only he was worse, more unstable, than I thought. And I hurt him. And I would have—"

"Stop," he said, but gently. "Stop, stop, stop. You can tell me the whole thing, beginning to end. But first, a bath."

He stood up, and she did, too. She took his advice and after her bath told him the whole story. When she finished he was mostly scared to death about the enemy she'd stirred up against her. He didn't mention that, though. What he said was he didn't think she should feel so guilty about what she'd done.

"I guess you're right," she said, but he didn't know whether she really believed him.

And they went to bed and they were going to make love, but they didn't. Or maybe they did. If just holding on to each other and telling each other—without saying anything at all—that you're OK exactly the way you are, and starting to fall asleep that way . . . if that's a way love is made, he thought, then maybe they did.

NINETEEN

The weather was as nasty Monday as it had been glorious the day before. By eleven-thirty, the wind was driving a cold rain sideways, and Kirsten dashed from her cab into the lobby of a high-rise office building between Michigan Avenue and Lake Shore Drive, just north of the river.

It was part of a complex built up recently on land that years ago held rail yards and huge warehouses but had long been vacant. Park told her he'd heard once that the parcel stayed undeveloped so long because the ground was saturated with toxic chemicals and no one knew just how dangerous it would be to build there—or worse, to live or work there every day in what would be built. But nothing was ever said about that once the new buildings were on their way up.

At ten that morning the call had come from John Michael Hurley's secretary, very cool, very polite, with word that the king would receive her at his office at noon. "Would that be convenient for you?" the woman had asked.

"I'll fit it in," Kirsten said, and hung up.

Hurley's suite number was 2700, and the twenty-seventh was, of course, the top floor. She was early but decided he could make whatever he wanted to of that, and headed for the elevators. She couldn't find one that went above twenty-six. She headed back to the marble counter in the lobby, where an arrogant-looking man in a Prussian general's uniform had offered to assist her when she'd passed him on her way in. She'd declined then with a wave, and now the man seemed even more obnoxious than before.

"The elevator to twenty-seven," she said, "where is it?"

"And are you expected, miss?" A British accent, for God's sake. "Have you an appointment?"

She considered asking him the difference between those two questions but instead gave him her name and he got on the phone. When he hung up he pointed to his right. "You may go through there, miss."

There was no sign on the door, but when she pushed on it the lock clicked and she went through and found an elevator. She rode nonstop to twenty-seven, and the doors opened onto a carpeted reception area full of expensive-looking furniture. A full-figured, attractive woman in a navy business suit intercepted her and took her raincoat, then asked to see her purse.

Kirsten handed it to her and then raised her arms. "You patting me down, too?" she asked.

"I'd love to, dear, but not while we're both working." By the time Kirsten realized she probably wasn't kidding, the woman had looked in the purse and closed it again. "Meanwhile," she said, "I'll just hang onto this until you leave."

Must have something to do with the Colt automatic, Kirsten thought, and walked across to the reception desk. The middle-aged woman there was very polite, and Kirsten recognized her voice from the phone call.

Sixty seconds later she was alone with John Michael Hurley. The desk between them was actually an antique, glass-topped library table, covered with carefully arranged stacks of papers and file folders. There was a phone, too, and a laptop, and she got the impression real work was done here. It was a large, wood-paneled corner office, comfortable, though not ostentatious. Windows looked north and east, but there wasn't much to be seen beyond the rain that slashed against the glass.

Beside her chair was a small table with a coffee service: carafe, sugar, cream, and one cup and saucer. "Help yourself," Hurley said. "If you prefer a nonsugar sweetener . . ."

"No thanks. How is Tommy's hand?"

"It was the wrist that took most of the blow," he said. "No permanent damage."

"I . . . didn't know he was your son."

"I'll relay your apolo—"

"I said I didn't know he was your son." She'd had it with pleasantries. "I didn't say I was sorry."

He flinched, visibly, and for an instant she thought his eyes showed something of the ferocity she'd seen in his son's eyes the day before, but it vanished so quickly she may have been mistaken. All she saw now was a weary sort of sadness. "Father Rooney gave me your card," he said. "You wanted to talk to me?"

"Not so much talk, as ask. Why did you have a man following me?"

"I don't know what you're talking about." He rested his hands on the glass in front of him, and he seemed to have fully regained his composure.

"I think you *do* know, but I'll move on. Why is the man dead now?"

If he was surprised by what she said, he didn't show it. "I know nothing about anyone following you, or anyone dying. You've made a mistake." He shook his head like one of those ego-driven college professors who'd just been given the wrong answer—or, worse yet, been asked the wrong question. "Is there anything else?"

"Just one thing." Maybe the most important question, she thought. "Why did you agree to see me today?"

"Ah," he said, as though she'd finally gotten it right. He

looked down, studying the backs of his hands for a moment, then back up at her. "It's about your run-in with my son."

"You could call it that, although—"

"I've told him, and now I'm telling you . . . that's the end of it. There's to be no more contact between the two of you." He paused. "Is that clear?"

"Mr. Hurley, the fact that you're asking *me* to stay away from *him,* tells me you don't have a whole lot of control over your son." She stood up. "And, guess what? You've got no control at all over me."

"Sit down." He slid a bulging envelope out from one of the folders in front of him and centered it between them on the table. "You'll want to hear the rest of what I have to say."

He was right this time, and she sat down.

"There's cash in that envelope." Hardly a surprise. "Ten thousand dollars. It's yours."

"And?"

"And whatever it is you're . . . investigating, whatever led you to me yesterday, you drop it at once. Not because I'm afraid for myself. The very idea is ludicrous. But my son and I . . . we're often together, and I want to make certain there's no further contact between you and him. Is that clear?"

"What's clear is you're trying to buy me awfully cheap."

"Fine." He spread his hands wide. "How much then?"

"I don't know. Why is it so important to you?"

He sat quietly for a moment, then sighed. He might have just reached a decision—or not. She had no idea how much of all this was an act. "My wife died young." He spoke slowly, as though picking his words carefully. "We had three sons. There's the oldest, Jack, who blames me for his mother's death and thinks I'm interested in nothing but money. He despises me; we never communicate. There's Tommy, the youngest, who went bad despite everything I did for him. He went to prison and now he's out and on probation. And then there's Kieran, my middle

98

boy, who for some reason has always loved his brothers and me—all three of us—equally well. Kieran . . ." He paused and swallowed hard. "Kieran's a priest. Kieran's . . . dying. A brain tumor."

"I'm sorry," she said. She meant that, even though the information didn't improve her opinion of Hurley. "But none of that explains buying me off."

"I'm not 'buying you off.' " He pressed the tips of his fingers against his forehead, as though fighting a headache, then lowered his hands. "I've lost my wife. I have one son who'll soon be dead. Another might as well be, as far as I'm concerned. That leaves Tommy. Damaged as he is, he's what I've got left. I won't allow you to harm him. Prison wasn't . . . wasn't good for him."

"It never is . . . for anyone."

"He had some problems when he went in, unresolved issues, but now . . . At any rate, he's not going back there as long as I have breath in me, or beyond that if I—" His phone rang. He picked it up and listened, then said, "I'll call him back in five minutes." He hung up and looked at her. "What will it take to get you to drop whatever it is you're doing and to . . . to keep away from us? Ten thousand seems reasonable, but you name your price."

She stared at him. "Try fifty million dollars. We'll negotiate from there."

"I have no time for silliness. What will it take?"

"Mr. Hurley, my sources tell me your net worth is ten times fifty million, easy, and rising fast with every new landfill, shopping mall, and gambling casino you have a hand in. What's a son worth? I don't know. Maybe you can't buy one with money. Maybe you've already tried that. Maybe you'd like to make a different kind of deal."

"What deal?"

"You ever hear of CREW?" she asked.

"Crew?"

"C-R-E-W." She spelled it out. "The Committee to Rescue Emerald Woods. They're fighting construction of a shopping mall south of Kan—"

"Emerald Woods Mall, of course. Near Miracle City. CREW. Another group of ill-informed people. They feed on the fears of those who fail to see the benefits of well-planned development. An irritant, certainly."

"An irritant, that's all?"

"One of many: the federal and state EPAs, the Department of Transportation, and on and on. There are obstacles to overcome with every project. But I still don't know what you're getting at."

"Someone's putting the squeeze on one of the principals in CREW, obviously trying to eliminate one of your 'irritants.' As soon as I'm brought in to see what's going on, some mope starts following me around. When I turn on him he tells me you hired him. Shortly after that, he's dead. So . . . here I am."

"You know," he said, leaning forward as though about to share a secret, "what you're doing is revealing how far out of my league you are. You better stick to hanging around motels to videotape philandering husbands." He sat back again. "This 'mope' you talk about, whoever he is, might have told you the queen of England hired him. Would you fly to Windsor Castle?" He smiled in a condescending way. "The Emerald Woods Mall? Just another project. A business venture. I, and others, will put a lot of money into it, and hope later to take a lot more money out."

"That's my point. The 'lot more money' part."

"Exactly. It's an investment. Some pay off, some don't. When one doesn't, you put it behind you, and turn to other projects. A minute ago you mentioned gambling casinos. Check things out and you'll see I lost over fifteen million on the last riverboat I had a piece of. At the level I'm working at, do you really think I'm about to send some hood to help 'squeeze' some local fly in the ointment? If someone's being harassed, honey, maybe it's because of problems you don't know about."

"Maybe. But I intend to poke around until I find out who's behind it, and why."

"Oh? Well, here's a suggestion. Call it a 'health tip.' " His smile was not at all friendly. "You better do your 'poking around' in a way that doesn't interfere with me and my business interests. I'm going to build that mall, you see. And no bunch of small-time, know-nothing environmentalists and radicals—with or without your help, my dear little lady—will stop me."

"Gosh," she said, "and here I thought it was your *son* you were most interested in." He opened his mouth, then closed it, as though realizing he'd said too much already, so she went on. "I'd been suggesting a deal with a loving father, who—"

"You fucking ball-busting bitch." So much for his holding back. "What kind of *deal* are you talking about?"

"Tommy slapped me. Slapped me hard. And he made the first move." She leaned forward. "I *know* what he went away for." She'd just gotten the word an hour earlier. "Home invasion and aggravated battery . . . for savaging an ex-girlfriend. She managed to survive, or it would have been homicide. If I press charges, they'll violate his probation and send him back to jail."

Hurley's eyes narrowed. "You'd have to prove your case . . . and I'd see to it that you don't."

"Oh? What about the witnesses? Let's say you and Tommy both lie, and the two cops say they must have stepped away before it happened. What about Father Rooney? You able to buy *him* off?" She really didn't want to know the answer to that, so she threw in the kicker. "But it doesn't matter. The tape won't lie."

"Tape? Someone lurking behind the bingo tent with a video-cam? You expect me to believe that?"

She smiled. If he wanted to think videotape, that was fine

with her. "My, my, Mr. Hurley. Now it's you, revealing how far out of *my* league *you* are. Those telephoto lenses, you know, they're useful for more than just wayward spouses. You can be sure there's a tape, all right, and it's in safe hands." She stood up. "I want my client's problems to go away . . . now. Call it a show of good faith on your part, and maybe then we'll discuss the rest of the deal. You need to decide what's important to you. You need to think about it."

"You're bluffing," he said, looking up at her. "I can see it in your eyes."

"Oh, no you can't, my friend." She stared right back at him. "You can't see any bluff, because it isn't there."

She turned and left. Passing through the reception area, she retrieved her purse from the woman in the navy business suit— avoiding eye contact as she did—and went downstairs and out of the building. The rain had stopped.

She headed for Dugan's office on foot. It was a long walk, and there was still a surprisingly chilly breeze, but she wanted to be certain no one was following her. Besides, she needed to un-wind. The recorder in her purse at the carnival had captured the whole incident. But all it gave her was an audiotape that didn't actually prove a damn thing about what Tommy had done, no matter how many times she listened to it.

Still, if Hurley wanted to worry about a possible videotape, all the better. She didn't mind causing a few sleepless nights for a creep who called her degrading names.

"Fucking ball-busting bitch" she didn't care about. "Honey," though, and "my dear little lady" . . . that sort of stuff made her mad.

TWENTY

Monday mornings were usually productive, but when Mollie buzzed to see what he wanted for lunch, Dugan realized noon had come and gone and he hadn't made a dollar all day. He'd have settled a few cases by now if he'd stuck to the phone, but Chief Frawley had called at nine o'clock. He wanted to talk to Eudora about the fire at Mama Dee's, but she and her kids weren't around. Frawley wanted to know if Dugan knew where she was.

After that he hadn't done much but mope around his office and wonder what the hell Kirsten had gotten herself . . . themselves . . . mixed up in.

His two workers' comp lawyers—Fred Schustein and Peter Rienzo—waved from the hallway as they headed out somewhere for lunch. He'd inherited them when his dad dropped dead, running up a ramp at Wrigley Field with Old Styles for his buddies, and he left the state's attorney's office to take over the law firm. Fred and Peter still covered his workers' compensation cases, and until recently he'd been the firm's only other lawyer, working the personal injury cases by himself with a great secretarial staff. He'd quickly given up going to the courthouse, and any case he couldn't settle without shortchanging the client was referred to some other lawyer to file suit, and they split the fee.

Since he'd hired Larry Candle, though, he'd begun filing suit on a few cases himself. That was Larry's idea, and since the guy worked his tail off every day, why not keep him happy? Dugan wouldn't let him take any significant case to trial, of course—he'd still bring in someone else if it got that far—but Larry loved going to court to argue pretrial motions and attend status hearings. He said he had a reputation among the lawyers and judges and didn't want to lose it by dropping out of the game.

Dugan stood up and stared out the window. As far as he knew, Larry's reputation was for being a fast-talking pain in the ass. But then, maybe any recognition is better than none. After all, he himself enjoyed being known as the kind of free-swinging gonzo who'd hire someone like Larry in the first—

"If you're thinking of jumping out that window, don't." It was Kirsten. "A lawyer did that last week. Tied up traffic on LaSalle Street for hours."

He turned to face her. "I may look like I'm not getting a damn thing done," he said, "but remember Einstein's advice about creative thinking and gazing out the window."

"Actually," she said, setting her purse on his desk and dropping her very attractive body into one of his client's chairs, "I don't remember that particular piece of advice."

"Well, maybe it wasn't Einstein. Anyway, what are you doing here?"

"I've just spent a half hour with John Michael Hurley, and I've come for a dose of sanity."

"How about half a corned-beef sandwich and a Pepsi, instead? Mollie—"

"I know. I was there when she buzzed you. She ordered tuna salad on whole wheat toast for me."

While they waited for lunch she described her meeting with

Hurley, even including the Prussian general with the British accent and the woman who searched her purse.

"Our forefathers had half the worries we modern men have," he said when she'd finished. "They only had to watch out for *guys* hitting on their women."

"At least," she said, "that's what they thought."

He changed the subject and was telling her about Frawley not being able to find Eudora when Mollie came in with their sandwiches and two cans of Pepsi. "One's diet," she said, "for Kirsten." Then, looking at Dugan, she added, "I suppose you're going to be *out* this afternoon."

He grinned and made a point of speaking to Kirsten. "What Mollie means is, are you gonna drag me away again, and leave the firm to flounder on the brink of financial ruin?"

"People don't 'flounder' on the 'brink,' darling," Kirsten said. "They *teeter* on the brink, or else fall over and flounder in—"

"Sorry, Mollie," he said, "but whenever Kirsten says 'darling,' it means she has plans for me."

"I was merely checking," Mollie said. "Actually, the firm's income has been up the last few months."

"Really?" He was shocked. "How could that . . ." But Mollie was gone.

"Don't worry, darling." Kirsten was either stifling a laugh or choking on a bit of tuna salad. "Your firm still needs you. It's probably just that Larry doesn't feel free to cut fees or refund money to clients, like you do."

He concentrated on his sandwich for a while, then changed the subject again. "Do you believe Hurley? About the mall being just another deal, and CREW and Eudora not worth worrying about?"

"I really don't know. I discovered CREW has a website. Not bad, either, and they claim to be growing all the time. On the other hand, Hurley may have no money of his own at risk in the deal at this point. So what he said might make sense."

"Right," he said. "Or it could be total bullshit. He might need this deal to save his ass from absolute ruin, and CREW might be a major threat."

"But one thing seems awfully clear. Stealing the money from Eudora's refrigerator was designed to get her in trouble. When we step in to help, I get followed around. Then someone wallops the follower on the head and kills him, shuts me in with him, lures you out there and locks you in the pantry, and then torches Mama Dee's place."

"Was that the cause of death? A blow to the head?"

"Yep, and they ID'ed him as Alfred Brownley. Paper says he was a Chicago cop for a few years. Worked undercover, narcotics. Then they caught him shaking down the dealers, and he went to jail for a bit. Most recently he's been living in Kankakee." She finished up her sandwich. "Darn, I could eat another one of those."

"Whoever killed this Brownley guy at Mama Dee's couldn't have known you'd be showing up, right?" She nodded, so he went on. "So getting rid of you and me wasn't part of the original plan."

"I'm with you on that. But something else bothers me. They locked you in the pantry before they torched the place."

"Actually, that bothered *me* a little, too."

"No, really, think about it. I got locked in, too, but *outside* the house. And with just an old bolt through the hasp, not a padlock. Coral told me that. I mean, unlike you, it's quite possible I'd have survived the fire. The news reports don't indicate how badly Brownley's body was burned."

"My guess is he got pretty hot, though."

"I suppose, but the point is . . . they made your death a sure thing—or that's what they thought, anyway—and didn't do that with me."

"So . . . what does that mean?"

"I don't know. Just thought I'd bring it up." She stood up and grabbed her purse. "Let's go see if we can find Eudora . . . and, come to think of it, we ought to check on Coral, too."

They had to take a cab home to pick up the Camry, so it was midafternoon by the time they got out of the city. It was dark for that time of day, raining like hell again, and traffic was heavy and slow. Dugan stared out the window and let his mind wander while Kirsten drove. Then, halfway to Miracle City, he suddenly thought of something. "Didn't you tell me you stopped at a gas station and asked a couple of guys how to get to Till's Creek Road?"

"I wondered when you'd bring that up," she said.

"When they heard about the arson, why didn't they go tell the police? Can't happen every day, a babe like you dropping in. They'd have remembered."

"Thanks for the classy 'babe' compliment, but their forgetting is what I'm counting on. They were both in their seventies, easy, and looking like they'd been in a chronic chemical haze for the last ten years. I doubt they can distinguish one day from the next, or one person from another." She paused. "Anyway, that's what I hope."

"Jesus, if Frawley finds out we were there and didn't report it . . ."

"That's the thing. Frawley's one of the people I trust the least. Maybe he *does* know we were there."

"You mean maybe he *saw* us there?"

"Sure. Maybe he's the one who called you, or had someone call you."

"I think you're going off the deep end. Next you'll be saying it was that state's attorney, Wankel, who stole CREW's money from Eudora, and then—"

"Hey! Now you're getting into the flow. Maybe Einstein was right—or whoever." She reached over and patted his thigh. "You just keep looking out the window and let me know what pops up."

He tried, but by the time they got to Miracle City it was almost four o'clock, and the only ideas he'd had weren't worth mentioning. They were even more depressing than the traffic and the slate gray sky and the never-ending rain.

Then, when they arrived at Eudora's house, things took a turn for the worse.

TWENTY-ONE

udora's Ford Escort was parked in the driveway behind a huge yellow Chrysler, 1970s vintage, which Kirsten figured must be Mama Dee's. There was a third car, too, pulled in behind Eudora's. A mid-nineties four-door Crown Vic, solid blue. With its antennas, its plain black tires, and its rear end sticking into the street, it was as obviously a police vehicle as the two black-and-white Miracle City squad cars sitting nose to nose at the curb with their strobe lights flashing in the rain.

Just as Kirsten pulled up behind one of the black-and-whites, Eudora's front door opened and a uniformed cop came out. It was Galboa, the one who'd found the envelope in Eudora's garbage. He reached back through the door and yanked someone out onto the cement stoop. It was Eudora. She stood there in the cold rain, in pants and a short-sleeved top, no jacket, her hands cuffed behind her back.

"Jesus Christ!" Dugan said. "What's going on?" He pushed open his door.

"Calm down," Kirsten said, and put a hand on his shoulder. "You might make things worse."

A second uniform came out. He grabbed Eudora's other arm, and the two cops hauled her across the front yard. She had to struggle just to keep her footing as they dragged her through the long wet grass and puddled rainwater.

Before Kirsten could stop him, Dugan was out of the car, charging at the cops. "What the hell are you doing?" he yelled. "What's with the goddamned handcuffs? She's not resisting."

They stopped, and Galboa let go of Eudora's arm to face Dugan. "Police business, sir." His hand dropped to his waist, not-so-casually close to his service revolver. "Get back in your . . ." He leaned forward and peered through the falling rain. "Oh, you're the lawyer, right?"

"That's right, dammit!" Dugan was still yelling. "And if you keep on abusing my client, you'll be—"

"Take my keys, Dugan." She was right beside him now. Galboa stayed where he was, but the other cop was walking Eudora—more gently, Kirsten noticed—toward one of the patrol cars. "Why not just follow them to the station," she said, "and make sure she's treated right?"

"Goddamn right I will," he said, and grabbed the keys. She wasn't used to him acting this way, but he'd be fine by the time he got to the station. At least she hoped so.

"Meanwhile," she said, walking him back to the Camry, "I'll stay and talk to Mama Dee."

"Good idea," he said, in a surprisingly normal tone. He got behind the wheel and looked back up at her. "See you later." Then he grinned and gave her a wink and she suddenly realized she didn't know whether he'd really lost it for a minute or whether it was all a show for the cops . . . and—worst of all— she knew she'd never get the truth out of him.

One squad car, with Eudora in the backseat "cage," was already pulling away as Galboa got in the other and drove off, too, with Dugan right behind him. Turning back to the house, Kirsten saw Frawley standing in the open front doorway, his huge torso filling it, in fact. "You're getting wet," he said, which was an understatement. She waded through the grass to the stoop.

110

He didn't move. "I'd invite you in," he said, "but it's not my house."

"It's my client's house," she said, and he backed up into the house as she walked straight at him and went inside, too. The living room was empty, but she could hear a woman's voice and what might have been a child crying softly—maybe two children.

"A hothead, that husband of yours." In a rain-soaked uniform hat and a black slicker that would have covered three ordinary people, Frawley seemed to take up half the room. "Tell him he oughta be careful. Not all law officers are as well-disciplined as mine. Man could get hurt interfering with an arrest."

"People get hurt in lots of ways." She didn't like Frawley. "Does it take two well-disciplined goons to drag a handcuffed woman to a car?"

He smiled. "Your Miss Ragsdale's a difficult woman; very . . . hostile. Also a criminal and a fugitive."

"What are you talking about? She's on bond and awaiting trial. She has the same rights as anyone else."

"Not any more. She skipped out on her bond."

"She skipped, and you arrested her in her home?"

"She came back. Who knows for how long? We can't take a chance. Woman shows she can't be trusted to follow the law, she goes to jail. Tomorrow Wankel's asking the judge to revoke her bond." He headed for the door. "Now I'm on my way. Gotta make sure your husband doesn't get in trouble at the station."

He left the door open and she slammed it behind him. When she turned around there was a woman standing in the dining alcove off the living room. "You're Eudora's grandmother?"

"I'm Mama Dee. And you must be Kirsten." The woman was soft-spoken, and even though she wore an old-fashioned apron with large pockets, she was hardly the little old lady Kirsten had been unconsciously picturing. And no resemblance at all to Eudora, either. Pushing sixty, she was maybe five-ten, broad beamed, and full figured without being fat. Her skin was dark, and her hair was sprinkled with gray and cut short. "The children are in the kitchen," she said.

"It must have been traumatic for them, their mother being arrested."

"Yes, but they're pretty well calmed down now. They trust me when I say everything's gonna be okay . . . and besides, you can't beat good ol' tomato soup." Her smile broke out when she said that, deepening the lines in a face that had lots of them.

Mama Dee was an attractive, strong-looking woman, but what drew Kirsten's attention were her eyes. They were very hard to read. Was that kindness and the wisdom of experience? Or was it a deep, deep sadness? They reminded her of her own mother's—

". . . the twins?" Mama Dee was saying.

"What? Sorry," Kirsten said, "I missed what you—"

"I said would you like to meet the twins." Kirsten nodded and Mama Dee turned toward the kitchen and called, "Jeralyn? Jessica? Come on out here and meet a friend of your mama's." She went to the kitchen door and said, "Y'all say hello to the nice lady who's helping your mama."

When she turned back around she was flanked by two of the cutest little five-year-olds imaginable, wearing matching pink gym shoes, blue bib-overalls embroidered with Minnie Mouse, and pink sweatshirts. They had beautiful brown eyes—bright, inquisitive eyes—and the same smooth, tawny skin as Eudora. Their dark brown hair was pulled back into ponytails.

They said hello, and Kirsten told them their outfits were pretty and they smiled and told her shyly they'd been to Disney World and were careful to say, "Yes, ma'am," and "No ma'am," when she spoke to them. Pretty soon Mama Dee said their soup must be getting cold and they could put the Mary Poppins tape on the TV in the kitchen, and they left the room at once.

"They're so beautiful," Kirsten said, and as soon as she did

Mama Dee's eyes filled with tears. She turned and went into the living room and sat on the sofa.

Kirsten pulled a chair up close to her and sat there until she finally dropped her hands away from her face. "It must be terrible, all this on top of losing your house and all your belongings like that."

Mama Dee shook her head. "That old house don't matter," she said. "That's just . . . *stuff*. World's full of stuff. But Eudora . . ." She pulled a tissue from her apron pocket and blew her nose. "I didn't know noth— I didn't know anything about it. . . . I mean about the money being stolen and her being arrested. She didn't tell me and it wasn't on TV and none of the church ladies said a word about it." She shook her head again. "They wouldn't. They'd think it wasn't none of their business and I wouldn't want to talk about it."

"She should have told you."

"I don't fault her for that. She thought I'd try to talk her out of going on that trip she and the girls been planning for months, what with her bein' out on bond. And I would've, too. Disney World's not going anywhere: it'll be there next month, next year. But I understand. I might have done the same."

"What did she do, leave Friday and come back today?" Mama Dee nodded and Kirsten stood up and suddenly noticed she still had her raincoat on and was dripping water everywhere. She slipped it off and draped it over a chair by the door. "I'm surprised they even found out she was gone."

"They might not have, except for me." Mama Dee shook her head again. "When I got back into town last night they told me my place was burned down and I told the police I'd be here if they needed to talk to me, and I told them Eudora was in Florida, and . . . well . . . that's how they found out. From me."

"So Frawley already knew that, this morning, when he called Dugan."

"What?"

"Just thinking out loud," she said. "Do you . . . uh . . . know why anyone would want to burn down your house?"

"I sure don't. Except there's been times I wanted to burn the rickety old place down myself. Hard to keep clean, things always needing fixing. Place like that takes a whole lotta hard work . . . and money."

Kirsten almost said the house looked in pretty good shape to her, then remembered no one should know she'd been there. "Does anyone, well, have a grudge against you or something?"

"Not as I know of. I keep to myself, except for the church and the ladies' group there. It's a Catholic church. My folks been Catholic for three generations. Eudora's not a churchgoer, but she's Catholic, too. I keep telling her she should have the twins bap—" She stopped. "Listen to me. How did I get off on that?"

"That's okay. Did the police say they have any leads?"

"The police haven't hardly said one word to me. Except Frawley pestering me about Eudora. I *am* s'posed to go out there tomorrow, when the state fire investigators are going through what's left. They said they'd probably have some things—"

"Mama Dee?" It was one of the twins, standing in the dining alcove.

"Yes, honey?"

"The Mary Poppins tape stopped playing. Must be busted."

"You mean *broken*," Mama Dee said.

"Yes ma'am. Broken."

"I'll be there in a minute, Jessica honey." She stood up.

Kirsten stood, too. "I should get to the police station, anyway," she said. "Oh, I don't have a car, do I?"

"You take Eudora's car," Mama Dee said, and gave her the keys. "Eudora can drive home, if they let her go."

"They'll probably keep her overnight in Kankakee and take her to court tomorrow. I think the judge'll let her go then. Anyway, I'll bring the keys back tonight." She paused. "Oh, one more thing. There's this little girl . . . Coral? Have you seen her to-day?"

"No, can't say as I have. Which is funny, come to think of it. I'd have thought she'd be right up here under us as soon as Eudora and the twins got home. She's got no family herself, not to speak of. How do you know her?"

"Oh, I just talked to her a couple of times. She's a sweet girl. Thought I'd stop and say hello to her. She lives across the street, right? The green house?"

"Yes, with that poor cousin of hers who's not much more than a child her own self. She's sure no one to take care of a child, not—"

"Mama Dee!" One of the twins was calling. "Come help us, pleeeease?"

"You better go," Kirsten said. "I'm on my way."

She grabbed her raincoat and automatically looked for her purse, then remembered she'd left it in the car. She hoped Dugan had locked it in the trunk, or at least hid it under the seat. Her gun was in it.

She also hoped she'd find Coral Hancock Stitch at home.

TWENTY-TWO

Eudora sat on the edge of the steel cot that stuck out from the wall and stared at her feet . . . but she did not cry. That was the most important thing. Oh, sure, she knew in one way it didn't really matter, since nobody with any sense would think bad of her for crying. But she had made a promise to herself in the police car: *She would not cry.*

Snatched away from her children, dragged barefoot like some damn animal through the rain, shoved this way and that at the police station . . . and finally hauled here to Kankakee and stuck in the lockup to face the night all by herself in this little cell. All that and still: *She would not cry.*

It wasn't to prove anything to Frawley and them. They didn't care, anyway. And she wasn't just being hardheaded, either, or none of that. It was because not crying was the thing that came to her mind, riding in the back of that police car. She knew she couldn't control what *they* did, or even what they made her do— all that *stand up, sit down, sign this, get over there* bullshit—same as the first time they arrested her. She had cried that time and had felt so hopeless. So this time when she tried to think of one thing she would not let them do to her, one place she would not let them touch, that's what she came up with: *She would not cry.*

And she didn't, dammit. Dugan was a big help, too. He yelled at the police a lot outside her house, and it seemed like he didn't really know what he was doing. But they sure as hell stopped dragging her, didn't they? And then he came to the police station and watched everything, not letting them keep him away from her like they wanted. He had calmed down some by then, but he didn't back off. Uh-uh. Kept saying he'd sue Frawley and the mayor and the whole town and everyone. Even when they put her in the squad car again to drive her here to Kankakee, he made sure they didn't put the handcuffs on too tight.

And even if it turned out that Dugan was wrong about what he told her would probably happen tomorrow, even if the judge *didn't* let her go, she'd still keep her promise to herself. She would not cry. Not even in the middle of the night. Fact is, she was glad she was so tired from the weekend—all that flying and changing planes and chasing after two five-year-olds. All she thought about driving home from the airport was how her and the girls would eat a little something and then go right to bed. How she'd have to send Coral home, because she'd be watching and be over there right away for sure.

Instead, there was Mama Dee, telling about her house getting burned up and the man getting killed and all. And Coral never did show up. They'd kept their trip a secret from her, so she wouldn't feel bad. Now maybe she was angry or . . . Anyway, Eudora had been dead on her feet even before the police came, and that was hours ago, and now she would surely sleep.

She lay down on the hard cot. It was too damn hot in here, but she was glad of that because she didn't wanna use the blanket. She didn't know who might've used it last and what kind of nasty germs might be on it. Damn, she wished they'd turn the light out, but she wasn't about to ask. She turned over on her other side.

She didn't have a watch, but it was probably only about seven or eight o'clock or something. Still, it surprised her that she couldn't go right to sleep. That bothered her and she noticed she was starting to shake a little, then fighting to keep from shaking, and then shaking a lot. All of a sudden she thought she *was* gonna cry, after all. Damn! She sat up again and thought up a list of things to say to herself in place of crying.

There were only two cells in this room and nobody in the other one, so she started reciting her list out loud: "Damn you, Chief Frawley," she said. "You're as fat as a pig." Hearing her own words made her mad, which was better than scared. "Damn the rest of you police, too; Galboa and everyone. So dumb you think it helps you to suck up to Frawley. And damn the mayor, too, and the village board, fightin' for a stupid mall 'cause some rich white man throwin' you a few scraps. And damn whoever you are took that cash money and called me on the—"

Wait a minute! The phone call?

No way! It couldn't be. That nasal white man's voice she didn't recognize, but had somehow sounded familiar. She could hear it in her mind again, right now. All of a sudden she knew why the whole house wasn't torn up looking for that money. She knew who it was stole it, and he would know where she had hid it. But why *him*?

Oh my God! Had somebody somehow found out her secret . . . and told? Could that have something to do with Mama Dee's house getting burned down and that man getting killed? Maybe she should tell Kirsten. But if she did . . . how much would she have to tell?

TWENTY-THREE

By the time Kirsten got to the police station, which was in the basement of the Miracle City village hall, it was nearly seven o'clock and Eudora had been processed and sent to Kankakee to spend the night in the lockup. Dugan said he was sure the judge would release her the next day. Kirsten wanted to go see her, give her some encouragement, but decided against it. She had something new on her mind . . . something more disturbing.

With Dugan following in the Camry, she drove Eudora's car away from the police station. The sun was going down, but the rain had finally stopped and the sky was clearing. She'd hardly gone two blocks when she pulled over and stopped. Dugan parked behind her, and she walked back to the Camry and got into the passenger seat.

"What's up?" he asked. "I thought we were returning Eudora's car."

"We were, but . . . we need to decide what to do." Actually, she'd just reached a decision, but she wanted to see if he agreed with her.

"What to do about what? We're going—" He stopped, then shifted around in the seat and stared at her. "Are you . . . okay?"

"I'm fine."

"Really. Well, you don't *look* fine. You look tired, beat up, discouraged. In fact, you look like—"

"Coral's missing."

"What?"

"I stopped at her house to see her before I went to the police station. She's not home. No one was there."

"That doesn't mean she's *missing*. Just because she's not home. I mean, maybe her mother . . . I mean her aunt—"

"Cousin. She lives with her cousin. Her name's Raynelle Johnson. I went back and asked Mama Dee. She says Eudora told her Raynelle just got a new job—Eudora didn't know where—and she works afternoons, like three to eleven or something. Eudora told her it's a shame how late the woman gets home every night."

"Who the hell takes care of Coral?"

"She gets herself up and off to school every day—when she goes—and gets most of her own meals. Mama Dee was surprised she wasn't at the door the minute Eudora got home this afternoon. She likes to play with the twins, but basically it's Eudora she clings to. Raynelle has legal custody, gets paid something by the state, but I take it she's not very . . . not parentally inclined."

"Jesus."

"The main thing is," Kirsten said, "she's not home."

"Maybe she was asleep, didn't hear you."

"No. I rang the doorbell, then pounded on the doors, front and back. I know she's not there. And why didn't she show up this afternoon at Eudora's?"

"We better go to the police."

"They'll just say the same kinds of things you said, that for all we know she's with her cousin or a baby-sitter." She paused. "Plus, what if they ask about when we last saw her or something else we don't want to answer?"

"Why would they think of that? We'll tell them Mama Dee was concerned because she hadn't seen Coral, and you went to check and there was no sign of her and you got worried, too. Maybe they can locate Raynelle." He put his hand on her shoulder. "Let's go. We have to report it. If something bad *were* to happen to her, and we hadn't reported it . . ."

So he *did* agree with her.

They left Eudora's car parked where it was and went back to the station. Galboa was the only one there. He said the cops all knew Coral and that she skipped school a lot and had run away at least once, but she showed up the next day and said she'd slept out in the woods. He didn't seem interested in helping, but he finally tried Raynelle's home number. Her phone was disconnected. Then he tried Frawley but couldn't reach him. Finally he said they'd keep an eye out for Coral; and they'd watch for Raynelle to come home, and check with her.

"That's all I can do for now," Galboa said. "I'm off at ten tonight. I mean I can't call in the state or the county when we don't even know if she's missing."

"Thanks, anyway," Kirsten said, and they left.

"Galboa's not that bad a guy, actually," Dugan said, "at least when Frawley's not around."

"I don't like him, no matter who's around."

When they got to the car, he went straight to the trunk, opened it, and took out her purse. "My, Grandma," he said, "what a heavy pistol you have!"

She took the purse from him without a word, and they got into the car. "I have to find Coral."

"But you have to find out, first, whether she's really missing. The cops will do that."

"Maybe they will and maybe they won't." She stared out the front window, not seeing anything. "I let her go home alone Saturday night, then didn't even check to be sure she'd gotten there."

"*We* let her go. Not just you. And *we* agreed we couldn't grab her and take her against her will."

121

"I could have tried harder to convince her. But no, I wanted her to feel she could trust us. I wanted her on our side, dammit, so I didn't do what I should have done . . . and now she's missing."

"You're not thinking straight." He started the car and pulled out of the lot. "We're going home. Tomorrow—"

"No. Take me to Eudora's car. You drive home. And when you come back for court tomorrow, come early and bring me a change of clothes." He didn't argue with her, and she was glad. "I'll stop and tell Mama Dee where Eudora is," she said. "There's a Motel Six on the interstate, just south of Kankakee. That's where I'll be. I'll leave my room number on a card on the dashboard, so you won't have to ask at the desk."

"And what will you do in the meantime?"

"Watch for Raynelle Johnson to come home, I guess. What else *can* I do?"

He pulled to the curb behind Eudora's car and she opened her door to get out, but he grabbed her arm. "I'll stay and wait with you and—"

"No. She'll be more cooperative if it's just me. Besides, we both need a fresh set of clothes." She knew she should give him something else to do, too, other than worry about her. "Plus, Parker Gillson may have dug up more about John Michael Hurley. You should call him when you get home. Except it'll be late, so maybe you should wait until morning. And oh, see if he knows anything about Hurley's three sons, too."

"Let's see if I can keep my assignments straight," he said. "One, I'm to go for clothes. Two, I'm to make a phone call— and with multiple questions to ask, at that." He still held her arm, and leaned and kissed her on the cheek. "Three, and most especially, I'm not to worry about the little woman."

"You're such a quick study," she said. She turned and kissed him back. This one was on the lips—and then beyond that.

Finally, she lifted his hand—oh, so reluctantly—from where it was inching up her thigh, and slipped out of the car.

By eight-thirty Kirsten was back on Till's Creek Road again, driving Eudora's car and wearing a dry pair of jeans and a sweater from Eudora's closet. Turned out she was right; the two of them wore the same size . . . except Eudora's jeans must have shrunk—just a smidge. Eudora's running shoes were a little tight, too, but without socks they were fine. She had her own clothes in a plastic bag and her raincoat draped over the seat beside her. Mama Dee had loaned her a flashlight from Eudora's kitchen, and she promised to stay up and call Kirsten on her cell phone as soon as she spotted Raynelle.

Kirsten thought of going to the other two houses on Raynelle's side of the street to see if anyone knew where she worked, but Mama Dee said Raynelle and her neighbors didn't get along well and they wouldn't know. Besides, Kirsten didn't want to get people talking. Coral's bicycle wasn't in either her front or back yard, which might mean only that it was inside the house. But maybe it was with Coral.

If Mama Dee was right, Raynelle wasn't due home until eleven, and Kirsten had two or three hours to kill. She drove through the dark all the way back to Mama Dee's burned-down house but didn't turn into the driveway. Instead, she drove right up to the barricade and got out of the car. There might have been enough room, between the left side of the barrier and a drop-off into the ditch, for her to drive around and get onto the dirt road Coral said was part of her shortcut. But barely.

She couldn't take a chance on getting the car stuck out here, though, miles from help, so she got her raincoat and purse from the car and went around the barricade on foot. The sky had cleared and the moon and stars were out, but . . . at night, after a long, hard rain, the chance of her finding any sign of Coral was about zero. Still, she had to try. What else was there to do?

Besides, it wasn't some footprint or shred of clothing she was looking for. It was a bicycle . . . or a little girl.

TWENTY-FOUR

By the time he was back on I-57, Dugan had made up his mind, and he was paying close attention as he drove.

Damn, there *was* a Motel 6, just this side of Kankakee, visible from the road. How the hell did Kirsten remember that? He'd driven the same route she had, the same number of times, and he had no idea what motels were there. He wondered if she remembered the Arby's just beyond the motel, and then the shopping mall past that. He wouldn't have bet against her.

By nine o'clock he was sitting on the edge of the bed in a room at the motel. He could have called Kirsten and told her where he was, but he'd already made one call she might not like, so why make it two? Instead, he tapped out Parker Gillson's number. His suit was on a hanger on the shower rod in the bathroom, wet and wrinkled as hell. He'd found an Abercrombie & Fitch in the nearby mall and had taken just fifteen minutes to outfit himself and get the hell out of there. He hated shopping in the first place, and it hadn't helped to realize that he was the oldest one in the store, by five years, easy.

He had Kirsten's sizes written down, and he used his favorite technique for buying clothes for her. That meant pointing at the nearest mannequin that looked casual and classy and asking for one of each item. He let the clerk pick out the underwear on her own. Simple. All you needed was a sys—

"Hello?" It was Park.

Dugan gave his name, then braced himself for what he knew was coming.

"Hey, man," Park said, "we don't get to chat often enough." Actually, once a decade would have been more than enough. Frequent contact with a senior investigator for the attorney disciplinary system could be hazardous to his law practice. ". . . see today's *Law Bulletin?*" Park was saying, referring to Chicago's daily paper for lawyers.

"Missed it," Dugan lied. "Much too busy."

"Take a look at the story about how we're gonna get Zane Preeble's license yanked. Man has a string of ambulance chasers as long as your arm, and we're finally gonna be able to prove it."

"Congratulations," he said, wishing Park wouldn't always keep bringing up the same topic. "But I called because—"

"You should be happy." Park chuckled, and Dugan—as always—wondered just how much he knew about Dugan's police officers. "We pull the tickets of those bums who pay to get cases, and it evens the playing field for the rest of you guys."

"Really?" He knew he should shut up, but . . . "And what about the big firms? I hear the annual golf outing Brynston, Carey, and Vogel sponsors for members of the Illinois Medical Society is next week. You should check it out. Tell them you're a neurosurgeon and get a choice of tee times. Have your picture taken with Tiger Woods. Sign up to win a set of Arnold Palmer irons. During cocktails they'll describe their firm's aggressive new approach to squashing malpractice claims. Then dinner and dancing to a live orches—"

"Dugan?"

"Yeah?"

"You call for any particular reason?"

So they talked about multimillionaire John Michael Hurley and his three sons. Park would send a detailed report about Hurley himself. The oldest son, Jack, the one who hated his father, was a professor at the University of Illinois and was twice divorced. The youngest, Tommy, a sociopathic ex-con who got along with no one, was employed by one of his father's companies. The job apparently didn't include doing any work, but at least he seemed to be living up to the terms of his probation. Kieran, the middle son, had been a priest eleven years. He'd been assigned to a South Side parish about half that time and also worked at a local community center, putting on plays with mostly poor black kids. Then his order transferred him to somewhere down near St. Louis, to help run a combination monastery, farm, and home for elderly clergy. His recently diagnosed brain tumor was malignant and inoperable.

He didn't have many details on any of the three sons, Park admitted, but he wanted to be sure Dugan told Kirsten he'd keep digging.

"Don't worry, I will," Dugan said. "I know how much she appreciates your taking time from leveling all those playing fields and . . ." But Park had hung up.

Park would do anything for Kirsten, and with good reason. When he'd finally drunk himself down to the very bottom and dropped out of sight a few years ago, she'd searched long and hard and finally found him facedown in a filthy, stinking bug-infested flat near Belmont and Halsted. He'd had more alcohol than white blood cells packed into his circulatory system, and the filth and stink and bugs were mostly clinging to the open sores on his wasted body. He'd have died, for sure, except for Kirsten. She claimed all she did was haul him to the hospital and that it was he who saved his own life—and was still saving it every day—by sticking with each step of his recovery program.

Kirsten's disclaimers notwithstanding, Park would do anything for her. Dugan figured that that was the thirteenth step in his program.

He went to the desk to explain that Kirsten was on her way and wouldn't be expecting him to be there yet, so they should tell her what room he was in and give her a key. "She uses her own last name, but we *are* married, so . . ." He stopped explaining. The polite young man at the desk couldn't care less.

Then Dugan headed back toward Miracle City.

He stopped first in front of Eudora's house. Eudora's car wasn't there, so he drove up and down the nearby streets but didn't see it anywhere. He went back to see if there was any car in the driveway at Raynelle Johnson's house—Coral's house—but there wasn't. No lights on, either, and no sign of anyone at home. He saw no reason to bother Mama Dee, so he drove away.

The only business he found open, besides the town's two taverns, was a Quik Mart, a twenty-four-hour gas station and food store, where a squad car sat near the entrance. Eudora's car was nowhere in sight.

So where would Kirsten have gone? With Raynelle not due home until eleven or something, she'd have been antsy, worried about Coral. All he could think of was that she might drive out to Mama Dee's place and see what she could find. It would be past ten by the time he could get out there, though, and by then she'd be headed this way again.

Back at the Quik Mart the squad car was gone. He filled the tank of the Camry and went inside to pay cash. He got coffee and a couple of ham-and-cheese sandwiches at the deli counter and took them back to the car.

He'd meet Kirsten at Coral's house at eleven.

TWENTY-FIVE

At about nine-forty-five Kirsten was back behind the wheel in Eudora's car, facing the barricade at the end of Till's Creek Road. She stared down at the card she'd set on the seat beside her. It was one of her own Wild Onion, Ltd., business cards. It was the card she'd given to Coral.

Earlier, when she'd started walking and looking for any trace of Coral, the three-quarter moon had been so bright that she hadn't needed the flashlight to see her way. Leftover shreds of storm clouds raced across the sky, throwing eerie, fleeting shadows as they crossed the moon. It hadn't been that windy on the ground, though, and the air was crisp and cool and laced with . . . well . . . farm odors.

Just as Coral said, the dirt road was smooth and flat and would have made for easy bike riding. Kirsten was tempted to break into a run but didn't want to miss any paths leading away from the road. About a hundred yards past the barricade the weeds on both sides were replaced with plowed fields and long straight rows of tiny shoots—showing pale white against the ground in the darkness, but certainly green in the daylight.

In less than thirty minutes, maybe two miles, she'd reached a T in the road. To the right was a gravel road; to the left, more of the same hard-packed dirt tracks. Straight ahead was a barbed-wire fence and what she guessed was a cow pasture. She figured Miracle City to be off to her left, so that's the way she'd gone. In another half mile the dirt road ended abruptly, but a footpath angled off toward a row of trees. Within the trees was a stream and a cinder path, which must have been the bike path Coral had mentioned.

It was on the bike path that she'd finally started running and had come quickly to a blacktopped highway. The stream ran through a culvert under the road, but the bike path didn't pick up on the other side. She thought the road must lead back to Miracle City and would have followed it for a while, but she couldn't tell whether to go right or left. She decided to go back to the car.

It was after she'd turned around and gone maybe ten yards that she spotted something off to the side of the path, something metallic, reflecting the moonlight. She walked closer. It was the handlebar of a bicycle, and she had to force herself to keep going, terrified of what she'd find.

It was only a bike, though, lying in the weeds behind a ragged bush. Not very well hidden, really, although certainly not visible from the road.

Coral's bike, for sure. She crouched beside it. There was a small white card jammed between the coils of one of the springs under the seat, where it would have been protected from rain.

Now she sat in the car by the barricade and tried to stay calm. She'd left the bike where it was, hadn't touched it, had taken only the card that lay now on the seat beside her. WILD ON-ION, LTD., *Confidential Inquiries—Personal Security Services.*

That's what it said on the front of the card, along with her phone and fax numbers.

But she was staring down at the back of the card, and at the two little dark splotches there. She believed they were blood, believed they were a message for her, even believed she knew the meaning of the message.

She backed the car away from the barricade, all the way to Mama Dee's driveway, and turned around. That's when the cell phone rang.

It was Mama Dee. "I been watching out the window, you know," she said, "and, well, I didn't know if I should bother you, but—"

"Is it Raynelle? Did she come home?"

"No. It's a man, in a car. He keep drivin' up and down the street real slow, you know?"

"What man? What kind of car?"

"Hard to tell at night, but looks like the same car you was in this afternoon with that big, loud-talking man. Fact is, looks like the same *man*."

"Don't worry about it," Kirsten said. "You just go on to bed. I'm coming back there, and I'll watch for Raynelle."

She broke the connection, thought a minute as she drove, then tapped out Dugan's cell phone number.

"Hello?" he said.

"I thought you were gonna go get us some dry clothes."

"I did," he said.

"No way. You haven't had time." She couldn't keep the anger out of her voice. "I know just where you—"

"Hey, are we talking code here? I mean because we don't trust cell phones? So 'dry clothes' means—"

"Stop it, Dugan," she said. "Driving around town like you are, you probably have the entire Miracle City police force on the alert."

"Which is what? Two cars? Let me check." There was a pause, and she heard a siren over the phone. "Look at that," he said, "I think you're right."

"What're you talk—"

"Gotta hang up now," he said. And he did.

She didn't call back. He obviously had other things on his mind, and besides, she was mad as hell at him for getting in the way, maybe killing her chance of talking to Raynelle.

She drove back to town and decided to go past the police station on her way to Raynelle's . . . and was glad she did. The little parking area was crowded. There were two squad cars, her own Camry, and a white Camaro that had seen better days.

She went in the side entrance of the building and down the steps. Through the window in the door that said *POLICE DE-PARTMENT*, she saw Dugan and Galboa, both perched on the edges of gray steel desks on the police side of a waist-high railing that cut the little room in two, drinking from paper cups, neither one facing the door.

They seemed on friendly terms, but she wanted to be sure. The door was open a crack and she stepped close to it to listen.

". . . for sure." Dugan was saying. "Always lotsa horny chicks around colleges, man. Young, hot chicks, with—"

"Plus, there's this Hooters, man," Galboa cut in, "in Champaign, by the university? They got waitresses there got jugs out to here, man. And they ain't supposed to, y'know, but some of 'em, if they know you're a big tipper, they'll kinda lean over, y'know, or even brush one of them big, bouncin' globes against—"

She pushed through the door and they both jumped up and spun around, Dugan spilling coffee on what looked to her like a brand-new shirt. "I thought you were off at ten, officer," she said.

"Yes, ma'am. But . . . things came up."

She didn't like Galboa. Even the way he said "Yes, ma'am" sounded phony. "Have you found Coral?" she asked.

"Sorry, ma'am, that's police business."

Her heart beat faster, from fear for Coral . . . and from anger at both these men. "What the hell are you two—"

"Raynelle's here," Dugan said. "Back with Chief Frawley, in his office."

She started through the swinging gate in the railing, but a door slammed and Frawley came around a corner. "Galboa!" His fat face was turning red. "What's this civilian doing on the police side of the railing?"

"Sorry, Chief. We was just—"

"My fault," Dugan cut in. "I didn't realize I shouldn't be on this side and the officer was just telling me to go back. Sorry." He pushed through the gate and she had to back up as he did. "It's okay," he told her, his voice very low, "sort of. I'll explain."

"Miss Raynelle Johnson will be going home pretty soon," Frawley said, looking straight at Kirsten. "And if either of you attempt to contact her in any way, about anything, you'll be arrested and charged with interfering with a police investigation. You'll spend the rest of the goddamn night with that Ragsdale girl. The fucking *week*, if it's up to me."

"But what about Coral?" Kirsten stepped toward Frawley. "Where—"

"That's not your business," Frawley said. "Now I want both of you outta my sight, and outta this town. I swear I'll have you locked up if that's what it takes."

"But we haven't done anything. We're not interfering with—"

"Call it disturbing the peace. Call it whatever the hell you want. You got three seconds to move, dammit."

They moved.

She went straight to Eudora's car without even looking at

Dugan. Because of him she wouldn't be able to talk to Raynelle, and she was so mad at him she really didn't care what he did. But he followed her in her car to Eudora's house, where she parked in the driveway and shoved Eudora's keys through the mail slot. She walked back to the Camry, got into the passenger seat, and slammed the door—hard.

They drove in silence until finally Dugan said, "Do you want to hear what—"

"No." She could hardly breathe, she was so angry. "If you hadn't interfered, they wouldn't have seen you, and I would have gotten to talk to Raynelle and maybe I'd have found out . . . Damn! Just forget it, okay? I don't want to talk."

"You're tired."

"I thought I said I don't want to talk. Can't you ever—"

"Kirsten," he said, "shut up." His voice was low and firm.

She was so stunned she couldn't have spoken if she'd tried.

"I'm sorry," he said. "I never said that to you before and I hope I never do again. But you're making me mad. Just listen, god-dammit." He was driving so fast they were out on the highway already. "Please," he added.

"Okay."

"Thank you." She was deliberately not looking at him, but she heard him sigh. "What I was trying to tell you was that—"

"Wait," she said, and she did turn toward him then, but he was staring straight ahead through the windshield.

"Wait *why*, dammit?"

"Wait . . . because I'm sorry. I'm getting the feeling I was wrong about what I thought happened, and about whether it was your fault."

"Oh." He paused. "So . . . did you hear me tell you back there that it's okay, sort of?"

"I . . . yes, I guess I did, but—"

"I meant Coral's alive, and not hurt. The thing is, she's in police custody. I got that out of Galboa. He wasn't supposed to tell anyone and he's sure Frawley'd fire him if he knew he told me."

"Police custody? What police? Where? Why?"

"State troopers. In Kankakee, probably. She was picked up after she left us Saturday night. I guess they stopped a speeder and then spotted her. Walking, Galboa said. I don't know what happened to her bike. They were taking her home, when calls started coming in about the fire, and then about the body. Somewhere along the line they decided she'd probably been out at Mama Dee's and might know something."

"What has she told them?"

"I don't know. I had to take it easy with Galboa. I couldn't just openly interrogate him. I got the impression, though, that she hasn't been cooperative. Apparently, her cousin Raynelle hasn't been any help in dealing with her."

"Coral's tough." Kirsten closed her eyes. "Let me think for a minute, okay?"

"Sure." They were on the interstate and he switched lanes. "There's the Motel Six, anyway."

"No," she said. "We better go home. I need a change of clothes, and—"

"Aha! And of course you think I don't know how to follow orders, right?" He was grinning now. He told her about the clothes he'd bought, and his phone call to Parker Gillson, while he drove to the motel.

When they got to their room she explained how she'd found Coral's bike. "She must have known they saw her, so she hid her bike and . . . and left a message." She showed him the drops of blood on the card. "She swore she wouldn't say anything to anyone. 'A blood oath,' is what she said. I think . . . well, I think she pricked her finger and left the card to assure me she'd keep her promise."

"Jesus."

"I bet she hasn't spoken one tiny word about what happened."

135

Kirsten crawled into bed while Dugan was still in the shower. She was so tired she could hardly move, but couldn't fall asleep. She was facing the wall when she heard him come out of the bathroom and felt the bed sag as he sat on it. She waited a long time, but he didn't move.

"You just gonna sit there?" she finally asked.

"I thought you were asleep already. I was wondering if I should wake you up to . . . well . . . to tell you I'm sorry, for what I said."

"You mean for telling me to shut up." She rolled over and grabbed him from behind around the waist. "Don't worry. I already forgot about it."

"Good," he said, and leaned backward until he was lying on his back on top of her, crosswise.

"However," she said, wriggling out from under him, "what's this crap about colleges and young, hot chicks? And waitresses with jugs out to there that lean over and rub—"

"All part of my interrogation technique," he said. "When in Rome, y'know, you gotta talk Roman . . . or Italian or something. So we were talking macho-guy talk." He kissed her on the cheek and turned over. "And you were right. Galboa's sort of a bastard."

She thought a minute and decided she loved him more than ever, even if he *had* told her to shut up. Plus, worn out and worried as she was, she suddenly felt as young and horny as any of those college chicks. She reached for him, but he'd wrapped himself in the sheet and . . . damn!

He was asleep already, the creep.

TWENTY-SIX

The hearing Tuesday, on the state's attorney's motion to revoke Eudora's I-bond and keep her in custody until trial, went pretty much as Dugan thought it would. Judge Harold Jones told Eudora that her leaving the state without permission, even for a prepaid trip to Disney World with her children, was "reckless and inexcusable."

Then he excused her and denied the motion.

"This Court is cognizant of the fact," the judge said, "that this is the defendant's first interaction with the criminal justice system and finds that the defendant's fear that a request for judicial relief would be denied was understandable under the circumstances, albeit misplaced. That being said, I must admonish the defendant that this Court will not tolerate additional violations of its orders. Requests for deviations from the terms of defendant's bond should be presented to this Court, through defendant's counsel, and will be given due consideration." He leaned forward over the bench. "In other words, my dear, go on home. And the next time you need something, just ask."

"Thank you, Judge," Eudora said, and Dugan decided he'd better withdraw their jury demand and let Judge Jones decide this case on his own.

After court, the three of them got into Kirsten's Camry to head for Miracle City. Dugan took the backseat for himself so he could stretch his legs the width of the car if he wanted. They were passing a McDonald's a few blocks from the courthouse and he was surprised when Kirsten abruptly turned in, then more surprised when she pulled into the drive-through lane that began at the rear of the building.

"I suppose if we eat in the car," he said, "we'll save time."

"I never go in these things," Eudora said.

Dugan was amazed. "You don't like McDonald's?"

"McDonald's is okay," she answered. "I guess."

"Actually," Kirsten said, "you can get a fairly nutritious and low-fat meal. Of course, you have to order carefully."

"Which means," Dugan said, "you can't order the stuff everybody—including me—always orders."

"It's not the food I'm talking about," Eudora said. "It's the drive-through. I mean, like now, there's five or six cars ahead of us before we can even make our order."

"Drive-throughs can be handy, though," Kirsten said. She pulled forward in the line and they got to the corner of the building.

"Maybe," Eudora said. "But since I got involved with CREW and started reading a lot of environmental stuff, I've stayed away from them."

Kirsten kept looking in the rearview mirror and Dugan turned around to see what had her attention. What he saw were about six or seven teenagers crammed into the car behind them, bouncing the whole vehicle to the beat of some music he was probably happy he couldn't hear. "Good thing we're not trapped behind that bunch," Dugan said. "This is exactly the sort of drive-through I don't like. Once you're in line you've got a wall on one side and a high curb on the other and you can't get out, no matter how slow the line moves. Drives me nuts."

"But the bad part is," Eudora said, "you end up with all these cars sitting in line for five or ten minutes or more, with their motors running. It wastes gas and creates an awful lot of unnecessary pollution."

"I agree entirely," Kirsten said. By this time she was pulling up beside the intercom to place their order. "But like I said, they can be handy."

The intercom squawked with static that probably meant, "Can I help you?"

"One coffee, black," Kirsten said. "That's all."

"What?" Dugan said.

"Second window," the squawk said.

The car in front of them was just leaving the first window, and Kirsten pulled past that window and the second one, too, and kept right on going. To get out on the street she took a left that Dugan thought was a little overconfident, considering the traffic coming on from both directions, and then turned right at the next corner.

"You're not a McDonald's fan, and I've never seen you use a drive-through lane," Dugan said. "But I think I know now what you meant by them being handy sometimes."

"Right," Kirsten said. By this time she'd driven around the block and was pulling into an Amoco station across the street from the McDonald's they'd just left. She ignored the gas pumps and parked near a public phone. "Handy sometimes."

"What are you two talking about?" Eudora asked. "Handy?"

"Uh-huh," Kirsten said, "especially when the guy that's been following you is hungry enough—and dumb enough—to get himself trapped two cars back, in a slow-moving line."

"A man?" Eudora seemed at a loss and Dugan didn't blame her at all. "He's following us?"

"No," Kirsten said. "He *was* following us. At least he had enough sense to realize he'd lost us, and he might as well eat his lunch. See? A red Camaro." She pointed. "Those teenagers took a long time, and he's just now picking up his food at the service window. I suppose at this distance it's hard to tell if you've ever seen him before."

"Actually, I *can* tell," Eudora said. She was leaning forward, peering through the windshield. "I've seen him before, all right. He's the one stole the money outta my freezer, then called me on the phone."

"Wait a minute," Dugan said. "You said you had no idea at all who did it and didn't see anyone, dammit." He didn't like clients holding out on him. "You said it was a white man's voice on the phone. What the hell kinda games are you—"

"Relax, Dugan." Kirsten pulled out onto the street, and despite how mad he was, he noticed that now it was they who were tailing the red Camaro. "Why not stop for a breath," she said, "and let Eudora explain?"

"Bullshit." He sat back. "How the hell can I help a client who lies to me? I mean, she—"

"Look here, man." Eudora was suddenly right up in his face, twisted around in her seat, poking a finger at him. "Don't you be callin' me no damn liar!" He hadn't heard that cold tone, or seen that fury on her face, since she'd stood ready for Chief Frawley with a baseball bat.

"Well," he said, "I know you—"

"You don't know nothin', man. You don't know one goddamn thing about . . ." Then all at once she stopped, pulled back her hand. She turned around and slumped down in her seat. "I . . . I'm sorry," she said. "It's . . . I guess sometimes I forget where I'm at."

"My fault," he said. "Maybe I'm hungry or something."

"Let's start over," Kirsten said. "But first . . . you're certain, Eudora? You know who that man is?"

"For sure. He was my boyfriend when . . . when I came up pregnant with the twins." Her voice was very soft, almost a whisper, as though she were speaking to herself. "I nearly married that boy."

"Well," Kirsten said, "he's about to head north on the interstate, and I don't see any reason to follow him if we know who he is. Let's go to a *real* restaurant and get some lunch."

They went past an Applebee's and a Denny's, neither of which Dugan thought was any more 'real' a restaurant than McDonald's—although he'd have been happy to stop at either one of them—and finally found sort of a deli place that had corned-beef sandwiches.

They ordered at the counter. Eudora got a chili dog and said she'd never eaten a corned-beef sandwich in her life, which he found startling. There were only a couple of tables and no privacy at all, so they took their sandwiches and drinks back to the car. It was a beautiful warm day and they sat with all the windows open and ate their lunches.

And he decided to shut up and let Eudora talk.

He sat in the backseat behind Kirsten, and Eudora leaned back against the passenger side door and faced them both. She set her half-eaten chili dog on a napkin on the dashboard and sipped some diet Pepsi through a straw. "I really didn't lie to you, y'know?"

"We believe you," Kirsten said. Dugan wasn't quite so sure, but he nodded his agreement.

"First off," Eudora said, "I didn't know who it was. I told you it *sounded* like a white man's voice but familiar, too, somehow. Now I know why. Clyborn—that's his name, Clyborn Settles—and he and I were in plays together in high school. He was a good actor, too. I mean he could play old people, people with different accents, all that. Anyway, we got to be friends. Course, Clyborn, he kept wantin' to . . . you know . . . be more than just friends." She stopped and gave them an inquiring look.

"We get the picture," he said, and didn't blame Clyborn one bit.

"I liked him, too, pretty much, but I just . . . for a long time I never . . ." Her voice trailed off. "Anyway, when I got pregnant it was twins, and I didn't want them not to have a daddy and I asked Clyborn what're you gonna do and he said he'd go ahead and marry me, but . . . well . . . I could see that wasn't gonna work out, so one day—after the girls were born—I told him I wasn't gonna go ahead with it." She stared down at the soft-drink cup she held cradled in both hands in her lap. "He was glad, I could tell. We split up, and I haven't seen him now in maybe two, three years."

She didn't say anything for a while, and Dugan finally couldn't wait. "So, is that it? Based on a voice on the phone you didn't recognize at the time you heard it, now you're saying he's the one who stole the money? That doesn't make a whole lotta—"

"Dugan," Kirsten said, "relax, will you? Let her take her time."

"It just came to me last night," Eudora said, "when I was locked up and couldn't sleep and everything was going through my mind. I *know* it was him on the phone, for sure. And it's not just the voice. I wondered why whoever took that money didn't tear up the place looking for it. But if someone told Clyborn there was money in the house, he'd know right where to look for it. He'd know, because he's the one told me the freezer was the best place to hide stuff. Back when I was pregnant, he had got hold of some pot and he brought it to me to hide for him, and I said my aunt would find it and she would kill me. He said put it in the freezer, way in the back. And I did, and my aunt never did find it, and he came back in a few days and it was still there." She sipped more of her drink. "So he knew where the money would be."

"Eudora," Dugan said, "the freezer is about the first place *any* crook looks in *any* house for money hidden away."

"It is?" She was looking at Kirsten, as though she might disagree.

"I think he's right," Kirsten said. "That or the toilet tank."

"Doesn't matter." Eudora shook her head. "It was him on the phone, so it was him took the money."

"That's not enough," Dugan said. "At least not to prove it to a judge."

"No," Kirsten said, "but it's enough for me. We know he's involved somehow in this business. His following us from the courthouse today proves it." She started the car. "We should get moving and get you home to your kids."

"Wait a minute," Dugan said. "Who told him you had some money hidden in your house? It's obvious the theft was intended to discredit you because of your fight against that mall. So what's Clyborn got to do with that?"

"I been thinking about that since last night," she said, "and . . ." She lowered her head and swished the drink around in her cup.

"And what?" He leaned toward her. "What were you going to say?"

"I was . . . I was gonna say I don't know why, and I miss my girls and I wanna go home now."

"But dammit, Eudora, you—"

"Let it go, Dugan," Kirsten said, and he did, because there were tears running down Eudora's cheeks, and she was wiping at them with her hands.

TWENTY-SEVEN

Eudora's tears seemed honest tears, and she certainly seemed like an honest person to Kirsten. So, even though it was clear she'd stopped short of telling them everything she might have, Kirsten decided not to push her right then and changed the subject.

"You said you don't always lock your doors."

"Yeah, I know it's stupid, but—"

"What about Mama Dee? Does she always lock hers? Like on Friday, when you picked up the kids and she followed you into town?"

"Probably. It's hard to . . . Oh, wait. Yes. I mean I was the last one out the door, and she was in the yard. She reminded me, and I locked it myself."

Kirsten couldn't think of anything else just then, so she just drove on to Eudora's home. When they got there they'd barely had time to say hello to Mama Dee and the twins, when Mama Dee said Eudora's boss had called and said she was fired because she didn't show up for work at the video store that day.

"That's good," Kirsten said. "I was ready to tell you to take some time off. There's way too much going on right now."

"But how will I pay you?" Eudora asked. "I mean, do you think Mr. Candle will keep on advancing—"

"Oh, he'd be happy to keep helping," Kirsten said, which wasn't *exactly* a lie. "You'll talk to Larry, won't you Dugan?"

"Absolutely. And don't bother calling him, Eudora. I think he's gonna be extra busy at the office."

"Anyway," Kirsten said, "you have the kids to worry about and Mama Dee here'll be busy with her house and insurance and things, and I'll need you available to—" A car door slammed outside and she looked out the window. "Oh, one other thing. Dugan told me this morning that he called a friend of his."

"Actually," Dugan said, "more a friend of Kirsten's. I wouldn't want people to think—"

"Someone both of us know and trust. He's going to be, well, watching over you all for the next few days. He's here now."

"Watching over us?" Mama Dee moved to the window and looked out. "Like a bodyguard?"

They all swarmed around the window then—Eudora and Mama Dee and the twins, and she and Dugan, too—and peered out at the man leaning against the side of a Chevy Blazer at the curb.

"Oooo-eee," one of the twins cried. "Lookit him!"

"Hush, child," Mama Dee said. "But he sure is kinda big, ain't he, and kinda mean lookin', too."

"His name's Radovich," Kirsten said, "and I guess I wouldn't call him just 'kinda big.' " Actually, Cuffs Radovich was a huge rectangle of a man who made the Blazer look insubstantial, as though it might flip over on its side if he actually leaned too hard against it.

"And I wouldn't just call him 'kinda mean lookin', 'either," Eudora said.

Cuffs had dark, deep-set eyes and a face full of angular creases and lines—none of them looked like laugh lines—and a shaggy, drooping mustache like a walrus. Kirsten had asked him once if his ancestors were Gypsies, and all he'd said was he hated Gypsies—which didn't answer the question, of course. Today he wore black shoes, black pants, and a long black raincoat hanging open over a gray sweatshirt. On his head was a sort of Swiss mountaineer's hat that was green and a little too small and would have made the ordinary man look silly. It made Cuffs look like he didn't give a goddamn what anyone thought about how he looked—which Kirsten thought was not quite the truth.

He neither nodded nor waved, merely crossed his arms across his chest and stared back at all of them, clustered in the window, with a look on his face that seemed to say he despised them. Kirsten had come to believe, though, that it meant that these people he'd been hired to watch over would turn out to be the sort who would never be decent or honorable or tell the truth if it were the least bit inconvenient to them. In other words, as far as he was concerned, they'd be like pretty much everyone else in his world.

She felt sorry for Cuffs, but she trusted him to follow through on his word, too, as much as she trusted Dugan or herself. Maybe more than herself. "He'll pretty much stay out of your way," she said. "Probably sleep in his car, if he ever sleeps—which I doubt. He'll need a house key, though."

"Of course," Mama Dee said. "Even a man don't sleep needs a bathroom."

They went outside and she made introductions. The family all called him "Mr. Radovich," and he, although his usual surly self, immediately convinced them somehow that they were incompetent, if not very friendly, hands and they'd be better off doing whatever he told them to do.

The twins seemed especially fascinated by him, whispering to each other and giggling, and then running back to the house to get something they wanted to show him.

He stared after them, then turned to Eudora and Mama Dee.

146

"The deal is you do what I say. If you don't," he said, "that's your problem, and I don't give a shit. But if that happens, and if anyone gets hurt because of it—even them two little girls—it won't be my goddamn fault and I won't waste one fucking minute feeling bad about it."

The only thing that surprised Kirsten about his statement was that he hadn't made it with the twins standing right there. Maybe he was mellowing. When the girls came back they had a Munsters videotape and asked him if he wanted to watch it. He scowled and said no . . . but at least he didn't crush the box.

Half an hour later Kirsten and Dugan were headed for Chicago. She was having second thoughts and told him so. "Not so much about your calling Cuffs in," she explained, "but . . . maybe we shouldn't have sprung him on them so suddenly, you know?"

"That's always the problem," he said. "How do you *ease* Cuffs Radovich into someone's life?" He paused. "It'd be like easing a tub of tarantulas into a bridge party. You try to explain, 'No, really, they *never* bite—almost.' And pretty soon there's no party."

"Did you warn him the clients were black? I mean you know how he feels about—"

"Yes, I told him. And yes, I know how he feels. About the same as he feels about Asians and Arabs and Jews, not to mention his take on 'those fucking micks on both ends of Ireland.' Who the hell *does* he like? Not women. Not people in authority, either—cops, clergy, elected offi—"

"Okay, okay!" she said. "I give."

"He does kinda dig *you*, though."

"Which I won't put on my résumé," she said. "So forget Cuffs. Let's figure out who framed Eudora and burned down Mama Dee's house and killed that guy under the cellar doors."

"And tried to kill you and me."

"You, anyway. I'm still not sure they tried to kill me."

"Fine," he said. "Tried to just . . . braise you a bit?"

"Whatever. Let's figure out who it is."

But by the time she dropped him at his office, they hadn't figured out who . . . or even why.

TWENTY-EIGHT

By five o'clock that same afternoon, Tuesday, Kirsten had called a cop she used to work with, who'd helped her find Clyborn Settles, or at least the address the red Camaro he'd just purchased was registered to. She called Dugan's office and asked Mollie to tell him she didn't know what time she'd be home. Mollie probably knew why she didn't want to talk to Dugan directly. He'd just want to know where she was going and want to go with her.

The old, familiar dilemma. She wanted his help, wanted him around. At the same time she needed her freedom, no one telling her what to do, not dependent on anyone. Oh, maybe the occasional freelancer like Cuffs Radovich, when she couldn't be in two places at once. Otherwise, though, on her own.

With time to kill before dark, she sat in her tiny office and would have stared out the window, if there'd been a window. Instead, she stared at a painting she'd bought a few weeks ago at a neighborhood art fair. She'd come across a woman she'd run with in college, showing some lovely watercolors—which was a surprise because the woman had spent her student years partying and studying with equal intensity, with an MBA as her goal. One of her paintings in particular had struck Kirsten. It was a

149

view looking out through an old-fashioned screen door and down the length of a narrow porch toward some distant, hazy woods. It seemed exciting—as though luring the viewer out the door toward some journey—yet also hauntingly sad, lonely.

The price seemed quite high and she asked the woman, who looked happier and more at peace than she ever had in school, whether she actually made a living through her art.

"Oh God, no!" The woman laughed. "My husband's the sort that can't seem to help but make money. I've got two kids and a nanny and hours of time to spend on my painting. If I hadn't met Jerry and learned to let him take care of me, I'd never have discovered my true passion. I've studied in France and the Netherlands and . . ." She went on and on and sure didn't seem to be faking it.

Now, staring at the painting, Kirsten wondered how a person could be true to her own dreams, and also totally dependent on someone else to carry them out. She herself wasn't even comfortable with Dugan's having called Cuffs without asking her.

Yes, it made sense to bring Cuffs in; and yes, she'd been considering it herself. But still, it bothered her. It was *she* who owned Wild Onion, Ltd. Eudora was *her* client. She enjoyed having Dugan help her, but—

The phone rang.

She let the machine answer, and it was Dugan. "Hey, it's me. Are you there?" She didn't answer. "Damn," he said. "Well, if you retrieve this before I see you, call and let me know when you'll be home. I . . . uh . . . I was gonna ask where you were going. I'd have gone with you."

She thought about hitting the button to answer, but then he hung up.

At eight-fifteen she was sitting in the Camry on the South Side, near Seventy-ninth and Jefferey Boulevard, down the block from the six-flat where Clyborn Settles lived. According to the directory in the little foyer, he had the first floor north. A while ago she'd pressed the buzzer beside his name, quite a few times, but there was no answer. Faint light showed through drapes drawn across his apartment windows, and she'd decided to go back to the car and wait. If she saw him come home, she'd try to talk to him; if he was already home, and came out, she'd follow him.

It seemed a quiet, mostly middle-class neighborhood. There were lots of three- and six-flat apartment buildings on that particular block, though, and she'd been lucky that the only place she'd found to park was one where she could watch the front of the building. It was past dark, a chilly evening and threatening rain, and not many kids or teenagers went by. Lots of adults did, though. Most of them hurried along, paying no apparent attention to parked cars. Still, as time passed, she felt more and more conspicuous. There may have been a handful of other white persons within a square-mile area, but probably none of them a woman who'd been sitting in her car at the curb for more than an hour.

Her cell phone rang. She answered and it was Dugan. "Where are you?"

"Working," she said. "Go ahead and eat without me. There's leftover pizza in the refrigerator."

"I'm not calling about eating. I've been watching the news and—"

"Damn!" she said. Clyborn had just stepped out the door of his building. "Can't talk now. Gotta go."

"Wait!"

"Gotta go," she repeated, and broke the connection.

She was parked on the east side of the southbound one-way street, which put the driver's seat—and her—directly beside the sidewalk. Clyborn was walking in her direction. She leaned way over to her right, pretending to search through the glove compartment. He went right on by.

She sat up and her phone rang again. Instead of answering, she turned it off. "Sorry," she said, knowing it had to be Dugan again, and got out of the car to follow Clyborn.

He was tall and nicely put together and sporting a wide-brimmed fedora and a gray—or maybe light-blue—knee-length coat that had sort of a shine to it under the streetlights. The metal taps on his heels clicked on the sidewalk, and so did the tip of his slim umbrella.

He turned west on Seventy-seventh Street and she hung back, waiting at the corner. Maybe he was headed for the bars and clubs along Stony Island Avenue, a few blocks farther west. Maybe she should have just stopped him on the street and told him she wanted to talk to him. Maybe lots of things, but for sure she didn't want to wander the streets of the South Side on foot very far, following this dandy who twirled his umbrella as though he were Fred Astaire—but playing a pimp in *Cotton Comes to Harlem*. Not that she was afraid, but even in black jeans and a lightweight leather car coat, and her cloche pulled down to her eyebrows, she didn't exactly blend into the environment.

Halfway down the block ahead of her he turned, stepped off the curb between two cars, and then went around and opened the driver's door of one of them, his Camaro—which she realized now she should have looked for when she first got there. She turned and hurried to her own car, hoping he'd come back around the corner. He did, and she pulled away from the curb and fell in behind him.

He headed south to Seventy-ninth Street, west to Stony Island, then north. She stayed half a block back, but he hadn't gone far before he parked by a fire hydrant and went into a tavern. "Jesus, Clyborn," she said out loud, "you could have gotten here sooner on foot."

A parking place opened up right in front of her. It wasn't that tight a fit, and she slipped the Camry into it. She turned off the ignition, thinking what a great parallel parker she was, when she got the creepy feeling someone was watching her. She leaned and looked out the window to her right. Three young men, crouched on their haunches on the sidewalk outside a pool hall, were leering at her, commenting to each other and laughing.

Two in warm-up jackets, the third in a long cloth coat, they were . . . how old? Twenty? Maybe twenty-five? Who could say? Not a one of them, though, had more than a few years left, at least not this side of a prison wall . . . or the grave. Young black men: one with long dreadlocks; another—the fat one with the cue stick in his hand—with stubby braids sticking out of his head in every direction; the third with his scalp shaved clean. As a cop she'd seen them a thousand times on a thousand corners, aggressive and angry and hopeless, until it got hard to remember they were individual persons, with individual mothers who maybe still loved them—or maybe never did.

She hit the button that locked all her doors, and they must have seen that, or heard the *chunk* of the four locks falling into place, because they jostled each other and laughed. She turned away and stared through the windshield, pulling her purse up from the floor beside her feet and onto her lap without looking at it. She wanted to start up the car again and get out of there, but she had a job to do, dammit. She reached, as though adjusting the car radio, and glanced out the window again. Good. Two of them were gone and the only one left, the one with the shaved head, was standing and not even looking her way. She pulled her hand back from the radio.

Then a sudden shadow darkened the passenger-side window, and the fat end of a cue stick came punching through, exploding tiny cubes of safety glass inside the car. Before she could move he was smashing out the rest of the window. A face appeared, the man with the stubby braids. He was short and grossly overweight.

"Gimme the purse." His voice was soft and low—and very powerful.

She shrank against the door behind her and stared straight back at him, trying not to look down at her cell phone, which she suddenly noticed was lying easily within his reach on the passenger seat.

"Gimme the purse, bitch!" Still not raising his voice.

When in Rome . . . she thought, like Dugan said, and answered him in the same low tone. "Get outta my face, you fat asshole."

He hesitated, just slightly, and then a grin, wide and mean and full of crooked yellow teeth, spread across his round, pock-marked face. "Well, ain't *you* somethin'?" He leaned the cue stick against the side of the car and crouched lower. He saw the cell phone and grabbed it. With his other hand he was fumbling with the inside door handle, but she kept her finger pressed on the lock button. "Look here, bitch," he said, pointing the phone at her face, "unlock the doors."

Instead, she started the car and pulled the shift lever into reverse. The man raised up and slid the cue stick across the roof of the Camry, and that's when she first realized that someone was standing right beside her, outside the driver's door. It was the man with the dreadlocks, and he started yanking on her door handle, over and over, as though pretty soon she'd give up and it would open. Meanwhile the shaved head had stationed himself on the sidewalk near her front fender, looking first one way, then the other. People passed by, and one elderly woman even stopped and stared, but the lookout leaned close to her and said something, and she hurried away.

The first man looked in at her again. "Do like I say, or my man gonna do your window like I did this one. And that pretty face might get in the way when the stick poke through."

"Hold on a minute." She kept her finger on the lock button, but moved the shift lever into park. Meanwhile, the man right beside her kept working the door handle. Pull . . . release . . . pull . . . release. Over and over. "Let's talk about this," she said.

The man across from her grinned again through the broken-out window. "Just unlock the motherfuckin' doors."

Beside her it was still *pull . . . release . . . pull. . . .* On *release* she hit the unlock button and he pulled and the door beside her flew open—with her shoulder pushing it—and slammed against the man with the cue stick. His arms flailed helplessly, and he stumbled backward toward moving traffic, and she almost fell out onto the pavement.

Brakes screeched, car horns blared, someone shouted and cursed.

Keeping a grip on her purse, she righted herself, pulled the door closed, and hit the lock button. Traffic was moving again, and there was a crack as a car ran over the cue stick. The man she'd shoved into traffic was limping across the street, maybe hit by a car, and the lookout from her front fender was hustling after him.

But the fat man who'd broken her window wasn't going anywhere. He was sitting right beside her in the passenger seat. He pulled his door closed. "You one crazy bitch," he said. He reeked of stale cigarette smoke and cheap wine, too many days without a shower, and way too much cologne. "I like that," he added, and chuckled.

"Your friends have run away," she said, and started easing the car out of the parking space. "You better go find them."

"Uh-uh. I jus' wanted your purse, is all. But now I see you like the rough stuff, so we gonna go for a ride." He slid his right hand out from under his coat. "Some place more private." There was a knife in his hand, and the blade snapped open. "Drive."

She had the car angled out and could have pulled into traffic, but slipped the gear shift back into park.

"Drive, bitch!"

"Nope, 'cause the cavalry's here," she said, and pointed with her left hand toward the sidewalk. He turned to look and she said, "Not there, stupid! This way!"

155

He swiveled his head back and she shoved the barrel of the Colt hard and deep into the side of his throat, driving it through folds of fat, up against his trachea. "Shooting an unarmed man could be big trouble," she said, "even a jackal like you. But a man with a knife, and inside my own damn car . . ." She pressed harder with the gun, angling upward now, and he gargled in pain and struggled to lift himself up off the seat to ease the pressure on his injured windpipe. His breaths came in short, hacking gasps. "Put the blade on the dashboard," she said. "Then the cell phone."

He gagged and tried to say something, but couldn't get it out, and she just pushed harder against his windpipe. This was a guy who wouldn't know she couldn't pull the trigger with the barrel pressed so hard against him.

"The knife first," she said. "Then the phone. And then get your sorry ass out of my car. Otherwise, my friend, you're gonna feel your teeth tear their way through the top of your head."

He flipped the knife, then the phone, onto the dash and got out of the car, slamming the door shut behind him.

"Have a nice day," she said, and as she slid the lever into drive, the man leaned down and spat, and a huge wad of yellowish, blood-specked foam landed on the passenger seat. "Hey, I empathize," she called out, knowing he couldn't hear her as she pulled away. "I'm a little pissed off, myself."

And she was, too, mostly because Clyborn's red Camaro was nowhere to be seen.

TWENTY-NINE

Dugan wasn't angry when Kirsten hung up on him, or even when she turned off her phone. Uh-uh, not at all. He'd gotten past that long ago—or mostly past it.

It did no good, anyway.

Guys sometimes said things to him like, "I sure as hell wouldn't let *my* wife get involved in that sort of dangerous stuff." They didn't understand, though. He didn't allow Kirsten, or *not* allow her, to do anything. She was who she was, did what she did. Oh, he'd give her the needle sometimes, tell her she ought to get an adult's job, stop playing cops and robbers; but that was just talk, like her telling him he was crazy for working sixty or seventy hours a week at a job he didn't really like, that he ought to get a life. He simply couldn't imagine either of them seriously trying to *make* the other do anything. "Encourage, yes," he'd say. "Try to compel? I don't think so."

It did get a little irritating, though, when she'd ask him, or even *trap* him, into helping her—like this time—and then he'd get caught up in it and she'd suddenly turn him off when she felt like it. When she was inconsistent, even arbitrary, that did piss him off, dammit. So maybe he *was* angry, just a little.

Mostly, though, he was worried. All she'd said was she was

working and couldn't talk just then, so there was nothing specific to worry about. But it bothered him. He'd have been better off not knowing anything about what she was working on. Not knowing she was interfering with the economic designs of a hugely powerful man like John Michael Hurley; not knowing she'd humiliated Hurley's violent, psychopathic son in public; not knowing that someone, whether Hurley or not, was having her followed around and was willing to kill people—including people like, say, Dugan himself—to get whatever it was they wanted.

There was something else he wouldn't have known, too, or at least wouldn't have paid much attention to when it came on the news. Someone had confessed to killing Alfred Brownley, the man found under Mama Dee's cellar doors. The person was in custody, and though the name wasn't being released, she was a minor . . . an eleven-year-old girl from Kankakee County.

Dugan had taken in his rented Neon and traded it for a full-size Dodge, so he was ready to roll, and about two hours later he was in an interview room at state police headquarters in Kankakee. The detective across the desk from him was named Terrapin. He was a thin, dark man who had to be in his mid-sixties and gave the impression he'd been handling these cases since about the time Dugan was born and he'd never be surprised again. Dugan himself had been surprised, though, that Lieutenant Francis Terrapin was so willing to sit down and talk to him so late in the evening, since it was clear from the outset that the man had no intention of letting him in to see Coral.

"No sir," Terrapin was saying, "I'm not telling you she's in custody. What I'm saying is you can't visit the girl, whether she's here or not."

"But she needs a lawyer, for God's sake. She's just a kid."

"The offender is a juvenile with a legal guardian, and she has a lawyer already," Terrapin said, "the public defender. Bottom line is . . . you haven't got a chance of getting in."

"Then why the hell are we sitting—" Dugan stood up. "I'll talk to the PD in the morning."

"Fine." Terrapin didn't move, just sat there staring up at Dugan.

"Guess that's it." Dugan turned toward the door.

"There *is* just one more thing," Terrapin said. Dugan turned slowly back to him. He didn't like the feeling he was beginning to get. "Even if this juvenile offender, or her legal guardian, wanted a private lawyer—which so far nobody's mentioned to anybody—no judge would let *you* represent her." He paused. "There's this . . . conflict of interest thing, you know?"

"Conflict of interest? Because I represent the granddaughter of the owner of the house where the victim was found, in an unrelated matter?"

"You're the one's saying the matters are unrelated." Terrapin shrugged. "But that's not what I'm talking about, anyway."

"What then? What's the conflict?"

"The conflict is that there's this other person we're looking for now, someone we haven't had the chance to talk to, yet."

Dugan's stomach started churning. "Really?"

"Uh-huh. A possible witness and . . . maybe even a suspect." Terrapin paused. "On the record, you know, that last part I didn't tell you. But, off the record, I think you got a right to know."

"And why is that?" Dugan's heart was sinking.

"Because you're gonna help us find this individual."

"Oh?" That's all he was able to say.

"I think you're getting my drift." Terrapin pointed to the chair Dugan had just vacated. "Why don't you sit down for another couple of minutes, counselor."

When Dugan left Kankakee, he went to Miracle City and drove first past the gas station where Kirsten said she'd gotten directions from two old drunks. Obviously, they hadn't been quite as forgetful as she'd hoped they'd be. The place was closed, though, so he drove to Eudora's and banged on the door until Eudora and Mama Dee both appeared.

They had no idea where Kirsten might be. They obviously hadn't seen the report on TV and wanted to know what the emergency was. When he told them Coral had confessed to killing the man at Mama Dee's house, they both stared at him, wide-eyed, and then Eudora burst into tears.

"That's not possible," Mama Dee said. She walked Eudora across the room and sat beside her on the sofa, holding the younger woman close to her. "I don't know what they done to her to make her say somethin' like that," she said, "but that child didn't do nothin' of the kind."

He pulled a chair from the table in the dining alcove and sat opposite them. "The state police don't know her the way you do," he said.

"Chief Frawley knows her," Eudora said. She lifted her head and wiped at her tears with a tissue Mama Dee put in her hand. "All the Miracle City police know her. They know Coral's not the type of person's got killing inside her. Isn't that right, Mama Dee?"

"I just don't know," Mama Dee said. "Maybe most everybody's got killin' inside 'em, you give 'em the right reason. Bible says even Jesus got so mad he whipped them people for sellin' animals inside the temple."

"I don't read the Bible like you," Eudora said, "but I never heard of Jesus killing anybody."

"But he got mad. Righteous anger. That's what I'm sayin'. I ain't sayin' killin' that man was right, and I *sure* know Coral didn't do it."

"I don't even know just what she told them," he said. "But I have a feeling they don't really believe her. They're still looking for . . . for witnesses, people who might know something."

"They already talked to me and Mama Dee," Eudora said. "They weren't here very long."

"They know where both of you were all weekend."

"Right," Eudora said. "And neither of us knew anything about him. What other witnesses could there be?"

"For one thing, they want to talk to Kirsten."

"Why?" Mama Dee asked.

"I have no idea." He stood up. "It's late. I should—"

"Wait," Eudora said. "Shouldn't we go see if Coral's okay?"

"They won't let you see her. There's nothing any of us can do tonight. Except . . . if you hear from Kirsten, tell her what I said. Tell her she needs to talk to me before she talks to the police." They both looked terribly worried. "And don't worry about Coral. There's no way anyone's gonna believe she really killed that guy."

He hurried out and down the sidewalk. He must have left his cell phone in the car, and Kirsten might have been trying to reach him. He was almost to the car when he suddenly remembered that Cuffs should have been around somewhere, watching. He turned to go back in, to see if Eudora knew where he was, but then, from inside the car, he heard his cell phone ring. Probably Kirsten. He struggled with the damn key and finally got the passenger door open and grabbed the phone off the seat.

He flipped it open. "That you?" he said, slightly out of breath.

"Who the hell'd you think it was?" It was Cuffs. His voice on the phone seemed very loud, as though he were standing—

"Shit!" he said, and spun around.

"Gotcha!" Cuffs was standing about ten feet from him, wearing the same black clothes, but with a black knit cap on his head in place of that silly hat he'd had on earlier—Tyrolean or whatever.

"Nice cap," Dugan said.

"Uh-huh. Kirsten just called me, while you were inside there, talking to the ladies. Said she's been trying to get you but got no answer at home, and your cell phone was turned off."

He'd had the phone turned off at home and actually couldn't remember turning it on. "But it must have been on," he said, "because it rang just now when you called me."

"Well, hey then, let's see. First the fucking phone is *off* when Kirsten tries to call you. Then you go in the house, and then it's *on* when I call." He grinned—not what you'd call a good-natured grin. Dugan doubted the man had a good-natured cell in his body.

"You're telling me someone turned my phone on," he said. "You're telling me *you* turned it on. But that's bullshit. This car was locked when I went in, and it was locked when I came out."

"I know. I'm real quick at that sorta thing."

Dugan got in the car and drove away. He'd have punched Cuffs if he hadn't been so astounded to discover the sonovabitch actually engaging in a little humor—and if he'd been sure he could get a punch thrown before suffering some serious pain.

THIRTY

Eudora couldn't get to sleep. What could Coral have told the police? What was that Brownley man doing out at Mama Dee's anyway? The news reports never said for sure how he died, just that it was a head injury and the police weren't treating it as an accident. Was he hit with something? Was he pushed down the cellar steps?

She wondered if Mama Dee was right. Could it be true that just about anyone could kill a person, if they had a strong enough reason? Surely not a little girl like Coral. Then she remembered some of those little boys in the projects; there were some who were so far gone by the time they were ten or twelve years old that she could believe they might kill someone. Coral wasn't like them, though. Besides, even *they* had to have *some* kind of reason, and what reason could Coral have to kill some unknown white man?

She knew in her heart that Coral couldn't have killed anyone—not on purpose, anyway. Such a sad, lonely little girl. Your heart couldn't help but go out to her. Raynelle sure wasn't much of a guardian, but otherwise it would have been some foster home, and Coral said she would have run away for sure. A hardheaded child, independent. A serious child, too; a child who *thought* about things. That's one thing made her so different from most other kids—and especially those little gangsters in the projects who'd do whatever evil thing the bigger boys said, without thinking one bit. Seemed like Coral would never do anything just because someone—even if it was Eudora—told her to. She always had to think first. Then, if it seemed right to her, she'd do it.

Anyway, it couldn't have been Coral. What would she have been doing out there, with Eudora and Mama Dee both out of town? It didn't make sense.

Only one thing made sense, and that was that all these evil things that were happening—that man killed, Coral locked up in jail, Mama Dee's house burned down—it was all her fault. If she'd have stopped working with CREW against the mall when she got the first phone call, back before the carnival, all this wouldn't be happening. For sure she wouldn't have been accused of stealing CREW's money, because she wouldn't have had it to steal.

Funny, she never even thought to tell Kirsten about that first call. She really didn't take it seriously. Some man on the phone saying there were people who didn't like other people messing in important business, and if she kept it up she'd be sorry. Something like that. And that call was *not* from Clyborn, for sure. She mentioned it at a CREW executive committee meeting, but nobody else said they got called. They mostly agreed it was just some sick joke or something.

The caller had been right, though. She hadn't paid attention to him . . . and now she was sorry. On the morning of the day she went to Florida she called some of the other CREW people and explained what really happened with the carnival money. She told them she'd decided to resign as treasurer and stay away from meetings until the court case was over. They all listened; they all said they believed her. But not a single one of them believed her enough to say she should stay on as treasurer, or even that she should keep on coming to meetings.

164

Dugan kept saying the judge wouldn't find her guilty of anything, but that didn't mean people wouldn't still believe she took the money. Most of the people liked her, and they'd think she always intended to pay it back as soon as she could. But for sure most everyone, whether they liked her or not, would think she took the money and spent it. That's what she would have thought about some other person.

So someone was trying to get her to stop fighting the mall. With her out of the way, there'd be no one to make sure the CREW people got their letters written, their phone calls made, their flyers out. Things wouldn't get done. Whoever took the money knew that, and they figured pretty soon there'd be a million cars parked, seven days a week, right where Emerald Woods used to be.

On the other hand, she'd already sent out letters to bigger groups, like the Sierra Club and the Wilderness Society, asking for help. If some of them got involved, there'd surely be someone who'd take her place in CREW and keep people on their toes. "Ain't one person in this here world can't be replaced, no matter how important they think they are." That's what Mama Dee always said.

Whatever happened, though, it was obvious she wasn't going to be much help to CREW, not after her arrest. So, then, why did those other bad things happen? Mama Dee's house being burned down could have been because she was against the mall, too, and was so close to Eudora. But why was that man killed right there at Mama Dee's?

And Clyborn. How was Clyborn involved?

She started to shiver again, same as she'd shivered in that jail cell in Kankakee. She rolled herself tighter into her blankets. She was so scared she almost wished she'd die. She knew what she was afraid of, too. She only had one real secret, and that was it.

She got up out of bed and went out to the kitchen and put some water on for tea. She didn't really wish she'd die. Jessica and Jeralyn needed her too badly. Mama Dee needed her. Shoot, even Coral needed her. She would not die, and she would not give up the fight for Emerald Woods.

She'd been foolish to believe she could keep her secret forever. If it got out, there was no telling what might happen. Maybe nothing. But maybe what was most precious to her would be terribly hurt, or even snatched away. She'd promised herself she'd keep that secret. Now she was afraid it might come out, afraid she might even have to reveal it herself. But she'd need an awful strong reason to make her—

"Eudora, honey."

She jumped. "Oh, Mama Dee, you oughta be sleeping."

"That kettle 'bout to start whistlin', child, and be wakin' up the little ones." Eudora watched as the older woman turned the burner off. She put tea bags in two cups and poured the hot water over them.

"Thank you, Mama Dee," she said, pulling one of the cups across the table toward her.

"You're welcome, child." She sipped her tea right away, and Eudora wondered how she could stand it so hot. "I s'pose we both oughta be sleepin'."

"Soon as I lie down, I get to thinking," Eudora said, "and the more I think, the less I'm able to sleep."

"It's that way, sometimes."

"That man getting killed, your house getting burned down— all that's on account of me. You know that, don't you?"

"I don't know nothin' of the kind," Mama Dee answered, but Eudora didn't believe her.

"And Coral being in jail, that's on account of me, too."

"Drink your tea, child. Things won't look so bad in the mornin'."

"I don't believe Coral killed that man, Mama Dee. But I been thinking, and I think what you said might be right."

166

"What did I say?"

"You said most anybody might do anything, if they had a strong enough reason."

Mama Dee drank more tea. "People get my age," she said, "sometimes they talk just 'cause they got somebody who'll listen. That don't mean they always right."

Eudora tried her own tea. Still too hot. "I think it's true, though," she said. "A person might do something they didn't ever want to do . . . if they have a strong enough reason."

THIRTY-ONE

When the phone rang it was only inches from her hand, but Kirsten let it chirp a while before she answered. "Hello?"

"Hey." It was Dugan. "You're home. How things goin'?" Maybe just a tad too cheerful sounding. Probably still mad at her for hanging up on him a few hours ago.

"Fine," she said, "but I'm afraid I'm in nearly over my head."

"Why? What happened? Are you all right? Damn, I—"

"Dugan," she said, "listen." She dipped her chin below water level and blew bubbles near the phone.

"What's— Hey, are you in the tub?"

"Uh-huh. In nearly over my head. Immersed in mountains of soothing, aromatic suds. Surrounded by softly glowing candles. Johnny Mathis on the CD player."

"You're lying. You hate Johnny Mathis."

"I know." She blew some more bubbles at the phone. "But everything else is true."

"You stay right there," he said. "I'm on my way."

"I'm not going anywhere." She sighed, loud enough so she knew he could hear. "Where are you?"

"Dammit, I'm—" She heard the blare of a horn and the roar

of what sounded like a huge truck. "Dammit!" he repeated, much louder this time.

"Not very romantic, darling. Where *are* you?"

"I'm . . . hell, I just passed Kankakee."

"Oh, my. That's . . . awfully far."

"I'm going as fast as I can, though," he said.

She stretched out her left leg and turned on the hot water with her big toe, just the thinnest of streams. "I'll be turning off the phone now," she said. "I know it's the second time tonight, but don't be mad, okay? It's so you can concentrate on your driving. You don't want to have . . . an accident or something."

"Dammit, I—"

"I'll be here. Bye, darling." She put the phone down, then took a deep breath and sank a little deeper into the warm water, shifting and sliding her bottom on the slick, smooth surface of the tub. She'd be in bed and long asleep by the time he got home. "Too bad, too," she whispered. "Dammit."

It was the loveliest of mornings, and only when they'd gotten dressed and out to the kitchen did Kirsten notice it was raining outside. "Let's eat," she said. "And you can tell me what you wanted to tell me when I hung up on you last night—the first time, I mean." She switched on the coffee maker. "You want toast or a bagel?" she asked.

"What I want is a ham and cheese omelet with hash browns. Or better yet, pancakes and sausages. In other words, how about the good ol' Blue Sunrise Cafe?"

"But this is Wednesday." If she sounded too enthusiastic, he might change his mind. "You have to go to the office."

"It *seems* like Sunday, though. Besides, I'm thinking of starting a new regimen . . . including Wednesday afternoons off."

"It's a long time till afternoon."

"I know, but I'm behind in getting my new regimen operative." He frowned. "The thing is, we need to talk over some recent developments . . . and what we're going to do about them." His tone was getting more serious. "First, though, I'll go downstairs for the paper." She sensed reality closing in again.

By the time he got back she'd poured out two mugs of coffee. He took one but didn't seem much interested in drinking it. He spread the paper out on the kitchen table and quickly paged through it, then looked up. "Nothing here," he said.

"About what?"

"I take it nobody called before I got home last night?"

"Nope. Just you. And no messages on the machine when I got here."

"I erased the messages," he said, "from outside."

"Really? What were they? And what's not in the paper?"

"What's not in the paper is that Coral confessed to killing that man at Mama Dee's."

"What?" She could actually *feel* the stupefied look come across her face. "That's crazy!"

"I don't think the cops believe her, either," he said. "Actually, they're looking for . . . someone else. A witness, maybe."

"Oh?"

"Someone Officer Galboa puts right there in Miracle City on the Saturday afternoon in question. Someone two old drunks seem to recall asking directions to Mama Dee's." She stared at him, amazed at how calm he seemed, wondering if he felt as foolish now as she did, for thinking they'd get away with not reporting the dead man and the arson. ". . . the Blue Sunrise first," he was saying, "and then drive down to Kankakee while we figure out what to tell them."

"So the message you erased was for me to call the state homicide dicks?"

"Two messages, actually. A Lieutenant Terrapin. Bright, tough, experienced. He and I got along pretty well, and I don't

170

think I told him any outright lies. Decent enough guy. He warned me you were a possible suspect."

"He can't be serious." She shook her head. "And why didn't you wake me up and tell me all this last night?"

"Why?" he said. "We couldn't do anything about it until to-day, anyway. And I'd say Terrapin is at least moderately serious. I could tell he has doubts about Coral's having done it. And that's why we should think hard about what you're going to tell him."

"How about the truth, the whole truth, and nothing but the truth?"

"Always a possibility. But a big breakfast might give us strength to think of other alternatives." He paused. "For example, we might omit the fact of *my* being there."

"Oh?"

"Because otherwise, how can I be your attorney?"

They did opt for breakfast out, but first Dugan called Lieutenant Terrapin and told him they'd meet him at noon. Then he called Larry Candle and told him he wouldn't be in all day.

"Hey, Doogie pal," Larry said, "I can handle it. I'm making us buckets of money here while you're gone."

"That's great, but all I ask is you don't get either one of us disbarred." He paused. "Because . . . Larry? You might have to handle a criminal case in Kankakee, after all."

"Whoa, partner. I told you, my luck hasn't been—"

"Larry?"

"What's up, buddy boy?"

"If you ever say that again, you're fired."

"You mean . . . don't say 'buddy boy,' or don't talk about bad luck?"

"I mean don't ever use the word *partner* in my presence again."

"Relax, Doogie pal. It's just a manner of speak—"

Dugan hung up, and they went for breakfast.

First they dropped the Camry at a glass repair shop and paid way too much because they wanted the passenger window replaced by the time they ate and came back. Then they took a cab to the Blue Sunrise. It was too crowded there to speak confidentially, so they ate in silence.

They went back and picked up the car. Kirsten drove, and he waited for her to start the conversation. Finally, when they were on the interstate and headed toward Kankakee, she asked, "How do you suggest we handle this interview, counselor?"

He'd been through it in his mind and knew just what she should do. "I tell Terrapin I'm your lawyer, and therefore I sit in on your statement. You answer his questions, but you pay very close attention to me, and do whatever I—"

"Hey, hey, hey. Hold on a minute. You're my lawyer, right?"

"Sure."

"Good. So my lawyer's job is to give me his best lawyerly advice." She reached out and patted him gently on the shoulder. "His job is *not* to decide for me what I should do."

"Relax. It's just a manner of speak—" He stopped. Christ, he was sounding like Larry Candle. "You're right. Let's discuss the possibilities."

THIRTY-TWO

got no problem with your hus . . . I mean your lawyer . . . sitting in," Terrapin said. "Thanks for coming."

Kirsten nodded but said nothing. There was something about this cop that she already liked, but even though Dugan and she had gone over it a dozen different ways, she still wasn't certain how she wanted to play this.

The office was small, the wall behind Terrapin's desk made of concrete blocks painted green, with one dirt-streaked window. The two side walls were plaster, the same color green, and the wall behind them was glass from about waist high to the ceiling. There were file folders and papers stacked on top of file cabinets along the wall to their left, and more of the same in piles on the floor. The top of Terrapin's gray steel desk, though, held just one paper cup, half full of coffee, and one slim folder.

"Can I get you something?" he said. "Coffee? Soft drink?" She was sure he expected her to say no.

"Yes," she said. "Coffee, black."

"Nothing for me," Dugan said.

Terrapin raised one hand high over his head, first with the index finger pointing up, and then making an "O" with that finger and his thumb. Almost immediately the door behind Dugan and her opened. A middle-aged woman in a tan uniform brought in coffee in a paper cup. She set it on the edge of Terrapin's desk, near Kirsten, and walked out again without saying a word.

"Thank you," Kirsten said, and let the cup sit there. She had no intention of drinking it, and no intention of saying anything at all she didn't have to say—not until she had a better handle on this guy.

Terrapin drummed the fingers of both hands on the folder in front of him. "Do you want to make a statement," he asked, looking straight at her, "about your activities in and around Miracle City on Saturday afternoon and evening?"

"No."

"Funny," he said. "It was my understanding that you came in today to make a statement."

She turned her head toward Dugan and he said, "Is my client a suspect?"

"Not at this time. She's being interviewed as a witness."

"Is she free to leave if she wishes?"

"Yes."

"Good." Dugan stood up. "Let's go home."

She stood, too, but when they turned toward the door Terrapin said, "What the hell are you doing?" He seemed more surprised than angry.

They both turned back, and she let Dugan speak. "My client is being cooperative," he said. "She's here to answer questions in connection with the investigation of an apparent homicide. Your only question so far—does she want to make any statement?—has been answered."

"Sit down," Terrapin said. She sat, and Dugan followed suit. "Were you in Miracle City this past Saturday afternoon, ma'am?"

"Yes."

Terrapin waited, and when she didn't elaborate, he asked, "Do you want to tell me what you were doing there?"

"No."

Terrapin's eyes narrowed, but Dugan said, "Again, I suggest you ask your questions more carefully, Lieutenant."

"What time did you arrive in Miracle City, and what did you do when you got there?"

"I drove my car directly to the home of Eudora Ragsdale. I tried the front door and the back door and got no answer. As I was leaving, I had a conversation with a little girl. Then I had a conversation with a Miracle City police officer whose name is, I believe, Galboa. After that, I left. I don't know exactly what time. You can get that information from Officer Galboa."

"Why did you go to Ms. Ragsdale's home?"

She looked at Dugan. "My client's motives and thought processes," he said, "are not relevant, in my opinion, to the death investigation. Also, they're private and confidential."

"I'll decide what's relevant," Terrapin said. "Answer my question, ma'am."

"No, sir," she said.

He turned back to Dugan. "Are you instructing her not to answer?"

"Nope. I'm not instructing her anything. My client makes her own decisions. Occasionally, they're based on her careful consideration of my opinions."

"Jesus." Terrapin leaned back in his swivel chair and laced his hands behind his head. "Why are you two working so hard to piss me off? I talked to *you* last night," he said, nodding at Dugan, "and I thought we understood each other." He leaned forward and rested his hands on the file folder again. "Now what the hell's going on?"

"My client—"

"Forget it," she said. Her mind was made up. "I just wanted some time, Lieutenant, to observe."

"Observe *me*, you mean," he answered. "So?"

She gave him what she hoped looked like a friendly, apologetic smile. "So I think I trust you."

"I'm thrilled."

"I propose a deal. I tell you what I did on Saturday, and why—which I don't think I'm required to do. In exchange, you tell me what Coral Stitch said about killing that man. You've got nothing to lose there, surely. Any statement she's made will be given to her attorney, anyway." She smiled again. "I'll be candid, though. I can't promise that what I have to say will help you find any killer—if there is a killer. To the contrary, I don't know who the dead man is—other than the media say his name was Brownley—and I don't know how, where, or when he died."

"What's in any so-called deal for me? You have to cooperate, anyway. I can have you detained as a material witness. I can go after your PI license. I can even lock you up as a suspect."

"You could try all those things, and more. But you—and the state of Illinois—might eventually pay for a hasty decision on your part. What's in it for you is you get my information, such as it is, without all the hassle." He was drumming his fingers on the folder again. "Besides," she added, "if you get any evidence—from me or anyone—that convinces you I had any part in a homicide, you can always have me arrested."

"And I will."

"I should hope so, Lieutenant," she said.

They made the deal and she told him . . . well . . . *almost* everything, including Coral's being there and unlatching the cellar door to let Kirsten out. She'd intended at first to leave Dugan out of it but changed her mind. She really didn't know how much Terrapin already knew, either from Coral or from some other source.

Then Dugan had to describe how he'd been knocked out, woke up in the pantry, and got away with Kirsten's help.

When they'd finished, Terrapin said, "And you didn't call the police or the fire department?"

"I couldn't think of a single way in which we could have assisted in a police investigation. I still can't," she said.

"I can't, either," Dugan said. "I suppose I could have reported a battery against me, but I had no idea who did it and decided not to bother with it."

"The sooner we get to a crime scene," Terrapin said, "the fresher the evidence is. You know that."

"But we heard sirens in the distance as we turned off Till's Creek Road," she said, "and the media reports suggest that the authorities were there very shortly after we left." Terrapin just sat there and stared at her unhappily, but they did have a deal, and she gave him her best sweet smile. "Your turn," she said. "What did that little girl say?"

He opened the folder in front of him and stared down at the top page of what looked from where she sat like about ten pages of police reports. "She says she was out riding her bike Saturday and decided to go visit her neighbor's grandmother. When she got there no one answered the door, so she was leaving. Then a man grabbed her and dragged her to the backyard. She could tell he was going to, quote, 'take me down into the basement and do bad things to me.' She says he pulled open the cellar door and she broke loose and pushed him and he fell down the stairs. He didn't get up, or move, and she was scared and rode away on her bike." He looked up at her.

"She give you any time when all this happened?"

"She's unclear on the time."

"I bet she is," Kirsten said. "You guys picked her up Saturday night when? Ten o'clock? Eleven? You got any fix on time of death?"

"A preliminary."

"When?"

He smiled. "It's only preliminary."

"And you're not telling us," she said. He smiled again, so she answered it herself. "It had to be sometime before two P.M., because he was dead before I got there."

"Assuming you're telling the truth," Terrapin said.

"So it took her at least seven hours to go from Mama Dee's house to where she got picked up?"

"She doesn't mention seeing you there at all. Thing is, she says she pushed the man down the stairs the *first* time she was at Mama Dee's that day."

"What?"

"Uh-huh. Seems later, when it was dark out, she went back . . . to see if the man had gotten better and gone away. The house was on fire, though, so she turned around and went home again. And that's when she got picked up."

"You know the whole thing's absurd, don't you?"

"I don't know anything but what people tell me. Maybe both you and the kid are telling me the truth, in which case the kid could have killed the guy before you got there. Or maybe you're both lying."

"In which case what?" she asked.

"In which case the kid might be trying to hide the identity of the real killer."

"But why?"

"Maybe because she likes the person. We know she's real close to Eudora Ragsdale and her grandmother. Both of them, though, appear to have been out of town at the time of the incident. So maybe she's trying to protect someone else she's attached to."

"Really? Who?"

"All I can say is, ever since she made the statement I just told you about, she won't talk to anybody. Not her legal guardian; not even the public defender. Says there's only one person she'll talk to."

Kirsten looked at Dugan, and he looked at Terrapin. "Interesting," Dugan said. "And who would that be?"

Terrapin looked down at the report in front of him and turned a few pages. "That would be, in Coral's words, 'the nice white lady, the one who's helping Miz Eudora.'"

THIRTY-THREE

Kirsten couldn't fault Lieutenant Terrapin. He'd kept his word and told them what Coral had said. Of course, that's all he'd say about the investigation, and he was understandably unhappy with them for leaving a crime scene without reporting it. And he had to consider her a possible suspect, whether her being involved in either an arson or a homicide made sense to him personally or not—which she thought it didn't.

When Dugan was able to prove what time he'd picked up his rental car, Terrapin's reaction told her he knew Brownley had been dead before that. He'd sent them on their way, with a warning to keep themselves available.

Outside, she called Coral's public defender, who said he'd make arrangements for her to see Coral right away. He'd meet Kirsten when she got there and would have to be present for the meeting. Dugan wouldn't be allowed in.

The juvenile detention facility was part of a county complex not far from state police headquarters. She drove, and when they got there she turned to Dugan. "I'll be an hour at most. They must have a lobby, if you want to wait inside."

"Leave me the keys," he said. "I'll wait in the car."

"Okay," she said, "but don't disappear and leave me stuck here forever."

She watched him drive away. He hadn't said anything about her having told Terrapin that he'd been at Mama Dee's, too, even though they'd agreed to leave that part out. The problem was, with Terrapin asking questions here and there as she talked, she'd realized she couldn't really keep Dugan out of it without flat-out lying—which could have meant big trouble if things fell apart and Terrapin found out. She knew Dugan wasn't angry—she could always tell when he was—so he must have understood why she'd changed her mind.

"You're a bright guy, Doogie pal," she said, pushing her way through the door, "although we both must be out of our minds."

Reception directed her to the metal detectors and security directed her down the hall to the public defender's office. Coral's PD was out in about fifteen seconds. He was a tad shorter than Kirsten, a little pudgy, with smooth tan skin and lots of curly black hair. In his khakis and sport coat, and his tie pulled down from his unbuttoned collar, he looked like a freshly scrubbed college sophomore. Odd, how the people she dealt with kept getting younger and younger.

This particular young man was certainly full of energy; smiling, nodding, shaking her hand with enthusiasm. "Emilio Rodriguez," he said. "I got it all set up."

They rode up in the elevator with a woman about Kirsten's age who'd also come out of the PD's office and carried the same sort of brown file folder as Emilio did. She was attractive and nicely dressed, but her whole body seemed to slump, as though she needed a vacation.

"So, Emilio," Kirsten said, "how long have you been a public defender?"

"Three months. My first job as a lawyer; the job I wanted all through law school." He grinned. "A chance to really give back to the community, and get paid for it, too." The elevator door opened, and he was the first one out. "C'mon. Coral's this way." He hurried off to the right.

The other woman turned to Kirsten as they stepped together out of the elevator. "Jesus," the woman said, "I've been here five years and three months, and I'd kill to be able to smile again like that about what I do." She turned and went down the hall the other way.

Several locked doors and another metal detector later, she and Emilio Rodriguez stepped into a brightly lit room, maybe the size of a double classroom. It was clean and bright and cheerfully decorated, with chairs and sofas scattered around, and a couple of TV sets, but the only person in sight was a uniformed guard, a woman, who sat at a little table far to the right, paging through a newspaper.

Along the wall of the room opposite the door was a row of very small separate rooms, each of them completely visible from the large room through a clear glass wall. The small rooms were obviously designed so that kids could have private—although entirely visible—conversations with their relatives or lawyers. Each held a low round table and three low-backed upholstered chairs. The interview rooms Kirsten could see into from where she stood were all empty.

The guard looked up when they came in and nodded toward the last little room at the end, nearest her. They went that way, and Kirsten saw Coral sitting in one of the chairs and waved to her. Coral gave a sort of half wave back, then dropped her hand and stared down at the floor. She wore light blue denim pants and a short-sleeved white blouse. If it was a uniform, you couldn't tell—not without seeing lots of other girls in the same outfits.

They went inside. "Hi, Coral," Rodriguez said.

Coral nodded.

Kirsten said hello and leaned and kissed her lightly on the forehead. Coral flinched and didn't say anything. Her eyes filled with tears, but she rubbed them and no more tears came. "So," Kirsten said. "Mr. Rodriguez here said you wanted to see me."

"I ain't talked to him. He been to see me a couple times, but I ain't talked to him."

"That's right," he said, his voice kind. "But the police officers told me you said you'd only talk to the lady who—"

"You seen Miz Eudora?" Coral asked, ignoring him and looking at Kirsten. "And Jeralyn and Jessica?"

"Yes, they're fine. They can't wait to see you."

"How Mama Dee doin'? She real sad about her house?"

"A little, but she's already planning to buy a modular home and put it out near her old one. You know what a modular home is?"

"Nope." And she didn't seem much interested, either. "Can I talk to you?"

"Sure. Go ahead."

"No. I mean alone, without this man here."

"The problem is, Coral," Rodriguez said, "if this lady is here with me, and I say she's helping me help you, no one can make her tell anything you say to her."

"Why not?" Coral said.

"Because I'm your lawyer and no one's allowed to make me tell, and she's helping me."

"If they can't make her tell 'cause she helpin' you, why you gotta be in the room, too?"

Rodriguez looked at Kirsten and grinned. "Well," he said, "I guess she's got me this time. Thing is, you're not officially working for the PD's office, so I don't know if I can be sure you'll be covered by the privilege."

"I doubt it'll ever come to that," Kirsten said, and Rodriguez got up and left the room.

She thought Coral almost smiled.

"You're a very smart little girl, Coral."

"I ain't so little," she said, "and ain't nobody else thinks I'm smart. Teachers all say I'm slow."

"Well, teachers aren't always right."

Coral smiled, this time for sure, but it went away in a hurry. "I told the police I killed that man."

"I know that. Why ever did you say such a thing?"

" 'Cause I told you on a blood oath that I wouldn't say nothin' to nobody about you bein' there. And they kept on askin' and askin' and *askin'*. They wouldn't let me alone. I got real tired, but they wouldn't take me home and wouldn't let me go to bed."

"Didn't your cousin come and—"

"Raynelle, she ain't no use. She just come in and say she real mad 'cause she wanna go home and go to bed, and why don't I tell the police the truth. I told her just go away and leave me alone. And she did."

"Oh."

"Pretty soon they started sayin' maybe I killed that man my own self. Maybe I pushed him and he fell down the steps. They jus' kept after me and after me. The only way I could make 'em stop is to say yeah, I did it. But then they still wouldn't go away. Different ones, mostly all men, white men, and two ladies, too, kept comin' in and goin' out, askin' and askin', and pretty soon I hadda make up a whole big story about what happened. I made it up from a program I seen once on TV. But the part about goin' back a second time and seein' if he had got better? I made that part up myself."

"But why did you think you had to lie?"

"I *told* you!" She looked as though she thought Kirsten was a little slow herself. " 'Cause they wouldn't leave me alone, and otherwise I would've had to say I seen you out there by Mama Dee's cellar door by where that dead man was, and I told you . . ." She stopped for a moment, then added, "I left that little card, but you probably didn't—"

"Yes, I found it, and I knew it meant you were gonna keep your promise. Oh, Coral, I'm so sorry I caused you all this trouble. But it's okay, now. Dugan and I just told the police, today, that we were there." She patted the child's knee. "So you saw that . . . that man out there?"

"Yeah. I seen him when you ran inside Mama Dee's house and I was lookin' for water for the fire." She picked at a little scab on her arm. "I thought . . . you know . . . I was scared you had killed him because he was bad or was bein' mean to Miz Eudora or somethin', so—"

"Coral."

"Uh-huh?"

"I didn't kill that man."

"Okay. I won't say nothin'."

"No, Coral, I mean I really didn't kill anybody."

"You didn't?" Tears filled Coral's eyes again, and she didn't wipe at them. "For real?"

"For real," she said. She found a tissue in her purse and wiped the tears from Coral's cheeks. "And I don't think the police think I did. And I *know* they don't believe that story you made up."

"They don't?"

"They know you did no such thing. Now I want you to talk to Mr. Rodriguez and tell him just what happened." There was fear in Coral's eyes. "He'll help us get this all taken care of and get you out of here. But I'll stay here when you talk to him, okay?"

Coral nodded. "Uh-huh."

So she called the PD in, and Coral told him what happened, about talking to Kirsten and later to Dugan. And then how she

185

got curious and worried and rode her bike her own special way to Mama Dee's. On her way back home, when she got close to the road she heard the police siren and thought the police were after her, so she hid her bike and tried to sneak down the side of the road on foot, but they saw her. She didn't mention Kirsten's card and the drops of blood.

"And why did you make up that story about *you* killing the man?" Rodriguez asked.

"Because I didn't wanna get Miz Kirsten in trouble."

Rodriguez leaned slightly forward toward her. "Coral," he said, "did this lady ask you to lie for her, to make up a story?"

"No!" Coral was angry. "She didn't say nothin' like that! Her and the man said they'd take me back to town, and I just ran away on my bike and wouldn't let them. They didn't tell me nothin'. But I knew they was helpin' Miz Eudora, and I didn't want them to get into trouble." She looked down at the floor. "Miz Eudora, she my friend."

"That's okay, Coral," Rodriguez said. "I just had to ask, that's all." He looked at his watch. "We have to leave now. I'll be back tomorrow, and we'll go over it again, and then I'll tell the police that you want to tell them what really happened."

"They gonna let me outta here after that?"

"I don't know exactly how fast. Maybe not right away, but pretty soon."

Rodriguez stepped outside again and Kirsten said, "You do what he says, okay? He's a good man."

"He okay, I guess. I jus' keep on telling the truth then, is that all right?"

"Yes, Coral, telling the truth is just fine."

THIRTY-FOUR

They'd had no lunch, but Dugan didn't even notice he was hungry until Kirsten had gone inside to see Coral. He could wait, though. They'd pick a nice place on the way home and have an early supper. He drove around the parking lot until he finally found an open slot, but by then he was *really* hungry. Maybe something to read would take his mind off his stomach.

He drove out of the lot and had gone just a few blocks when he spotted a row of newspaper vending boxes on the sidewalk. He parked in the lot of a nearby Taco Bell and went to get a paper. Three of the four boxes were empty. No *Chicago Tribune* or *Sun-Times,* no local Kankakee paper. Just something called *InSighter,* one of those giveaway tabloids about what was happening on the local art, theater, and music scenes. In this case, "local" seemed to mean roughly a triangle from Kankakee eighty miles south to Champaign and the University of Illinois, and then west fifty miles to Bloomington-Normal and the universities there.

He couldn't resist the Taco Bell and ended up at a table by the window to toss down a Pepsi and a couple of *chalupas* while he read. *InSighter* was heavy on the rock scene, and the last four pages were classified personals and ads for escort services, phone sex, and the like. There were reviews of some art exhibits, though, and a story about a foreign film festival in Champaign, along with lists of dozens of events, most of them sponsored by the various area colleges, from lectures to concerts to live theater. He figured that if he ever lived outside a major city—God forbid—it would have to be in a university town. The U of I, for example, was—

Which made him think of something.

He finished eating in a hurry and took the paper out to the Camry. There was a listing for information about a lecture that Friday night at the U of I on "The New Cosmology," and he tapped out the number on his cell phone.

"Department of Philosophy," the woman said.

"Oh," Dugan said, "I guess I dialed wrong. Could you give me the dean's office or administration or something?"

"I can't transfer you, but I can give you the number."

"Thanks." He wrote the number down, then tapped it out and, after about ninety seconds of recorded messages, hit zero to speak to a living person.

"University of Illinois. How may I direct your call?" Another woman, this one very official.

"I need some information about one of your teachers there."

"What sort of information, sir; and do you mean a professor, an adjunct professor, an assistant pro—"

"Actually, I don't know that. I can give you his name, though, and maybe you can tell me what he teaches and what his schedule is. Oh, and where I'd find him. That's about it."

"I'm afraid I can't do that, sir. You'd have to talk to the office of the school to whose faculty the individual is assigned. They may or may not be willing to give you the information you request. However, most of them are closed this week because—"

"Thanks." He hung up and called the first number again.

"Department of Philosophy." Same woman as before.

"It's me again."

188

"Pardon me?"

"Anyway," he said, "could you give me the number for the library?"

"Sure. Which library?"

"The biggest one, I guess," he said. "Not medicine or law, though. Maybe arts and sciences."

"Well . . . here, try this one."

"Thanks." He took the number and tried it.

"Library." She didn't say which one.

"If one of the university professors had written a doctoral thesis, would it be in your library there?"

"That depends on a lot of things, but I'll certainly see what I can do for you." Like all librarians, and unlike most administrative personnel, she sounded determinedly helpful. "Who is the professor?"

"I'm assuming he's a full professor. His name is Hurley, Jack Hurley. He's—"

"That would be Professor Hurley. He's the only Hurley on the entire faculty. But it's not Jack. His name is John Michael Hurley."

"Really. You know him then?"

"Not personally, but he's something of an . . . activist, and rather well known here. And I can assure you," she added, in a rather conspiratorial tone, "*no* one here calls him Jack."

"Got it," he said. "And what does Professor Hurley teach?"

"Various courses. He's the Heidkamp Professor of Environmental Policy."

"I see." Which he didn't. "And by 'activist,' what did you mean?"

"Just that, apart from his research and classroom work, he lectures frequently on environmental issues and occasionally gets involved in what we call 'real-world affairs.' Environmental controversies, that kind of thing."

"Just the sort I'm looking for. I need to catch up with him for just a minute. What's his schedule tomorrow?"

"Oh, that wouldn't be easy to . . ." She stopped, apparently remembering the librarians' code of helpfulness. "Here, let me see what I can pull up." There was a pause, broken by the tapping of computer keys. "No." More tapping. "Nope." Still more keywork, then, "Ah, I did it! His final class of this session is tomorrow. It's a late class, four o'clock, an exam. Of course, I don't know whether he'll be available before or after class."

"That's all right," he said. "Hey, you know? You oughta get a raise."

"Tell me about it," she said.

Driving back to pick up Kirsten, he decided this detective stuff wasn't so hard—not nearly as hard as negotiating with all those stubborn, suspicious insurance adjusters. The problem was there wasn't much money in it—not nearly as much as in negotiating with all those adjusters—which might explain why they were so stubborn and suspicious.

THIRTY-FIVE

Sometimes what you've been chasing, and unable to catch, arrives in the simplest of ways. The next morning Kirsten was in her office, waiting to hear from Emilio Rodriguez about the reaction to Coral's changing her story, when the phone rang.

"Wild Onion, Limited," she said.

"Huh? Oh . . . yeah." A black man. Not a voice she knew. "This the private detective's office? The lady?"

"Yes." Unless he was a new client, who weren't exactly flocking to her door, she had only one guess who it was, so . . . "What can I do for you, Clyborn?"

"What?" Just one word, and she knew she'd guessed right.

"Clyborn Settles," she said. " 'Clyborn,' like the North and Clybourn subway stop, but spelled different, right?"

"Yeah, I mean, I guess so. But . . . but how you know who I am? I mean, I'm on a pay phone and—"

"Oh, I know who you are, all right. I also know you drive a two-year-old red Camaro, recently purchased from Tadmore Motors. I know where you live—first floor south. I know you work at a scrap metal yard near a Hundred-and-fifteenth and Torrence. I know you favor wide-brimmed fedoras, and you stop in now and then at Rico's Tap, on Stony Island."

"How you know all—"

"Like you said, I'm a detective." If he was inclined to talk, she didn't want him thinking he could back out later. "I know what your first payment was toward the Camaro." That was stretching it a bit. "And I even know where you got the money." That wasn't.

"Damn."

"Most important of all, I know you want to talk to me."

"What makes you think that?"

"Because, Clyborn, you *called* me."

"Yeah, well . . ."

They met at the Adler Planetarium, at the tip of a thumb of land built out into Lake Michigan at about Twelfth Street, part of the newly designed, parklike museum campus along with the Shedd Aquarium and the Field Museum. Just to the south was tiny Meigs Field, also built out into the lake, where commuter planes constantly battled the turbulent winds, and sometimes lost. . . .

She led him to a cafeteria-style lunchroom where she figured there'd be lots of hyperactive kids on field trips, yelling and laughing and racing around—and she was right. There were a few scattered adults, too, and she could tell which ones were the teachers. They seemed less bothered by the noise and confusion.

She told Clyborn she'd buy, and he ordered two cheeseburgers—the beef patties as thin as the cheese—two bags of Ruffles potato chips, a Cherry Coke in a cup big enough to wash your hair in, a cellophane-wrapped brownie, and a piece of apple pie. Not a terribly disciplined eater. The pie looked pretty good, actually, so she took a piece of that, too, to go with her pasta salad and diet Sprite.

"So," she said, "let's eat a little first, then talk."

"Fine with me." He was acting cool, disinterested, like he

could be there or not. But she knew better, because he *was* there. Maybe his conscience was bothering him; more likely, though, he was scared.

He was dressed far differently than when she'd followed him from his apartment: gray pants, a blue work shirt, and a darker blue windbreaker that was fraying around the cuffs. Even so, he was a strikingly handsome man—movie star material—tall and light brown skinned and terribly egocentric. But seen close up, the skin on his face sagged a little already, and there was a layer of fat showing up. He was neglecting the infrastructure that held the whole package together, and it was beginning to betray him. He'd step out of the shower one day soon and catch himself in the mirror and be stunned by how out of shape and soft he'd gotten—and how *old*. Of course, that day's on its way for all of us, she thought, but his was rushing at him in a hurry, and it would hit him harder than—

"Look here, you spaced out or what?" He was staring across the table at her.

"Just thinking." She sipped her Sprite. "So . . . why did you take that money from Eudora's?"

"What?" She'd clearly taken him by surprise. "I ain't said I did that."

"And I note, my dear Clyborn, that you ain't said you didn't." She leaned toward him. "Look, you may be a little broke right now, but you didn't call me up so you could con me out of a couple of burgers. What's the deal?"

He stared down at his tray and slid the little plate with the pie closer to him. "I seen you and Eudora—and that lawyer you was with—in court, you know? And I asked around, and one of them court sheriffs knew your name. I followed after you all 'cause I wanted to talk to you. But you got away. So I looked in the phone book, you know, and got your number." He cut himself a bite of apple pie with a white plastic fork.

"Congratulations. That's pretty much the same way I found

out things about you." He didn't answer, just chewed his pie and poked at the ice in his cup with a straw. "Look," she said, "you wanted to talk to me, and here we are. I already know part of what you can tell me. I know you took the money from Eudora's."

He looked up, as though annoyed at her saying that again, but he still didn't deny it.

"I know it," she said, "and I can prove it . . . *if* I ever want to. You tell me the truth, though, all of it, and I'll do my best for you." Intentionally vague. "Was the deal you could keep whatever money you found? And whose idea was it? Just tell me what happened, from the beginning."

"I . . . Damn, I don't know if I . . ." Then his shoulders slumped and she could tell that the fear that made him call her had won out over the fear of telling her. "Okay, me and another dude was, you know, like laid off from truck driving for the scrap yard, and they put us workin' nights, like security guards, but no gun or nothin'. Takin' turns. Like I work Monday, Wednesday, and Thursday. Saturdays, too, during the day. Only about half the pay as drivin', though, and—"

"Clyborn, let's get to it."

"Yeah. Anyway, there's a bar out that way that's open for night-shift guys, and I meet this dude there one morning and him and me get to talkin' and he buys me a beer or two. Then a few days later he shows up again and . . . anyway, one day he tells me he's got a way I can make some money. He says he knows, like, who I am and all, including stuff in the past, 'cause he's investigatin' Eudora. Like he knows me and her used to go together, and about her havin' twins, and . . . well . . ." He put down his cup and started rummaging for crumbs in one of the Ruffles bags.

"And what?" she pressed him. "Go on."

"So he say . . . he say Eudora had stole some money and he think she hidin' it in her house. He told me where she lived. He say he workin' for a man who's workin' for some people who want her to get caught, you know, get in trouble, 'cause she's like, messin' in somethin' she shouldn't. He say I'm just the man for the job. All I got to do is go in there and look. He say he picked me 'cause if I got caught I could say I was there to see Eudora about the kids. He give me some money up front, and if I find the cash money she stole, I can keep that, too. I wasn't s'posed to take nothin' but cash. He said it probably be in a brown envelope. After I got it, I had to call and tell him. That was it. Nothin' else."

"And you agreed, for God's sake?"

"Yeah, I agreed." He spoke with a sullen sneer that infuriated her.

"You said, 'Oh yeah, I'm the man for the job all right. I'll be happy to steal two thousand bucks from the woman who's struggling to survive and support my own two kids.' " She knew she should shut up, but she was too angry to stop. "When's the last time you sent her some support money, dammit? When's the—"

He was on his feet. "Fuck that shit! I ain't even— You don't know nothin'.'"

"Okay, okay." She raised her hands, palms up. "My fault. I'm sorry. Relax. You ain't even what?"

He sat down, which, she thought, said a mouthful about how he viewed his options. "I didn't even have to bust the door. It was unlocked. And I didn't hurt nobody. I knew she was at work. Besides, she *stole* the money, so—"

"Oh no. Some guy you already knew was dishonest *told* you she stole it, and . . ." She stopped. Why try to convince this grown-up preadolescent he'd done wrong, for God's sake? "Anyway, you were supposed to call her up, too. To frighten her?"

"Uh-uh. I done that on my own. I mean, the dude told me he had called her hisself a few times, tryin' to scare her away from messin' in whatever it was . . . but it didn't work. Anyway, I didn't call to scare her. I had took the money a couple days

days before, and I wanted to see did she find out it was gone yet. And warn her, you know? I didn't want her to know who I was, but I was gonna explain how come the money she stole got stole from her." His eyes turned angry again. "Then she gets all up in my face on the phone. I'm doin' the bitch a favor and she starts callin' me names and—"

"Okay, okay, relax a minute," she said. She took a bite of her own pie. It wasn't as good as it looked, and she washed it down with Sprite. "So . . . who was the man?"

"White man. Called hisself Bill Williams. I never did know what the dude's real name was."

"What his name *was*?" He didn't answer, and she leaned across the table. "He's dead now?"

"That's why I called you," he said. "I seen his picture in the paper."

"Brownley? The man they found at Mama Dee's house?"

"Yeah, but I didn't know his real name. I didn't even know whose house it was they found him at. The dude just told me we— I mean . . ." He sighed. "Man, I don't know how much to say."

"I already told you I'll do my best for you, with the cops, if it ever comes to that."

"Yeah, but the cops . . . anyway, cops ain't the only thing I'm scared of." He looked around the room, as though wishing he could slip off and join one of the tables of school kids, giggling and grabbing at each other's lunches. "I can't sleep. I keep dreamin' they gonna kill me."

"Who? Who are 'they'? And why do you think that?"

"After I took the money I figured that was the end of it and went and right away bought the Camaro. Then the dude meets me again. That was Friday. He say the dude he's workin' for— actually he say *we* workin' for him—that dude's tied up with some powerful people. I ask what he means and he say, 'real powerful people, connected people,' and I know he means like, you know, mob people—which he didn't never tell me before."

"Did he say 'Outfit' or 'Mafia' or what?"

"I *told* you, he just say 'real powerful, connected people.' But I know it's mob people and . . . and other people, too." Clyborn was back to stirring what was left of the ice in his cup. "Anyway, he reminded me he knew all about me, all about Eudora and her girls. Then he say he had gave the man all this information."

"Gave it to who?" When he didn't answer, she said, "This first man, Brownley, he told you he was working for a second man who was working for these 'powerful people.' Who was the second man? Did Brownley give you a name?"

"Yeah, he . . . I mean no . . . I don't know. I can't tell you. I'm scared, you know? Shit. I thought, you know, maybe if I gave the two thousand back, maybe you—"

"You don't have it."

"I know, but I mean, you know, I *would* pay it back as soon as I get it and . . . I just thought maybe you could help me. I don't know . . ." His voice trailed off and she realized he didn't know what to ask for. All he knew was he was frightened.

Her instinct was to reassure the poor bastard, but she beat that feeling back in a hurry. The more scared he was, the more useful. "So," she said, "Brownley worked for a guy, and that guy works for the Outfit, and maybe they *do* want to kill you. But why?"

"I don't know. Why they wanna kill *him*?"

"Maybe that had nothing to do with your deal with him. Maybe there was some other reason altogether."

"Uh-huh." It was clear he didn't believe that, any more than she did.

"So why did he come back and tell you this. What did he want?"

"He told me he . . . he had another plan. And if I helped him we could make a whole lotta money. But we couldn't tell anyone about it or they'd be pissed off, you know, at us havin' a side deal. He told me to meet him on Saturday at this farmhouse out near Miracle City and—"

"You mean at Mama Dee's?"

"Yeah, it musta been, but I didn't know for sure. I ain't never been out there. He just gave me directions and said I should be there at noon. I said . . . I said I would."

"And did you?"

"No. It was a Saturday, and I was workin'. I had told him I'd skip work. I was gonna go, but I didn't know if I could even find the place he talkin' about, way out in the country. And plus, I was . . . you know . . ."

"Scared."

"Yeah."

"No need to look so embarrassed, Clyborn. Not going was the first intelligent choice you made in this whole business." Unless his story was a lie, and she didn't really think it was. "What is it you want me to do?"

"I don't know. I just . . ." He stopped and pretended to cough, and for a moment she thought he might actually burst into tears, but he got control of himself again. "Thing is . . . what am I gonna do now? They gonna kill me."

"Maybe they'll try," she said, still playing on his fear. "And maybe I can help you. But first, I need to know, what was the new plan?"

"I . . . don't know." He stared down at the half-eaten pie in front of him. "The dude didn't tell me."

That made her mad again. "Clyborn, look at me." He didn't move. "Dammit, Clyborn, look up at me." He did. "What was Brownley's new plan?"

"I *told* you, he didn't tell me." He couldn't even keep his eyes on her and looked past her shoulder. "Besides," he added, "what difference it make?"

"It makes a difference," she said, "because I don't believe you."

He pushed his chair back from the table. "You callin' me a liar?"

"Use whatever word you like. I don't believe you." He stood up, but she stayed right where she was and stared up at him. "I can help you," she said. "And I will help you." She saw a flicker of hope in his eyes. "But not until you tell me what you and Brownley were up to. Was his new plan to get a lot of money?"

He leaned down toward her. "You said you'd do your best for me if I told you about taking the money." She swore he was trembling. "Now you say somethin' else. *You* the liar!" He was trying very hard to look tough, she knew, but to her he looked only frightened . . . like a lost child, alone, abandoned in a strange neighborhood, wondering what to do and how much to tell her.

"I think Brownley told you what his plan was. I also think you know who the second man was, the one who hired Brownley. And I think you're afraid of that second man, too, as well as the Outfit." She stacked their two trays and gathered up the empty plates and plastic forks. "Here." She handed him his unopened brownie. "You go home and think about what kinda shit you're in, Clyborn. And when you're ready to tell me the truth, you let me know." She stood up. "And then I'll help you."

He hesitated, but only for an instant, then spun around and walked away. She watched him and when he got to the exit he turned back toward her. It seemed as though he might come back, and she almost waved, to encourage him. Then he slipped the brownie into his jacket pocket and disappeared through the door.

She carried both their trays across the room and slid the plates and cups and forks through the swinging door of the trash container and put the trays on top. She told herself again that she was right, and that Clyborn really *did* know who Brownley worked for, and what Brownley's plan for a "side deal" was.

She hoped he'd change his mind and tell her. She hoped nothing bad happened before he did.

THIRTY-SIX

Dugan spent all morning at his office, catching up on an endless stream of paperwork that could never be caught up with. One bright spot was the call at eleven about Reuben Carillo.

When Kirsten came in at noon he told her about Reuben, how a scaffold had collapsed and now his legs were in braces and he sat home all day and yelled at his three kids and dragged himself with two canes from his sofa to the dining room table to the bathroom, and each day got more and more overweight. The lawyer Dugan sent the case to, a couple of years ago, had called to say it had settled that morning. Now there'd be money for the best physical and occupational therapy available, state-of-the-art prostheses if he needed them, and a decent education for his kids. He'd need every penny of it.

"It looks like a lot of money now, though," he said. "Just the one-third fee probably looks to Reuben like more than he would have earned in his entire life. And he could be right."

"And you get half the fee," Kirsten said. "Funny, you don't seem all that excited about it."

"Not half. The fee gets split four ways, which is fine with me, and I'm happy about the settlement," he said. "But Reuben still has his ruined legs . . . and his hopeless feelings. I'm telling him about all the therapy possibilities, and he's saying he'll never play soccer with his boys, and then saying maybe he'll buy a home entertainment system and a bigger sofa, and send the kids to Mexico this summer with his wife to visit her mother's grave." He shook his head. "He sounded a little drunk. Shit."

"Jesus, Dugan, if it wasn't for you the guy wouldn't even have a *possibility* for a future."

"Uh-uh. If it wasn't for me, some other lawyer would have gotten the case."

"And the fee," she said.

"There *is* that," he said.

He knew, of course, that only Reuben could save Reuben's life, and that all he could do was make it a little more possible. He'd have Mollie call an agency he knew that was good at staying after accident victims who found themselves suddenly wealthy—sort of—and had no clue what to do. He'd pay the damn agency himself, if Reuben would cooperate and—

"Hey!" Kirsten was waggling her fingers at him. "I came in to tell you about my lunch with Clyborn Settles. Take your mind off those big depressing fees."

She gave him a blow-by-blow description, and when she finished and asked him what he thought, he said, "I suppose whoever's behind this *could* be mob connected."

"Could be," she said.

"But Brownley's death doesn't have the feel of a mob hit." He suddenly heard what he'd said. "My God, listen to me! The latest expert on the *feel* of a mob hit."

"But you're right, you know."

"Maybe the guy just wanted Clyborn to *think* the mob was involved, to keep him afraid."

"If so, it worked. But he's afraid of the guy who hired Brownley, too." She stood up and walked around behind Dugan's desk to look out the window. She didn't look happy. "Not much of a view here, is there?"

202

"Nope. It hasn't changed since the last time you looked out it."

"I doubt I've actually looked out this window in years."

"My point, exactly. What's the trouble?"

"Well, I handled Clyborn just the way I should have. He lied to me, so I encouraged him to be afraid and then told him I'd do nothing to help him until he tells me the truth."

"Right. So . . . what's the trouble?"

"Just that maybe he actually *is* in danger, and I'm refusing to help him until I can get what I want out of him."

"Damn, you sound like me."

"I do?"

"Yeah. You just did the best you could for your client . . . and now you refuse to feel good about it."

"Except I was thinking more about *my* good than Eudora's. We need to find out what happened. I don't like being a suspect in a homicide."

"There's no possible case against you on that. Why would you announce to two perfectly respectable old drunks where you're going, and then whap somebody in the head with a shovel or something when you get there?"

"I still don't like being a suspect. Who knows what someone might cook up?"

"Well, that's true. The guy didn't come on to you or something, did he? And you got pissed off and—"

"Dugan!"

"Because then you could plead self-defense or at least get the charge reduced to manslaughter. With no prior convictions, you might serve just a few years and—"

"You're hopeless."

"Thank you. Anyway, you handled Clyborn exactly right. Keep him scared, the bastard, until he tells the truth. Thing is, though, what could you do for him, anyway? If someone's determined to kill him, I mean. Especially if it's the—what's Larry

Candle call 'em?—the 'big bambinos.' You can't offer him life-time sanctuary. And even on a temporary basis, we only know one Cuffs Radovich, and he's otherwise engaged."

"I know. That's why we have to find out what's going on."

"I wish you'd stop saying 'we.' I'm just the lawyer who got roped into handling Eudora's criminal case. It's *you* who's the de-tective." He hadn't told her yet about his own detecting work . . . checking into John Michael Hurley, the professor. "Hell, you don't even let me know what you're doing half the time."

"You're still mad because I hung up on you the other night."

"Who, me? I'm not angry. I'm just . . . reminding you of my role." Actually, he *was* pissed off—a little—now that he thought about it again. Maybe he—

The intercom buzzed, and Mollie's voice came over the speaker. "New client on line three."

"Give it to Larry," he said.

"Sounds like a good case," Mollie said. She always knew, so he had to fight off the urge to pick up line three. "The kind of cli-ent," she added, "you should talk to personally."

He leaned closer to the intercom. "Mollie?"

"Yes?"

"Give it to Larry and—"

There was a click from the speaker and he smiled at Kirsten. She smiled back—grinned, actually. Damn, she was cute!

"That takes care of that." He got up and grabbed his jacket. "Let's the two of us go find out what's going on."

They got Kirsten's Camry and headed for Miracle City. Dugan decided the time was right, so he said, "Brownley told you he was hired by John Michael Hurley, right?"

"Uh-huh."

"And Hurley says he has three sons?" She glanced at him and nodded. "And one doesn't like him?"

" 'Hate' was the word he used," she said.

"And that one's name is Jack, right?"

"Right," she said. "Which is often short for John. So I checked, and Jack's name is John Michael Hurley, Junior. I found out he's a professor of environmental policy at the U of I."

"Damn."

"What's the matter?"

"Oh, nothing," he said. "What else did you find out?"

"That's it. I haven't had time to—"

"Did you find out no one at the university calls him Jack? Or that he's considered an activist, which means he gets involved and takes positions in real-life environmental controversies?" She didn't answer, which he took to be a negative. "Did you find out his last class of the semester—or quarter or whatever they have—is this afternoon at four o'clock, and that it's an exam?"

"What are you—"

"Of course, my confidential source didn't know Professor Hurley's availability before or after class."

"Damn."

"That's what I said, a minute ago." He paused to savor the moment. "So . . . could *that* be the John Michael Hurley who hired Brownley?"

"I don't know if a professor would have the kind of money needed for that. Um . . . what kind of positions does he take?"

"You mean is it usually: 'Bulldozing everything in sight is the environmentally sound choice, as long as the developer pays my consulting fee'?"

"I guess that's a way of putting it."

"I don't know. But he certainly bears checking out, right?"

"Uh-huh."

From then on he was happy to let her drive and to agree with what she thought should be done next. He was, after all, only the assistant.

Eudora's car was in her driveway, but Mama Dee's was gone, and so was Cuff's Blazer. No one answered the door.

"After court on Tuesday I got a set of Eudora's keys, just in case something like this happened," Kirsten said. "I'll wait here for them to come back, while you drive down to Champaign."

Dugan's instinct was not to leave her there alone, but that would have infuriated her, so he kept quiet about it and drove to Champaign to interview the *other* John Michael Hurley.

THIRTY-SEVEN

The drive to Champaign and the U of I campus, then finding the right room in the right building, took about two hours. There was an index card taped to the window of the classroom door with a hand-printed message: "Exam. Please do not disturb. J. M. Hurley." Dugan looked in and saw twenty or thirty students, most of them hunched over their desks, apparently struggling with exam questions. A few simply sat and stared up at the ceiling; either they'd already finished or they were looking for inspiration. Women students outnumbered men, about two to one.

The man pacing back and forth across the front of the room, tapping a rolled-up magazine against his thigh, had to be Hurley. He looked like everybody's dream of a university professor. Tall, dark, and fortyish, he managed to look both rugged and scholarly, with thick black hair that he couldn't—or wouldn't—quite keep in place. He wore khakis, a blue chambray shirt, and a corduroy sport coat with the end of a pair of glasses sticking up from the breast pocket. Dugan would have bet the farm they were half-lensed reading glasses, so that he could perch them low on his nose, and then peer out over them.

Did the man look like that and then just happen to become

a professor? Or did he become a professor first and then work real hard at looking like that?

While Dugan was wondering, Hurley checked his watch and set his magazine on the teacher's desk—which was on a platform raised several inches above the floor. He faced the class and said one word—probably "Time," although Dugan couldn't hear it—and the students gradually gave up their writing and sat back in their seats. Hurley went up and down the aisles, gathering up the test papers, and Dugan was amazed at how much it seemed just like . . . well . . . school.

Hurley took the papers with him to the front of the room and made a few brief comments. Again, Dugan couldn't hear what they were.

Whatever he'd said, though, it brought a smile to many of the students' faces, and even some scattered applause—mostly from the women, at which Dugan wasn't surprised—and they all got to their feet and started toward the door. Dugan stepped to the side and watched them file out into the corridor, chatting with each other, comparing answers. When they were gone, he stepped into the room.

One very serious-looking young woman had stayed behind to talk to Hurley. As Dugan approached, Hurley glanced his way and then said to her, "Not to worry, Doreen. You'll do just fine. Right now, though, there's someone here to see me." Doreen turned and saw Dugan, then slipped quietly out of the room, looking embarrassed.

"Professor Hurley?" Dugan reached out his hand.

"Yes," he said, shaking Dugan's hand. "And thank you."

"You're welcome. What did I do?"

"That Doreen, she's a fine student, and a good research assistant. But worry, worry, worry. I mean, the exam's over." He grinned a just-between-us-guys grin. "Why doesn't she just go out and get drunk, or get laid or whatever?"

It seemed an odd comment, between strangers. On the other

hand, Dugan knew lots of crude professionals. "She'll probably move on to that later, when the panic has subsided." Dugan looked around the room. "It's been a while since I was in school. I'm surprised the kids don't take their exams with computers or something."

Hurley gathered up the exam papers and slid them with his magazine—it was a *Sierra* magazine—into his briefcase. "Oh, they do. For the take-home part of the exam, where they have to research issues and write essay answers. Today was the multiple-choice part." He started toward the door, then stopped. "Anyway, what can I do for you?" He held his head tilted back and to the side as he spoke, as though observing Dugan from a distance—or maybe from an academic height.

Dugan handed him one of his business cards. "I represent a woman named Eudora Ragsdale. She's been charged with felony theft of—"

"I know," Hurley said.

"You do?"

"Well, I didn't know the precise charge, or who her lawyer was, but I know her. And I know she's been accused of stealing money from the Committee to Rescue Emerald Woods."

"But . . . say, can you spare me five minutes of your time?"

"Well, I don't . . . Yes, I suppose so. We can talk right here if you like." He perched on the edge of the teacher's desk.

Dugan would have had to sit in one of the student's chairs and crane his neck to look up at the man, so he stayed standing. "So," he said, "you actually *know* Eudora Ragsdale?"

"I thought I made that clear," Hurley said, sounding like a teacher to a rather dull student. "I've been to some CREW meetings myself, and that's how I know her."

"Really?"

"I assumed you knew that already. Isn't that why you're here? I mean, I was at the carnival where they took in the money she stole."

"*Allegedly* stole."

"Oh, yes, of course. Presumption of innocence. Anyway, I stopped by toward the end of the day to see how they were doing. They had bad luck with the weather. Still, it was an important first step. A morale builder for the group. That is, until she . . . until the money was taken."

"So you're convinced Eudora actually stole the money?"

"Convinced?" He seemed surprised. "I'm not sure I gave it that much thought. I suppose I simply assumed she did. Apparently the police think so, or else why did they arrest her?"

"Why, indeed? Did you know she'd deposited the entire amount in CREW's bank account, *before* she was arrested?"

"I heard that, and I assumed she'd managed to pay it back somehow after she knew she'd been found out. She may have meant to use the money only temporarily in the first place. Return it later, you know. People do that and then realize they can't cover their theft. I assume that's what—"

"You do a lot of assuming," Dugan said.

"Well, don't get me wrong. I'm sure she's entitled to a trial, if that's what she wants. And, whatever happens, I don't think she should go to jail or anything. But they certainly had to arrest her, from what little I know about it. Obviously, she needed money, so she used CREW's money and then lied to cover it up. She's poor and . . . well, you know . . . she's . . ."

"She's black, yes." Dugan filled in the blank correctly, he was sure. "There *is* that bit of evidence."

"No, no, no. I didn't say that. I simply . . ." He paused. "So, just exactly what is it you want from me?"

"Well, I . . ." Actually, he wasn't sure, other than to keep the guy talking. "I thought maybe you'd make a good character witness, but now . . . well . . ."

Hurley's eyes narrowed. "You weren't even aware that I *knew* the woman. So, what are you *really* doing here?"

"Well, you got me there. So I'll be honest with you." Sort of, anyway. "The name 'John Michael Hurley' came up when I was investigating the facts, as the man behind the proposed mall at Emerald Woods. Then I discovered there's more than one John Michael Hurley."

"My father and I."

"Yes. I understand it's your father who wants to build the mall. But I figured I had to talk to you, too. You see, Eudora didn't steal the money. She hid it in her house and someone else took it. Why? Maybe just a burglary. But maybe more than that. Maybe someone's trying to destroy Eudora's credibility."

"By 'someone,' whom do you mean? Surely not me."

"Well, someone who has an interest in seeing that the mall goes through. I don't know what your position is, or even if you have one. Although, I mean, it *is* your father's project."

"Oh, I have a position all right, dear old Dad or not." He apparently couldn't keep the sneer out of his voice.

"And?"

"It's consistent with the position I generally take in such matters. My primary interest is to help stop the further degradation of the environment by these goddamn robber barons who have no goal other than to rape and pillage the planet so they can make a buck. My father being one of them."

"You mean you joined with CREW, in opposition to your own father's project?"

"To begin with, even if I was close to my father, I couldn't support that mall. Second, I've been, as you say, 'in opposition' to my father since the day I learned to think on my own, and probably before that. My father never has enough money, and never will, and he has no scruples about how to get what he wants. I have no interest in his succeeding in any project whatsoever." He stood up and walked a few steps away from Dugan, then turned back. "I do have another interest, though. I'm doing research for a book I intend to write, on the need for grassroots involvement in local environmental issues as they arise, if we're going to slow down the rampant destruction of life on earth."

"Did Eudora know who you were? I mean, that you're the son of the man who's the driving force behind the mall?"

"She doesn't know it from me. I introduced myself simply as 'John,' someone who'd like to help save the woods." He paused. "Eudora Ragsdale has definite leadership qualities, even charisma. CREW's core group is maybe twenty people, and she was right there at the heart of it. But they need financial and organizational support to fight local government and business interests—not to mention my father and his . . ." He shook his head. "I always hoped the mall wouldn't be a done deal before Eudora could get CREW off the ground and get some outside organization—the Sierra Club, for instance—involved."

"*You* must have a lot of experience, though. Weren't you able to give advice?"

"I was certainly tempted to," Hurley said. "But my role there is not as a leader, but as an observer. What works? What doesn't? Why? What's to be learned from CREW's attempts? In the larger scheme, I hope my book will be more important to the environmental movement than that particular tract of marsh and woodland."

"I see," Dugan said. And possibly more important to the man's reputation and career, too, which he *didn't* say because he wasn't certain it was fair. "And what do you think this accusation against Eudora will mean to CREW? Or to her being effective in the group again?"

"I'd say, to both questions, 'It doesn't look good.' They've had one meeting since her arrest, and I was there. She wasn't, of course. They did nothing but bicker and talk of her betrayal and each other's failures. CREW might have had a chance of success before, but that's evaporating." He looked at his watch. "I have to run. I have an appointment."

Dugan followed him out of the room and, when they got to the main entrance, thanked him for his time and help. Hurley went quickly down a sidewalk that led at an angle away from the building, and Dugan was about to head the other way when he saw someone stop Hurley. Doreen, the worried student. She and Hurley exchanged a few words, and Hurley suddenly waved his hand toward her, palm outward as though brushing her aside, and continued on his way.

Doreen stood on the sidewalk and watched him leave, then turned and cut through the grass toward her right.

Dugan went after her. Too far away to be certain, of course, but it sure as hell looked like she was crying.

THIRTY-EIGHT

Kirsten watched Dugan drive away and then went inside Eudora's house. She considered calling Cuffs on his cell phone but decided to wait on that. Right now she was hungry, and she had another call she wanted to make first. They must all have gone somewhere together, probably Eudora and the twins with Mama Dee in her car and Cuffs following in the Blazer.

After looking around the kitchen, she hoped where they'd gone was a grocery store, because there certainly wasn't much food in the place. She settled for toast and peanut butter, washed down with a mug of tea.

She got her cell phone out of her purse, then decided to use Eudora's phone and leave her own line open in case Dugan tried to reach her. She called Rodriguez, the public defender, and he said Coral had talked to the police that morning and he expected her to be released by noon the next day. She was doing fine.

Kirsten dialed Parker Gillson at his office at the Attorney Disciplinary Commission. "You have time now to talk?" she asked.

"Sure," he said.

"I'm not diverting your valuable talents and resources away from investigating wayward lawyers, am I?"

"Not to worry. That's an endless task, anyway, and I've done enough for one day. I'm glad, though, that no one in John Michael Hurley's immediate family is a lawyer. Otherwise, I might be accused of divulging information I got on the job, which of course would be contrary to my fiduciary obligations—not to mention it could get my tail kicked outta here."

"Look, Park, I don't want to—"

"Forget it. Thing is, though, I don't have a whole lot more than what I already told Dugan. I faxed some notes about John Michael Hurley to your office. I'm still working on the three sons."

"Anything about the deceased wife?"

"Maiden name Anna Carpaccio, raised on the Near West Side, with an uncle and a few cousins rumored to be, as they say, in the loan business. Died in a four-car collision in an ice storm on Lake Shore Drive back when the kids were quite young."

"Hurley ever marry again?"

"Nope. On the plus side, he has no criminal record and he's a big donor to a lot of charitable causes."

"Like Mother of Mercy Village?"

"Big time. That's his pet project, and he's sponsoring a big fund-raiser for the place in a few weeks. But other charities, too. He also digs deep into his pockets for political contributions. Lots of them. He's just your all-around basic philanthropic, politically connected businessman. Which isn't to say he doesn't still have way more money than you or I could spend in several lifetimes."

"So," she said, "would some of his well-known generosity be to offset stuff on his 'minus side,' which you haven't gotten to yet?"

"Could be. On the minus side, he's a mean bastard. You deal with Hurley, you gotta be ready to do things his way, or pay the consequences. You own property he wants to buy? You sell. Otherwise, maybe your top customers suddenly go somewhere else,

215

or maybe one of your buildings goes up in flames one night. On the other hand, are you and he bidding on the same contract? You drop out and maybe some big problem your daughter's been having with a guy goes away . . . for good. Stuff like that."

"Rumors, though."

"Right. Just rumors. And jeez, with a guy like that, always buys a table at your benefit, supports your picnic for kids with cancer, helps find a job for your nephew who's just out of school—or out of the slammer. Who you gonna believe? Some down-and-out loser with an ax to grind? No way. And if the loser complains to the U.S. attorney, or some regulatory agency, why hell, whoever he's talking to probably sat next to Hurley last month at an NAACP breakfast meeting."

"So . . . all that being said, what's your take on him?"

"My take, thoughtful and unbiased, is the guy's a slime bag, a crook who'd slit your throat, literally or figuratively, to make a buck. But by proxy, of course. And environmentally speaking? If there was enough money in the deal, he'd pour concrete over the last forest on earth in a minute, and over any animals—and any people—who didn't get out of the way fast enough. That's my take. Want me to clarify that for—"

"No thanks," she said. "It's pretty clear."

Half an hour later Kirsten was driving Eudora's Ford Escort, and because she had no specific destination, she was headed in the direction of Kankakee. Eudora was in the passenger seat.

Eudora and Mama Dee had come home with a carload of groceries that had to be carried in and stowed away. Cuffs and the twins were right behind them, and the girls were thrilled because they'd gotten to ride in the Blazer. Kirsten had wondered what new words they'd learned but hadn't asked.

As soon as she'd gotten Eudora into the car, Kirsten started pressing her for what she was holding back. Eudora resisted and Kirsten had gone after her—too aggressively, she realized—and Eudora immediately jumped in and yelled right back. She was ferocious when she was attacked, and she'd made it goddamn clear she took no shit from anybody.

Kirsten had been making it just as clear that she didn't, either, when she'd been interrupted—fortunately—by Dugan calling on the cell phone. He gave her a quick rundown on his conversation with John Michael, Jr., then told her he was on his way to interview someone else and had to sign off.

By the time he hung up, she was over her anger. Eudora was, too, and they exchanged apologies.

"Let's start again," Kirsten said. "All I meant to do was ask if there was anything relevant you might not have told me."

"But you didn't say it that way," Eudora said. "You accused me of holding out on you. You pretty much said I was lying."

"What I said was, 'How can I trust you if you don't tell me the truth?' That's not accusing you of lying."

"It's close enough." Eudora blew her nose. "I already said I'm sorry I got so mad at you. But understand, you grow up in the projects you don't let people call you a liar to your face. You gotta protect yourself. I . . . well . . . I guess I overreact when someone comes after me. It's like self-defense. Automatic."

"Okay," Kirsten said. "But I'm certain there was something you almost told us a few days ago, after the hearing when they tried to revoke your bond."

"There *was* something, but I don't see how it could possibly be connected with what's been happening. I promise you, I'll tell you if I ever think it means anything." Eudora made a sniffling sound, and Kirsten realized she was crying. "I'll have to, because if they build that mall . . . well, I don't know what I'll do."

"I guess I'll have to accept that," Kirsten said. "What's going on with CREW? Have you heard?"

"All I heard was they had a special meeting earlier this week and didn't tell me. I don't think the others want me involved any more."

"They'll feel different after you get found not guilty."

"No, they won't. They'll just think I took the money and got away with it. People still won't trust me."

"Yeah? Well, CREW or not, Emerald Woods was your land, or your grandmother's, anyway. So I was thinking. Maybe you could go back to court and void the deed from way back when Mama Dee gave the land to Miracle City. The deal was it had to be used for a park or something, right?"

"Right," Eudora said. "And we thought of that. One of the women in CREW works as a secretary for a lawyer in Kankakee. Says he's real smart and real honest. She showed the papers to him and he said it would be a long shot. Mama Dee had this old lawyer helping her when she did it, and he messed up or something. Now he's dead. Plus, the lawyer we asked said Hurley would have some huge expensive law firm, and we'd need a lot of money to go to court. Which we don't have."

"Damn!" Kirsten drove in silence for a minute, then spotted a Wendy's. "Are you hungry?"

"I guess so."

"Let's get a sandwich and go home."

THIRTY-NINE

D ugan stayed about a half block behind the young woman named Doreen, wondering how best to approach her without scaring her off. Not that he was especially scary looking, but he was a stranger to her—and way bigger than she was. He really ought to have shaved off about fifteen pounds or maybe—

Oops, where was she?

He hurried ahead and looked in the window of a tiny place called the New Day Cafe and spotted her standing at the food counter. He went inside. It was a vegetarian place: no meat, no dairy. It seemed mostly for takeout, but there were three small tables: two by the window—both occupied—and a vacant one off to the side.

"For here," Doreen told the man behind the counter.

Maybe, Dugan thought, with a little luck . . .

He had no idea what to order and thought he might just copy her. But when he heard the counterman repeat what it was, he changed his mind and decided on one of several strangely named green teas. "And two of those thick slices of whole grain bread," he said, "with extra butter."

Of course there was no butter. He'd start losing that fifteen pounds right now. When he turned away from the counter with his tray, Doreen was seated at the table by the wall. He went over and smiled down at her. "Remember me?" She looked up and he could tell she recognized him. "We met in Dr. Hurley's classroom."

"I wouldn't exactly say we met," she said.

"Well, maybe not formally, but . . ." He looked around the little restaurant, indicating he'd sit elsewhere if there were any elsewhere to sit. "You don't mind if I share your table, do you?"

"Well . . ."

He sat down his tray and pulled out the fragile-looking chair, resting his left hand on the table, trying to make sure she noticed the wedding band. "We veggie folks have to stick together, you know." She didn't scream or run away, so he sat down.

"Actually," she said, "I'm not a true vegetarian . . . but I'm pushing myself that way." The red in her eyes told him he was right. She'd been crying.

"Me, too. That is, my wife and I." He tore a chunk from one of his slices of bread. "That Dr. Hurley, he's sure . . ." He stopped and leaned toward her a little. "Gosh, are your allergies bothering you?"

"What?" she said. "Oh, you mean my eyes. I just have a cold, that's all."

"You shouldn't rub them, you know? Anyway, that Dr. Hurley, he's something, isn't he?" As noncommittal as he could think of.

"He's . . . an excellent teacher," she said. She looked like what she wanted to say was that Hurley was despicable.

"He's working on a book, you know."

"Yes, I know."

"It's on local grassroots participation in environmental decision-making," he said, "or . . . something like that."

"What?" She looked surprised.

"Local grassroots partici—"

"I'm not aware of that one. I've been working with him on

220

the research for a different book." She frowned. "He's a very busy man, I guess."

"If you wanna know the truth," he said, deciding to take a chance, "I don't like the guy."

"Really?" She sounded almost hopeful. "Do you know him well?"

"Not well. But I think he's pompous, way too filled up with himself. And . . . I think he has a mean streak in him that runs pretty deep." If she still liked the guy at all, this conversation was just about over.

"Gosh." Her eyes widened. She looked barely twenty years old, and just a short time away from some very small farm in the middle of some very large prairie. "Gosh," she repeated, "I . . . well, I guess I'd have to agree. With me, at least, he's been . . ." She stopped short and was blushing. "I've been with him—as a student and a research assistant, I mean—all semester. A lot of people seem to respect his work, and some admire the proenvironment stances he takes. But when you get to know him more personally, you find out that Professor Hurley . . . well . . . he's just not always very nice. He's sort of . . . *calculating*. I think he's angry inside, you know? And he's not a very truthful person."

"He's not?"

"Definitely not." She seemed to be on a roll now, eager to get some things off her chest. "For example, whatever he told you about some book he's writing? It might be true or it might not. I certainly haven't seen one hint of any research, or heard one word, about the sort of book you mentioned." She shook her head. "Sometimes I wonder if he has a real . . . conscience, or something. With him it seems like it's always, 'What's in it for me?' "

"Let me ask you something, Doreen. It *is* Doreen, isn't it?" She nodded. "I don't mean to get personal or anything, okay?" She nodded again. She was *so* naive. "Did Professor Hurley just dump you?"

Her eyes flooded with tears, and she wiped at them with her paper napkin, which was earth-friendly brown, and about as smooth as sandpaper.

"Here," he said, and gave her his handkerchief. "Use this. You're far too young for dermabrasion."

She smiled at that, just a little, and wiped away the tears. "Actually, he *did* dump me, but not, you know, not the way you might think." She blushed again. "He told me he didn't need me . . . I mean as a research assistant . . . next semester. I was *so* counting on that money. . . ." She stared down at the vegetables and tofu and whatever else it was on her plate. "I'm not hungry anymore," she said.

"Me, either." He sipped some green tea. Not bad tasting, actually. "Um . . . has Professor Hurley ever mentioned a project up near Kankakee?"

"No, he hasn't. At least I—" She stopped abruptly and sat silently for a while. Finally, she looked up at him. "You know, I shouldn't have said what I did. Really, I'm surprised at myself." She was obviously embarrassed and uncomfortable saying anything more about Hurley. "It's not as though I know you."

"No, but . . . here." He gave her his card. "I'm a lawyer, see? That's probably why you trusted me." She didn't seem to get his little joke, so he said, "I'm not suing anybody, and I'm certainly not hiding anything. I'm just gathering information to help someone. And you've been very nice." He laid a twenty-dollar bill on the table. "This is from my client, for your time and cooperation. If you want to tell anyone—even Hurley, I guess— that you talked to me, you go right ahead. It's no secret. Okay?"

She looked down at the money and then up at him. "I guess so," she said.

He stood up and left in a hurry.

Regardless of her denial, that girl had been way more than a research assistant—and way less than she'd thought she was— to Hurley, and Dugan hoped that if she did tell the sonovabitch about their conversation, it would worry the hell out of him.

FORTY

unny," Kirsten said, "I have the feeling we're making progress, but I can't get a handle on where we're going." She and Dugan were back in the Camry again, headed home from Eudora's. He kept shifting around, as though he couldn't get comfortable, and she wondered if she should get a bigger car.

"My problem," he said, "is keeping straight just what it is we're trying to make progress on. It seems we've got most things under control. Like, I'm confident of a 'not guilty' in Eudora's criminal case; Coral's okay, and they'll be releasing her pretty soon; and it's up to the cops to catch whoever killed the guy at Mama Dee's and torched the place. So, as long as no one's messing with Eudora and Mama Dee any more, what's left?"

"Who's to bother them, with Cuffs there?" she said. "They're still at risk, and will be, as long as Eudora keeps fighting the mall."

"From John Michael Hurley?"

"That's how it looks. If building his mall means the end of Emerald Woods, that's just business. And apparently, if it takes destroying a few human beings along the way, too, so be it." She went on to explain what Parker Gillson had told her. "Hurley claims the mall's just another deal, not something he'd soil his hands over," she said. "But, if Park is right, what's been happening is typical of Hurley."

"Park's always right," Dugan said, "which is why he makes me so nervous. Besides, John Michael, Junior, said pretty much the same thing: no matter how much money his father has, it's never enough, and he'd do anything to add to it. Junior thinks the mall's probably a done deal with Eudora and CREW out of the way."

"Damn," she said. "So what else did he say? And who was that other person you were chasing after?"

He related his conversations with Hurley and his student Doreen. When he finished he added, "I'd say I've given you those conversations verbatim, or as close as any court reporter would get."

"Not that you'd ever boast about your steel-trap memory."

"Nope. Not me. Or about my keen-edged appetite, either, which is telling me you should take the next exit so we can eat before we get into the city."

"Fine, and after that we'll go talk to one of our witnesses."

"You mean one of *your* witnesses," he said. "I'm just a tired, hungry lawyer. Plus, can't you wait till tomorrow to see whoever it is?"

"No," she said, "because it's Clyborn. He's in way over his head; he's scared, and he reached out for my help. My keen-edged conscience is bothering me."

Two hours later she was driving again. Dugan was dozing in the seat beside her, his head periodically jerking up and then dropping again, bit by bit, until his chin hit his chest to start the cycle over. They'd left the interstate at Route 30, gone east and eaten at a Bohemian restaurant near Sauk Village, and then headed north into the city.

"We're there," she announced, and saw his head jerk up. "Almost, anyway."

He rolled his shoulders around and craned his neck to peer out the windows in every direction. "Where?"

"In the city. That light up there is a Hundred Twenty-sixth Street."

"Jesus, what city? Where are we?" He paused and she heard a little hiccup. "And what was in those dumplings?"

"Ask not what, darling. Ask how many." She stopped at the light. "We're in Chicago, going north on Torrence Avenue, just past the Ford assembly plant."

"There sure aren't many cars around. I mean it looks like the east side of the Berlin Wall—when there was one. Does anyone *live* within miles of here?"

"There are rows of little bungalows off to the east a few blocks, but right here it's all zoned industrial." The light changed and she drove on. "With the steel mills mostly gone, a lot of the southeast side is vacant. But if you think it looks deserted around here now, you should have seen it a few years ago, before the economic upswing."

"Yeah, well, some swing. But I guess you have to have rail yards and warehouses *some*where."

"Absolutely." She threw a sudden right, went up over an embankment and across some railroad tracks, and stopped at a wide double gate in a tall cyclone fence. "And scrap yards, too." A metal sign fixed to the gate said

WISNIEWSKI AND RYAN SCRAP METAL CO.
MAIN ENTRANCE

She switched off the headlights, and they sat in the dark at the southwest corner of a huge scrap yard. The fence, capped by barbed wire, stretched east, to their right, along the south edge of the property until she lost sight of it—more than a city block, anyway. The property seemed to extend equally deep in front of them. Inside the fence, lights atop tall, widely spaced poles threw an amber light, very dim, bathing the yard and the half-dozen buildings clustered near the entrance in a sad, eerie glow.

For some reason she thought of a desert—a dismal, abandoned desert at night. The buildings, most of them made of rust-stained corrugated metal, looked like the huts and equipment sheds of a miners' camp. And beyond them were the mountains, huge mounds of metal scrap, like misshapen pyramids—some of them several stories tall—rising up into the darkness above the light poles. They were scattered through the huge yard, disappearing into the distance and throwing odd-shaped shadows on the ground and across the other mountains around them.

"Damn!" Dugan said. "Great spot for a shootout, huh?" She turned and looked at him and he added, "I mean, in a movie."

There was one building made of brick. It was closest to the gate—about twenty yards in—and to the right of the roadway that led deeper into the yard. Just past that building were two drive-on truck scales, one on either side of the roadway. Weight in, minus weight out; and you had the weight of the scrap. There was a sign on the side of the building that she couldn't read in the low light from that distance. "Look," she said, pointing, "that must be the office. There's a light on inside." She stared. "And see that shadow? I think that's from a car parked on the other side of it."

"Uh-huh," he said. "So what?"

"So . . . let's go." She grabbed her purse off the floor and opened her door.

"Kirsten, wait." He laid a hand on her arm. "We can't. The gate is closed. There's a chain *holding* it closed."

"But I don't see any *padlock* on that chain."

"Jesus," he said, and leaned forward toward the windshield, "you're right. Which is another reason why we shouldn't go in. It doesn't make sense. There's a very bad feeling growing in my gut—and it's got nothing to do with dumplings. It's . . . in the air, or something."

"I know. I feel it too. It's called fear." She pushed her door open and turned to him. "You wait here. I'll be all right."

She figured that would bring him along with her . . . and it did.

The chain was looped through both sections of the gate but not locked. They unwound it and pushed the gate open. When Dugan started walking straight toward the office, she grabbed his arm and pulled him with her. They walked at an angle from the gate until they could see the other side of the building. "See?" she said. "It *is* a car."

A red Camaro, in fact. Clyborn's red Camaro.

"Clyborn!" she called. Dugan hissed at her, but she ignored him. "Clyborn!" This time as loud as she could. "C'mon out!" But the night air was warm and humid, and it seemed to swallow up her words.

By this time the Colt automatic was in her hand and she was running toward the office with Dugan right beside her. She glanced into the empty Camaro as she passed it, and then stopped at the closed office door, motioning Dugan off to the side.

"Clyborn!" she called. "Clyborn?" But she knew in her heart he wasn't going to answer.

And he didn't.

Inside, he was face down on the floor beside a desk cluttered with the remnants of a meal from Burger King. There was a small bullet hole in the back of his head . . . and not very much blood at all. A cheap looking revolver lay on the floor beside him.

She went back out the door and leaned against the side of the building, struggling to get air down into her lungs. She had a vague sense of Dugan talking to her, but she waved him away.

Clyborn had come to her for help and she'd let him dangle.

Not so much because he was an insufferable, dishonest fool, but because she'd thought he was worth more to her scared. She'd refused to help him until he told her what he knew, letting him twist until he'd given her what she wanted. To her, Clyborn was there only to be used for her own purposes. Now he was dead.

Was she that much different from, say, John Michael Hurley?

FORTY-ONE

Of course there's a difference," Dugan said, "a huge difference."
It was five in the morning and the Chicago PD Violent
Crimes investigators had finally let them leave Area Two
Headquarters. Now he was driving home and listening to Kirsten
compare herself to John Michael Hurley, for God's sake.
"There's the little matter of intent, motive, purpose," he said,
"the reason you do something, or don't."

"You mean, 'The end justifies the means.'"

"Whoa! I'm not gonna get dragged into that. The fact is you
didn't use any means. You didn't put the gun to Clyborn's head.
You didn't *tell* anyone to put the gun to his head."

They drove for a while in silence, and then she said, "Maybe . . .
well, maybe it's just as bad when you *don't* do something, when
you could have."

The *maybe,* and a new tone in her voice, told him she was
coming out of it. "Maybe," he said. "But what could you have
done? Hired round the clock security for Clyborn? Hell, it's not
like he told you enough to—"

"Okay," she said, "I give." She leaned and gave him a little
kiss on the cheek.

"You know?" he said. "Sometimes I wonder why you keep doing this kind of work when it bothers you so much."

"Me, too. But it's not like my bag's full of other skills or useful experience." She sighed. "I suppose I could go to dental hygienist school."

"Hell, you could go to cardiovascular surgery school, and graduate summa cum laude."

"I wouldn't last three days at any school in the universe. Anyway, this is what I do, and as time goes on, maybe I won't be so—"

"Nope. I don't wanna hear that. Certain things—like cruelty and abandonment and murder—will always bother you. I love it that they bother you. I love you more because they *do* bother you."

She kissed him again, this time a longer kiss, and on the ear. "We need a car with a bench seat," she said. "These two-seaters inhibit a loving relationship."

He drove a little faster and when they got home they went to bed. This time the only inhibitor was fatigue, which they dealt with pretty well.

When Dugan woke up it was just past noon. First he called the office and gave Mollie another lame excuse, and then he dragged Kirsten out of bed and they went to the Blue Sunrise for breakfast.

It was a beautiful day and they sat in a booth by the window. Kirsten ordered orange juice, coffee, and a couple of waffles with powdered sugar. No meat. Dugan ordered two short stacks of pancakes—one blueberry, one strawberry—with sausage patties and coffee. "Don't forget," he told the waitress, "*short* stacks." The woman swished away and he said to Kirsten, "Last time she forgot, remember?"

"Right, and you had to eat three pancakes instead of two. Poor dear."

"I know, but that was just one order. Today it's more important."

"So . . . not to change the subject," Kirsten said, "did you notice anything significant?"

"Ah." He took a little spiral notebook out of his shirt pocket and laid it on the table, open to a blank page, then laid his pen beside it. They'd known the cops wouldn't tell them a damn thing about their investigation of Clyborn's murder, so they'd looked around for a few minutes—not touching anything—before they called 911. "I noticed the gun on the floor," he said. "No sign of a struggle. The remains of a late night Whopper with fries."

"Did you notice there seemed to be one meal, but two soft drink cups?"

"Yes," he said. "And one cup had a little water in the bottom—probably melted ice—and cigarette ashes in the water."

"How do you know they were ashes?"

"First, they *looked* like cigarette ashes. Second, it smelled like someone had been smoking in there, although there were *No Smoking* signs all over. Third, there was an empty matchbook in the wastebasket beside the desk. Was Clyborn smoking when you talked to him?"

"It was a no smoking cafeteria," she said. "But he didn't smell like a smoker, and he wasn't smoking when I saw him on the street out near his apartment." She paused while the waitress refilled their coffees, then said, "Did you see the padlock?"

"Nope."

"I did. One of the dicks pulled it from Clyborn's jacket pocket. That was before they made us get out of the building."

"So," he said, "Clyborn let him into the yard. If it was the guy Clyborn was scared of, he must somehow have intimidated him;

231

or maybe he tricked him. He brought the food, and they sat and talked while Clyborn ate. He was probably finding out what he knew, or didn't know. Then he took out the gun, made Clyborn lie down on the floor, and shot him."

"Cold."

"As ice," he said. "But not bright enough to be a true professional."

The waitress returned, this time with their food. "Short stacks," she said, setting Dugan's plates in front of him. "See?"

"Thanks," he said, and dug in.

"Incidentally," Kirsten said, after they'd eaten in silence for a few minutes, "what's all this about?"

"What?" He looked up to see her pointing her fork at the notebook and pen he'd laid out on the table, and which the waitress had pushed off to the side. "Oh, that. I just thought it seemed . . . investigatorial. That's all."

"Okay, investigator," she said, "what are your thoughts about that empty matchbook?"

"A couple of things. First, something I learned way back when I worked in the PD's office . . . that not many killers would get caught if they weren't either still on the scene when the cops got there, or else nervous and stupid enough to leave clues around."

"And second?"

"Second, like I told the cop who was interviewing me, they oughta be looking for a guy Clyborn knew, and who lights up his smokes with matches from a restaurant named Hooters."

"Except Hooters is a chain, and the matchbook didn't say which one."

"That's what the investigator told me. One of the things, anyway."

"Oh?" She seemed curious. "What else did he tell you?"

"Basically, that you and I ought to leave the investigating to the professional police, and that we were lucky they weren't throwing our asses in the can for murder." He speared a sausage patty and lifted it toward his mouth. "Words to that effect."

"Did you mention Officer Galboa, and his talking about a Hooters?"

"Actually, I did. I was explaining why we were interested in Clyborn, and Galboa's name came up, along with Frawley's. I just happened to mention that Galboa told me about a Hooters he'd been to, near the U of I." He paused. "What about you?"

"I brought it up, too. The dick looked like he thought I was loony. But they'll have to check it out. Look for prints on the matchbook, at least."

"There won't be any."

"No," she said, "life's not quite that easy. One thing I didn't mention to the cops was that Galboa knew right away where to look for the empty envelope."

"What?"

"The envelope the cash was in at Eudora's house. He found it about thirty seconds after Frawley walked in the door with the search warrant."

"Yeah, but he found it in the garbage, you said. One of the first places anyone would look for a discarded envelope."

"It was still pretty quick," she said. "And how would he know the thief discarded it? Which brings me to . . . why do you think Clyborn was killed?"

"To keep him quiet."

"What did he know?"

"He knew who it was who killed him." Dugan drank some coffee. "Whether that was the same guy who hired Brownley to harass Eudora, and whether that might be enough to . . ." He stopped and made a point of searching the plates in front of him. "Hey, didn't I have *three* sausage patties?"

"Three? Hell, you had six!"

"Well, yes, but I mean three with each short stack. Anyway, one's missing."

233

"I ate it. You *saw* me eat it."

"I know." He grinned. "But you looked so distracted when you did, I wasn't sure you'd even remember."

"I remember it, and I enjoyed it. Thank you."

"You're welcome."

"Anyway, Clyborn wouldn't tell me who Brownley was taking orders from, but I think he knew. I also think he was as afraid of the cops as he was of the Outfit. So let's say Clyborn knew it was Galboa who recruited Brownley, and Galboa killed him so he wouldn't talk. Being a cop, Galboa might have a throwaway gun to use."

"But who killed Brownley?" he asked. "Galboa? Did he kill him early in the afternoon and then go back to Mama Dee's later, to torch the place? We'll have to check where he was Saturday afternoon." He crumpled his napkin and dropped it on his plate. "Is this confusing to you?"

"Yes," she said.

"Good. Then I don't feel so bad."

"Assume John Michael Hurley—or, let's say, someone on his behalf—hired Galboa to get Eudora out of the way of the mall. Galboa knew Brownley and hired him to—"

"Go back a step. Wouldn't it be risky for Hurley to hire a police officer to carry out a criminal plan?"

"Depends on the police officer, I guess," she said, "and what you already knew about him . . . or her. I checked on Galboa. He was a Chicago cop. Worked the same kind of undercover unit as Brownley. Maybe they knew each other, I don't know. Galboa never got accused like Brownley did, but he did resign from the department around the same time."

"Okay," he said, "so we assume Hurley's people hire Galboa to dirty up Eudora. Galboa recruits Brownley. Then Brownley—using Clyborn—does a great job, and Eudora gets arrested."

"And then Galboa kills Brownley to keep him quiet, and then he kills Clyborn to keep *him* quiet."

"Sort of a stretch," he said.

"Yes. And there are other things that have to be factored in, too. Clyborn told me Brownley ordered him to be at Mama Dee's on Saturday, to help in some separate plan, a scheme Brownley didn't want Galboa and his supposedly 'connected' employers to know about. Clyborn doesn't show, and Brownley gets killed. Then I show up, you show up, and an arsonist shows up and torches Mama Dee's."

"Don't forget Coral. She was there, too."

"Right."

"Is this confusing to you?"

"You're repeating yourself," she said. "We're missing something. Let's go back to the beginning. We have a real estate developer who's working on a shopping center project—a major development, not a little strip mall. But a community activist is stirring up opposition to the project. He could try to buy off the opposition, give her a little piece of the action. But let's say he realizes that that won't fly. So he hires people to get her out of the way. They start with threatening phone calls, which don't work. Then they dirty her up. That does work. She loses credibility and isn't much use to her organization any more. Meanwhile, she—"

"Wait," he said. "When she's found not guilty, she'll get her credibility back."

"She thinks you give the public too much credit. But anyway, at least for now she's under a cloud. She gets a couple of geniuses to help her out—that's us—and suddenly the ante is raised . . . *way* up. Her grandmother's house is burned to the ground, and then even the guys who were brought in to get rid of her start getting killed, for God's sake. The theory of the geniuses—that's us—is that Brownley and Clyborn, after they succeed, are murdered so they won't talk. But that's a pretty risky scenario, even to make a multimillion-dollar project work. Like Hurley says, there are other projects."

"But we agreed there's gotta be a ton of money to be made in this mall deal," he said, "and that Hurley'd make sure none of this could be traced back to him. He merely expresses an opinion. Then someone contacts someone, who contacts someone, who contacts Galboa—who maybe never heard of Hurley. If it's Galboa who's directing Brownley and Clyborn, then it's his ass that's in a sling for whatever they do. If Brownley had some crazy side deal going, Galboa might think it worthwhile to kill him, to keep the whole thing from blowing up."

"Maybe," she said, "but once Brownley's dead, what's Galboa afraid of? That Clyborn, a guy who has zero credibility, might come forward and confess that he committed a burglary at Eudora's house and claim he only did it because a now-deceased man who worked for a local police officer told him the money was there and he could keep it if he found it and stole it?"

"Still, Brownley and Clyborn together, either intentionally or by screwing up big time, could have put Galboa away for conspiracy and arson."

"Brownley was dead before any arson, and long dead when Clyborn got it."

"I know," he said, "but—"

"That's the thing. There are too many buts, too many things that don't fit. That's why I say there's a piece missing. There's another whole thread running though this mess, one we don't know about, one that's got enough at stake, for someone, that it makes killing people seem reasonable."

"Fine," he said. "If there's a thread, let someone else pick at it. Why not just let me handle Eudora's criminal case, and let the cops handle the homicides?"

"What about the mall? We just let that go ahead and be built?"

"That's not our problem."

"It's not? Well, it sure is *my* problem. It has been ever since Hurley treated me like a little girl and guaranteed me that his mall was going to be built, no matter what. It's up to me to decide what my problems are, and this is one of them. And you know what? It's yours, too. That phone call to our apartment threatened both of us, and then both of us were nearly killed at Mama Dee's. I'm the one who had the run-in with Tommy Hurley—which I don't think is over yet, not in his mind—but we've both been ordered around by Frawley, we're both under a cloud with the state cops, we both found Clyborn and—"

"You know, I kinda get the point." He drank the rest of his coffee. "So, this 'other thread.' Got any ideas how to find out what it is?"

"Not really. But—" Her cell phone rang.

Their waitress wasn't in sight, so while Kirsten answered her phone he took their check to the cash register and paid it. When he got back she was flipping her phone closed.

"Parker Gillson," she said. "Looks like we know what Eudora's secret might be."

"Oh?"

"I'd asked him to check court records to see if Eudora ever sued Clyborn for child support. The answer is no. But Clyborn's name did turn up in the computer. A case a couple of years ago, called *Loretta Jones versus Clyborn Settles*. A paternity case. Park went through the court file."

"And?"

"And, whoever Loretta Jones is, Clyborn couldn't possibly have been the father of her baby . . . for the same reason he couldn't possibly have been the father of Eudora's twins. As the lab tech who did the tests put it in his testimony, Clyborn's 'as sterile as a fresh Band-aid.'"

FORTY-TWO

They were in the car, headed for Miracle City, and Kirsten knew she was driving too fast but couldn't help it.

"What the hell is going on here?" she said.

"I don't know," he said. "Is Eudora crazy or—"

The phone rang again.

"Damn!" She fumbled it out of her purse, answered, listened quietly, and finally said, "I'm on my way." She closed the phone.

"Sounded like Cuffs's voice," he said.

"Right. Eudora insisted on going to the store about an hour ago. She hasn't come back."

Eudora turned onto Till's Creek Road and then drove as slowly as she dared. When he complained, she reminded him it was a gravel road and, with all the rain they'd had, if they went in the ditch, they'd sink in the mud and never get out.

He was stupid enough to buy that, but so what? He was sitting right beside her, and he had a gun. He'd told her outside the store that he wasn't alone in this and her babies would be hurt if she didn't do what he said. She knew Cuffs was with the twins, but still she panicked and got into her car. He got into the passenger seat. He'd tried to touch her breast once, at first, but she went crazy and told him she'd drive right up onto the curb and through some store window if he didn't keep his fucking hands away from her. He stopped, and she realized he couldn't afford to be caught right there in town and she should have just turned her back on him and walked away . . . but by then it had been too late and they were already outside town.

Now he had the gun in his left hand, just inches away from her side. His right hand was in his lap. She stared straight ahead as she drove, but she knew he was stroking himself through his pants. She hated him. If he tried to . . . to touch her, she'd kill him. She'd use her hands and her feet and her teeth and she'd kill him—or she'd die trying.

Cuffs explained it pretty much the way Kirsten thought he would. "You want a jailer," he said, "you hire a fucking jailer. I got plenty of experience keeping people locked up. But you wanted a bodyguard and that's what you got. You heard me tell 'em on day one that—"

"Okay. Okay. I know." He was right, too. No matter how frustrated she felt, he hadn't been hired to keep Eudora in custody. "So," she said, "do you think she had a secret agenda when she left?"

"Shit. She's a woman, y'know? Who knows what's in any of their ratty little minds?" He shook his head and, despite his words, she thought he was as worried as she was about where Eudora might be. "She said she wanted to go to the store for milk and a few things. I told her to wait till the kids were up from their nap and we'd all go. She said no, and we went back and forth a little. Mama Dee said she'd go with her and Eudora got mad. You know how she gets. So I thought fuck it and let her go." He stared at Kirsten as though watching for her reaction. "And I'd do the same goddamn thing tomorrow. I do my job. That's it."

"Did she talk about going anywhere else?" Dugan asked. "Some other store?"

"Christ, I told you. She was going to the grocery store for milk and stuff and in five minutes she'd be back. I gave her almost an hour, knowing how broads are, and then called you."

FORTY-THREE

The sun hadn't been out all afternoon, and it was gloomy and getting dark when Kirsten parked beside the village hall. She slid the Colt from the holster on her hip, put it in her purse, and locked the purse inside the Camry.

She'd left Dugan at Eudora's. If Eudora called there, he could call Kirsten on her cell phone. Then, if he needed to get anywhere in a hurry, he could use Mama Dee's car, while Cuffs stayed with Mama Dee and the twins. At the same time, Kirsten could call Dugan if she needed to, or if she found out anything.

She went down the outside stairway to the basement corridor and pushed her way through the door marked *POLICE DE-PARTMENT*. Chief Frawley was alone in the room, sitting at one of the gray metal desks behind the counter. He heard her come in, of course, and glanced up, but then went back to reading the newspaper spread open in front of him. His massive body made the desk look small.

There was a bell on the counter, the kind with a button on top, and a little sign that said: *Please Ring for Service.* She slapped the button with her palm, three times . . . hard.

Frawley raised his head, slowly, and stared at her. "Didn't I make it clear the other night," he said, "that you're not welcome around here?"

"Very clear," she said. "But you know, Chief, this isn't Dodge City. You can't just run people out of town and shoot 'em down if they come back."

"I know. A shame, too." He wrapped his huge hand around a paper cup on the desk, lifted it to his lips, then set it down again. "Was there something you wanted?"

"Where's Officer Galboa?"

He shook his head. "Y'know? You caused that boy trouble for no reason at all, trying to tie him in to the murder of some damn nigger in Chicago."

That stunned her. "Jesus, Frawley, you're the chief of police in this town, which is . . . what? Seventy-five percent African American?"

"Seventy." He shrugged and looked around the room. "But it's a hundred percent white in here. At least," he gave a wink, "I *think* it is. Unless you know better."

"Where's Galboa?"

"I gave him a few days off, and if I knew where he was, I wouldn't tell you. You got a problem?"

"Eudora Ragsdale's missing."

"Missing from where? You mean she isn't home? Woman's free to come and go as she pleases. Fucking weak-kneed judge proved that to her. She can even violate her bond and get away with it. Probably because she's a . . . because she's black."

"Look, Chief, you don't like her, but she's in danger, I think."

"Is she? I thought you had Superman over there, taking care of her." He placed his palms flat on the desk and pushed himself up to a standing position. "I don't dislike Eudora Ragsdale. She's a troublemaker, is all." Folding the newspaper into a tight little club, he waved it at her. "This town's dying, lady, in case you didn't notice it. And that shopping mall's our chance for an eco-

242

nomic shot in the arm. If Eudora doesn't like it, she oughta go live somewhere else . . . not try to hold back progress."

"That has nothing to do with—"

"You got any evidence she's in danger? She been 'missing' more than twenty-four hours? Any sign of forcible detention? Violence? Did she leave home voluntarily?"

"She left home to go shopping. She was driving. That was around noon. She hasn't come back."

"Oh, my. Well, maybe she liked Disney World so much she went back." He moved up to the counter, slammed the paper down, and tore a sheet from a pad of preprinted forms. "Tell you what, though," he said. "I'll fill out this incident report with the information you provided and tell my officers to keep an eye out for her."

She turned and left. By the time she was up the stairs and outside, she was nearly running, with no idea where to go next. It was fully dark out now. She unlocked the Camry with the electronic key and yanked open the door.

"Hi."

"What?" She whirled around, arms spread, and nearly smacked Coral in the face.

"I said 'hi.' It's me."

"Oh, Coral." She bent down and grabbed the child and squeezed her tightly. She felt tears streaming from her eyes and didn't know if they came because of Coral being there, or Eudora being gone, or what. "I didn't see you. I'm sorry."

Coral wriggled free of her embrace. She seemed embarrassed to be held. "What . . . what you doin' at the police station?"

"I'm trying to find Eudora."

"Miz Eudora? She in trouble again?"

"No. I mean, I don't know where she is, and I was asking the police to help me find her."

"Maybe she just went shopping, is all. I seen her this noon, outside the grocery store, talkin'—"

"I know she went shopping, but she didn't come home."

"I don't know about that. I hadda go to school this afternoon. I can't skip so much, these days. They kinda . . . watchin' for me."

"That's okay, Coral, I'll give you a ride home. Or do you have your bike?"

"Bike's got a flat tire. Anyway, I don't wanna go home. My cousin Raynelle, she . . . she got someone there. A man. They be drinkin' and pretty soon they gonna be . . . you know . . . having *relations* an' all. I don't like them men she go with. They loud, and nasty, and walkin' around the house in their underwear and all. Sometimes some of 'em start messin' with me like . . . well . . . I usually stay outta there."

"I'll take you to Eudora's then." She shooed Coral in through the driver's door, and the girl climbed easily over to the passenger seat. "Mama Dee's there and—" She suddenly remembered what Coral had said. "Wait. Who was it Eudora was talking to, outside the grocery store?"

"She talkin' to that police officer. The one look like a TV gangster."

"Officer Galboa?" She backed out of her parking spot and pulled into the street.

"Uh-huh. I think that's his name. The one went inside Miz Eudora's house with Chief Frawley the first day you was there."

Kirsten pulled over and stopped the car. "Um, Coral, do you know where Officer Galboa lives?"

"Why?"

"Because if he was talking to Eudora, maybe he knows where she went."

"He ain't gonna help you. He too mean."

"Do you *know?*"

"He live here in town, on the white folks' side, in a real big house with his grandma, and I think his sister, and she got three kids, or four, and a buncha other old people I don't know. They *all* mean, though. Even the kids."

"You wanna show me where it is?"

"And he got a secret place, too."

"What?"

"A secret place. Where he go sometimes . . . by himself. Or sometimes he go there with . . . you know . . . a lady or somethin'. I seen him. It ain't even his place. It ain't nobody's place. He just go there and nobody cares. Maybe nobody knows . . . but I know."

"Really? Where is it?"

"Out on the way to Mama Dee's. You know them ol' trailers in Emerald Woods? On Till's Creek Road? Nobody lives in any of 'em. It's one of them. A raggedy ol' broken-down trailer house. It'll be torn down, too, when they build that big dumb mall. That'll be the end of them trailers. The end of Emerald Woods, too."

"There isn't going to be any mall."

"There ain't? Who said so?"

"I said so," Kirsten said. "Me."

"Oh." Coral looked out the window, as though she hadn't noticed before that they were driving again. "Where we goin'?"

"To Officer Galboa's secret place."

"Oh." She was silent for a minute, then asked, "Am I helpin' you to find Miz Eudora?"

"Yes."

"Good. I'm glad you didn't take me home." She paused, then leaned closer to Kirsten. "You think that policeman messin' with Miz Eudora?"

"I don't know. I just want to look."

"Okay." She sat up straighter in her seat. "He real mean, though. I guess we gotta be careful."

"I guess so."

Sometimes a thing the whole world would know is unwise, even foolhardy, just seems, with a feeling from deep inside—this time, under these circumstances—to be the right thing to do. This was such a time. Kirsten could feel it. But she knew, too, that sometimes you do it and it turns out to have been exactly the stupid, crazy thing your mind told you it was in the first place. Then you have to pay for trusting your feeling.

She kept going, though, driving through the dark with an eleven-year-old child beside her, to find a woman who might, or might not, be out here and in danger from a man who might, or might not, be a killer. Because if you never pay attention to that deep feeling, never trust it . . . it might curl up down there and go to sleep and never wake up again. And then you end up having to pay for *not* trusting.

She drove on. After all, she had her cell phone. If she found out that Eudora was really out here, and was really in trouble, she could easily call for help.

But only after she knew for sure.

FORTY-FOUR

The cloud cover was still hanging in there, but Kirsten knew it had to be past sundown as she turned off the highway. It was almost as dark as it had been the first time she'd driven so cautiously down Till's Creek Road. Once you've covered a route a few times, though, it somehow gets shorter and simpler, and this time she was surprised at how quickly she got to where the gravel road narrowed and entered the woods.

She stopped on the road and turned off the headlights. "Do you know which trailer it is, Coral? Will we be able to tell which one, in the dark?"

"Uh-huh. I'm in these woods a lot."

"There are three house trailers along the road, right? Is it the one closest to Mama Dee's?" That's where they'd found Dugan's rental car last Saturday. "Sort of a blue color?"

"Uh-uh. It's *four* trailers, and it ain't that one."

"Four?"

"Uh-huh. Three you can see from the road, and one you can't. That's the one that policeman go to sometimes. You turn in at the one before the blue one, and then go on through. It's a little path, sorta like a dirt road, goes through some weeds behind the front trailer and then turns and goes out to another trailer. It's like . . . silver or something." She stared straight ahead through the windshield. "How come we just sittin' here?"

"I'm thinking. Is it big?"

"I don't know. I mean, *pretty* big."

What Kirsten meant was whether it was just a little one-room travel trailer, like the blue one. "Bigger than the blue one?"

"Uh-huh. It have, like, two or three different rooms. I mean, I never been inside it, but it look that way from outside. It's all rusty and nasty looking, scary or something. I ain't never wanted to get too close to it. But maybe he got it cleaned up inside."

"Maybe. But—" Something flashed in the rearview mirror, and Kirsten swung around in her seat. "Damn!"

"What?" Coral said. She turned to look. "Oh."

In the distance, maybe a half mile or more behind them, a pair of headlights had appeared, coming their way. "There's nothing out past here but Mama Dee's, is there?"

"Uh-uh," Coral said. "And them old trailers we been talkin' about."

"Is there some place we can hide?"

"It's a little road the farmers drive on," Coral said, "up there by them weeds at the end of the field. See?"

She was right, and Kirsten drove ahead a few yards and turned in to her right. It wasn't really a road, but a set of ruts flanked by weeds not much taller than her wheel wells. The ruts got deeper and more uneven the farther in she went, and the Camry, though pulling well with its front-wheel drive, kept bouncing up and then hitting bottom. She had to get farther off the road. She pressed the gas pedal down, and the car surged ahead . . . and was suddenly out of her control. It bounced high, and when it came down this time there was a loud metallic scraping from right under the floorboards . . . and they stopped moving. She hit the gas again. The engine roared and the front wheels spun with a high-pitched whine, but the car didn't move. They were hung up.

The headlights were coming closer. Whoever it was, though, seemed to be driving slowly, just as she had the first time she'd come that way. This gave them a little more time, but it also meant the driver was far more likely to see the Camry, sitting there in the weeds not twenty yards off the gravel road, than if he just drove by at normal speed.

In fact, the chance of them *not* being seen was about zero. She switched the engine off and shoved her keys in her jacket pocket, then reached and turned off the ceiling light so it wouldn't go on when they opened the doors. "Let's go, Coral. We gotta hide." She grabbed her purse from the floor and jumped out of the car, slamming the door behind her. "This way!" she called. "Stay low! Head for the woods!"

The other car was so close now she could hear the crunch of its tires on the gravel.

"Hurry!" she called, but Coral was already ahead of her, bent over and running at an angle away from the road and toward the woods . . . running far more easily than she was. "Stay low," Kirsten called, but she was giving advice to herself.

They stopped just inside the first row of trees and crouched on the damp ground. As her eyes adjusted to the dark she noticed the sky wasn't really black, but gray, as though the clouds were reflecting ground light from somewhere miles away, maybe Kankakee. They watched the car on the road. The driver, apparently a man, was the only visible occupant, and he *was* driving slowly. He didn't turn his head, and there was no sign that he saw the Camry. He kept on going and disappeared into the woods.

"I guess it's on foot from here." She started for the road. "You go back and wait in the car, Coral."

"It's quicker the other way."

"What?"

"That road turns and winds around and stuff, but if we go through the woods and past the swamp, it's a lot quicker. Want me to show you?"

"But will you be able to see where you're going?" Then she remembered she'd gotten a new little purse-size flashlight. She fished it out and gave it to Coral. "Here, try this."

Coral turned the flashlight on, but the thin beam wasn't much help, and she turned it off and stuck it in her jeans pocket. "It ain't all that dark," she said. "Up ahead there's a path for a while, and then we come to a swamp where sometimes I catch frogs at night. And we go round the edge of that, and the trailer's a little ways past there."

Sounded awfully vague, Kirsten thought, but if they went by the road it could take them an hour or more to get to where a car might get in ten minutes. So they went Coral's way.

It was maybe fifteen minutes later—Kirsten couldn't be sure—when they got to the swamp. If there was a path, she sure didn't notice it. She noticed about a million trees, though—some slender, some bigger around than she—that loomed up haphazardly, everywhere, to block their way. She noticed the mushy, uneven ground that kept her off balance despite her high-end leather walking shoes, while thorns and tangled underbrush grabbed at her pants legs to trip her up. Mostly, she noticed the endless barrage of stinging branches. Coral would push them aside and they'd whip back and first slap Kirsten in the face and then tangle themselves in her hair.

So, if there was a path, she missed it. But she sure as hell didn't miss the damn swamp.

To avoid the constant slap and sting of branches in her face, she'd let Coral get a little ahead of her. She moved as quickly as she could—a fast walk—crouching, weaving, holding her forearms up in front of her face to push her own way through. Suddenly she broke out of the brush and into a clearing . . . and Coral wasn't in front of her. She hurried forward into the darkness and found herself on a steep downward slope. She lost her balance, rushing forward, out of control.

Only a couple of steps, though, when she stumbled and—arms flailing in wild, helpless windmill circles—toppled headlong. She landed facedown in six inches or so of foul-smelling water and, under that water, thick ooze. Sputtering, coughing, spitting, she raised her head, then pushed up to her hands and knees, even as her palms sank deep into the muddy bottom. She pulled her hands free, one at a time, the mud giving up each one with a reluctant sucking sound.

"Miz Kirsten?" She twisted around and saw Coral, standing on dry ground, right behind her. "You all right, Miz Kirsten?" She sounded scared.

"I'm okay. My purse flew out of my hand, though. I should have slipped it over my head." She crouched in the muck and felt around her. Rough, sharp, reedy grass rising out of the water. Something that felt like a log, covered with slippery, slimy moss-like stuff. And then something was slithering down the side of her neck, below her ear. She slapped it and crushed it and didn't know if it had been a glob of mud or some living thing, like a slug.

She stood up. She could see Coral, and the trees behind her, in the dim light reflected by the clouds. But when she looked down toward the reeds and water, it was very dark. "I need to find my purse," she said.

Coral reached into her pocket and took out the flashlight, and a thin light appeared, dancing around in the darkness. "Is that it, over there?" She bounced the weak beam up and down, a couple of yards farther out and off to the right, on the other side of the log that lay half submerged in the shallow water.

"That's it," Kirsten said. The Colt .380 was holstered on her hip, but her wallet and her cell phone were in the purse. She stood up and, moving carefully through the water and mud, stepped over the log and farther out into the swamp. The purse was small and had just a fold-over flap, no snap or clasp. It had landed bottom up among the reeds, in water which wasn't much deeper than where she herself had landed.

The shoulder strap was half-floating on the surface, and she reached out and grabbed it and pulled the purse to her. She turned it over and looked inside, but it had apparently flown open and was empty except for some tissues. She tossed it onto dry ground near Coral's feet. When she turned back around, she realized she'd already lost track of exactly where the purse had been. In the dark, everything looked the same.

She crouched among the reeds where she thought it might have been, and with both hands she felt around under the water. Nothing but slime. A little to the left and she tried again, moving her hands over the bottom, and found her lipstick and put that in her jacket pocket. She moved farther out, back bent, both hands sweeping around on the mud beneath the water. Nothing.

Coral waded in and leaned over and was feeling around, too, with one hand. She had the flashlight in her other hand, but it wasn't much help. If anything, it seemed to be getting dimmer. Pretty soon Kirsten knew that neither of them had a very clear idea where the purse had been and, even if they did, there was no way to tell where its contents might have landed.

"I don't know, Coral, I—"

"Here!" Coral said. She stood up and held something out. It was Kirsten's wallet, heavy and waterlogged, and she put it in her pocket with the lipstick.

The wallet gave her hope, and they spent a few more minutes crouching and wading and feeling around in the dark. But they found nothing. Then Kirsten noticed how far they'd gotten from the fallen log. "C'mon back this way," she said.

Coral followed her.

"It could have landed on the other side," Kirsten said, stepping back over the log. "I'll just look a minute, and then we have to—"

She tripped, and brought her right foot down hard on top of the log. It was rotten and her shoe went right through it, which startled her and she stepped back.

She heard a strange hissing sound . . . or did she? At once something—several things, like black fingers—seemed to slide through the water, making Y-shaped ripples on the dark surface. And then, just as suddenly, they were gone.

"Did you see something, Coral?"

"Uh-huh. Moc'sins."

"Moxins? What are—"

"Water moc'sins. They all over this here swamp. Ain't none of 'em ever bothered me." She stepped over to Kirsten's side of the log and started feeling around under the water again. "You wanna look on this side?"

But by then Kirsten was already up on dry ground, fighting back a scream and frantically stamping her feet. "Not on your life," she said. "Let's get going."

FORTY-FIVE

Another ten minutes or so and they'd skirted the swamp and come again to a clearing in the woods. A wind was blowing now, which wouldn't have been cold except that her clothes were sopping wet. She was wearing a lightweight leather jacket, and she buttoned the top button.

"Are you cold, Coral?"

"Uh-uh," she said. For a jacket she had on what looked like a man's wool hunting shirt that reached to her knees. "I like bein' outside. I don't get cold much."

They stood in the dark by an ancient, sagging barbed-wire fence. Behind them, the bigger, older trees stopped about six feet short of the fence, but smaller trees and ragged bushes had crept forward. Some had reached the fence, even grown over it in places, as the woods moved in to recover the cleared land.

Beyond the barbed wire, weeds grew as high as Kirsten's waist—or Coral's shoulders—with here and there a pine tree or a clump of tall shrubs. In the dim, shadowless light, everything seemed vague and uncertain, in black and innumerable shades of gray, whispering and waving in the increasing wind.

"There," Coral said. "See?" She was pointing over the fence and off to the left a little.

"Yes, I see it."

The house trailer sat about fifty yards away, its unwavering bulk and the straight edges of its silhouette setting it apart from the shifting, uneven surroundings. There were at least two cars parked near it, and she thought she could see faint light glowing around the edges of what was probably a dark curtain in one window of the trailer. "Is there some easy place to get through this fence?"

"It's a couple spots where it's . . ." Coral stopped and stared up at her. "We ain't goin' up in there, are we? It's people there."

"I have to find Eudora, and I didn't come all this way in the goddamn dark just to stand around and . . ." She stopped. "I'm sorry. I mean . . . yes, I'm going in to look around. But you're gonna stay here."

"Whyn't you just call someone on that little phone you got? Like . . . that big monster man you got stayin' at Miz Eudora's place."

"Because the phone's back there in the swamp somewhere, Coral. That's what we were looking for."

"Oh." The child looked around. "That policeman, you think he got Miz Eudora up in there?"

"I don't know. But I have to go and look."

"I be scared stayin' here."

"But I thought you were *used* to being alone out here."

"Yeah, but that's when I'm *alone* alone. Ain't nothin' but animals and bugs and stuff."

"And water moccasins?"

"Uh-huh. But here there's *people*. You go up in there and leave me here . . . What if you don't come back?" She started moving along the fence to their right. "I'm goin' with you. It's a hole in the fence along here some place." She went a little farther. "Here."

Arguing was useless. Kirsten held two strands of wire spread wide for Coral to pass through, and Coral did the same for her.

They waded through the weeds, circling the trailer from a distance, passing by a tiny falling-down shed that looked just like an outhouse. The door to the trailer was on the side away from where they'd come out of the woods, and it opened onto a small porch with a wrought-iron railing and three steps. The porch listed slightly to one side, as though sinking unevenly into the ground.

Like the ones she'd seen from the road, this trailer looked like it had sat on this spot for forty years, easy, and been vacant for the last five or ten. A TV antenna lay on its side on the roof, and there was a pole at one corner, sticking a few feet up above roof level. The pole must have been for an electrical hookup, but there were no wires leading to it.

They picked their way through years of litter that got worse the closer they came to the trailer. There were piles of wood and rolled fencing, a refrigerator, an old iron bed, dozens of pale plastic milk jugs, and a thousand other pieces of junk, unidentifiable in the darkness.

A rusted-out Thunderbird convertible from the sixties sat nearly submerged in the weeds—no wheels, no seats, no windshield—backed right up against the rear end of the trailer. But parked near the front end, where the hitch would be—she didn't know if these things actually had hitches—were the two other vehicles she'd seen. One of them was Eudora's Ford Escort, the other an Acura sedan.

The trailer was maybe twenty-five or thirty-feet long, and though the windows were all boarded up or curtained, from this close it was clear there were lights on inside. With no electricity, maybe they were kerosene lamps or something. She couldn't remember ever seeing the inside of one of these things, except the one on that California beach in *The Rockford Files*—of which Dugan had every last silly episode on tape. She figured this one must have a separate bedroom—maybe two bedrooms, one at each end—with a combined living space and kitchen in the middle, around the only door.

With Coral right beside her, she was moving in to check out the cars, when she stepped on something that was plastic and brittle and broke with a sharp crack. "Damn. Hope there's no dog around."

"I never known that policeman to have a dog with him," Coral whispered. "Besides, if there was, we'd been caught a long time ago."

"Good point." She went to the Escort and felt the hood with her palm. It was cool. The Acura, though, was still warm. "This must have been the car," she whispered, "that came up behind us on—"

The trailer door burst open and banged against the porch railing. Even as Kirsten dropped to the ground, pulling Coral with her, she knew the figure she'd seen for an instant in the doorway was a male. They crouched behind the Acura, and she heard him step onto the porch, not twenty feet away, but didn't hear him go down the steps.

"The sonovabitch," the man said. "I wish he'd hurry the fuck up and get here." It was Galboa, and then some other man answered from inside, but she couldn't make out the words. Over the mournful voice of a female country singer, coming from a radio or a CD player inside, Kirsten thought she could hear what Galboa was doing.

After he went back inside and closed the door, Coral whispered, "Sound like he emptyin' out some water."

"Sort of," she answered. "I think he was . . . you know . . . going to the bathroom."

"Yuck! Out on the front porch?"

They stood up again, but stayed behind the Acura. "There's at least two men in there," Kirsten said, "and another one on the way." She pointed. "See that little bit of light coming from the window at the other end?"

"Uh-huh."

"That's probably a bedroom. C'mon, I'm gonna try to look inside it."

FORTY-SIX

She dearly wished she'd left Coral back at the car, but at the same time knew she'd still be out walking in the dark along Till's Creek Road somewhere if she had.

They went around the trailer to the side that had no door. The window closest to the back was blocked with cardboard or something on the inside, and was too high above the ground to look into, anyway. Another window, not very large, faced straight out the rear of the trailer. This one was a louvered window, with horizontal panes that cranked open and shut—they were fully open now—and would have been too high to look through, also, except that she and Coral climbed up onto the trunk of the Thunderbird.

The dim light inside came from a little glass bowl of a lamp, filled with oil, the burning wick sticking just barely out through a hole in the top. The lamp sat on a shelf on the wall to their right—a shelf that had been part of a set of built-in storage cabinets, but now all the doors were broken off. Opposite the window was a door into the rest of the trailer—pretty insubstantial looking, but closed.

The louvered window was cheaply made, with just two panes of thin glass. Because they were open, the panes jutted out and made it difficult to get her face up to the opening, but Kirsten twisted her head sideways under the lower of the two and was able to see downward into the room. It was small, and littered with crushed beer cans and parts of newspapers. Ugly stains were splashed against the fake wood wall paneling, at least where gaping holes hadn't been punched through. Most of the floor space was taken up by a bed, up against the wall below the window. There was a bare, stained mattress on the bed, and lying on the mattress—wearing what looked like a man's bathrobe—was Eudora.

She lay on her side, facing the door, with her head to Kirsten's right. Her hands were tied behind her back with pieces of cloth torn into strips. Her ankles were bound together with cloth, too, and then apparently tied to something too close to the wall to be visible to Kirsten. Her hair was disheveled and matted. She was gagged, and Kirsten thought there were scratches on the side of her face.

"I can't see nothin' but that little candle thing and the ceiling," Coral whispered. She was standing on her tiptoes and could barely get her chin up to the lower edge of the window. "Miz Eudora in there?"

"Yes, she is."

"She okay?"

"Yes. She's . . . okay." She was conscious, anyway, because she'd obviously heard the whispering from the window above her. Kirsten watched as she twisted around, struggling to turn and look upward. She saw then that Eudora's face was badly swollen. Some of that was because her mouth had been stuffed with something to gag her; but the puffy, darkened skin around her eyes was clearly from being hit. She also saw that Eudora had no clothes on under the bathrobe. No underwear. Nothing. And she was in shadows, yes, but those dark splotches on her body were bruises, for sure.

Worse than that, though, was the look on her face. Her eyes

were wide open, reflecting the dim lamp light from above, and her expression seemed to say she'd gone way beyond fear, way beyond panic. As though she'd toppled over the precipice at the edge of sanity and might never be able to climb back up.

Kirsten didn't know if Eudora could see her face, but she stuck her hand through the open window and waved her fingers around. "It's me," she whispered, "Kirsten. Coral's here, too. We're gonna get you out of there." Uh-huh, but how?

A sort of yowling moan came up, surprisingly loud, from Eudora, as she struggled to answer.

Kirsten pulled her hand back. "Don't say anything," she whispered. "You—"

The bedroom door opened. It was a sliding door. That much Kirsten saw before she ducked below the window.

"Shut the fuck up in here, bitch." Galboa's voice. Too loud, as though he'd been drinking. "You ain't hurt so bad. Shit, you'd been willing to give it up with a more friendly attitude you wouldn't be hurt at all." He gave a barking laugh. "But I always *heard* you people like it rough."

Eudora made some soft sobbing sounds, but Galboa just laughed again, and the door slid closed.

Kirsten put her face back to the window and whispered, "Just relax, Eudora. You're safe now. I'm coming in."

She looked down at Coral, standing beside her. "Hop down onto the ground for a minute," she said.

Coral looked back at her with wide eyes but then did as she was told.

Kirsten stared at the window. The framing, and the cheap little brackets that held the panes at both ends and rotated them when the crank was turned, were metal, probably aluminum. The opening looked pretty small, but it might be possible, and she had to try. She hunched her shoulders and withdrew her hands up into her sleeves. Using the soft leather of the jacket sleeves as protective gloves, she grasped the lower pane of glass with

261

both hands. She yanked down, hard, and snapped the glass out of its brackets. It came out mostly in two pieces, one in each hand, although some glass shattered and fell onto the trunk lid.

She froze, but the wind was blowing much harder now, and apparently no one heard the glass. She handed the two pieces down to Coral, who put them on the ground.

She broke the upper pane out, too, but still didn't know if she could squeeze through. She twisted and bent the aluminum framing that held the brackets on each side, and the crank mechanism, but she couldn't get them completely out of the way. She'd have to have cutters, or else yank the whole damn frame out of the wall, which—even if it were possible—would bring Galboa and whoever else was there in a hurry. Even with the Colt she'd have a hard time handling two of them at once—assuming there were only two here now, and that whoever was on the way hadn't arrived by then.

She stared at the window again, measuring the dimensions in her mind, comparing the space to the width of her shoulders. The opening might be just barely big enough to squeeze through. Even if it was, though, she'd rip herself apart on those metal brackets. She could stand there and study it forever, but she wasn't going to get in through the window.

She stuck her head inside and looked down. "Eudora," she whispered, "don't say anything. Just listen. I'll be away for a little while. But don't worry. I'll get you out."

She climbed down off the trunk and rested her hands on Coral's shoulders. "Look," she said, "you have to run away now. Run all the way back to town, to Eudora's house. Tell Dugan to get the police out—"

"No."

"You *have* to. It's dangerous here, and we need help."

"Then why ain't you goin'?"

"I can't, because . . . because there isn't time."

"Time I get all the way back there, you might be dead. Miz Eudora, too. That's right, ain't it?"

"No, I—"

"Don't lie to me. I ain't never lied to you."

"Okay, it could be true. But *you* don't have to be dead."

"What I wanna be livin' for, if Miz Eudora dead? So I can go home to my cousin's? You try to make me go and I'll start screamin' and . . . Anyway, I ain't goin' nowhere." The poor child was shaking. "Tell me what to do to help."

"Okay," She helped Coral back onto the trunk. "You stay by the window. Eudora's very frightened, and you can help her. Count like this to yourself: 'One thousand-one, one thousand-two.' When you get to 'one thousand-ten,' put your mouth up by the window and whisper that we're still here and everything's gonna be fine. Then start over." She paused. "And . . . if something real bad happens, you run away as fast as you can. You promise?"

Coral stared up at her. "What's wrong with Miz Eudora? Why she don't come to the window?"

"Her hands and feet are tied up, she's gagged, and she can hardly move. She's been . . . beaten up. And she needs you to keep her from getting too scared. Okay?"

"She tied up?" Kirsten nodded, and Coral seemed to be thinking about that. But then she said, "*How* high you say I s'posed to count? Ten?"

"Yes, and then tell her she's gonna be fine. Loud enough so she can hear, but not *too* loud."

As Kirsten backed away, Coral stood there and stuffed her hands under her long shirt and down into her jeans pockets. Her lips were already mouthing the numbers. "One thousand-one, one thousand-two . . ."

Kirsten slipped the Colt from its holster and moved away, into the darkness. God, what the hell was she doing?

FORTY-SEVEN

taying on the side without the door, Kirsten crept back along the length of the trailer toward the front end again, thinking maybe there was a cell phone in either the Escort or the Acura. Then, near the front, she suddenly heard talking—a weather report on the radio—from inside, as though right though the wall.

She stopped and backed up a step, to a slotted vent, about four inches square, in the trailer wall. For a refrigerator? A gas stove? The floor of the trailer was about two feet off the ground, on a foundation of cinder blocks, which put the vent about shoulder high. She placed her ear against it as a new country song began, a male singer, but was cut off abruptly.

"I hate that fucking Ricky Skaggs," Galboa said. "Even his name sucks." She heard the sound of a bottle being opened, and then, "I hate this Mexican beer, too. Why'd you bring this shit for?"

"I don't drink beer." A man's voice. "I thought you'd appreciate it. It's expensive."

"Fuck expensive. I like beer out of a can. Gimme a Bud Light any day. Tastes great, less filling. Tastes great, less—"

"That's a Miller ad," the other man said.

"Fuck you. Where's your goddamn brother, anyway?" Galboa had had way too much to drink. "Asshole better show up."

"Don't worry," the man said, "Tommy'll be here. There's a lot for him in this . . . or so he thinks, anyway."

Tommy? Was the man's brother Tommy Hurley?

"A lot in it for him, huh? What the fuck's all this about, anyway?"

"That's my business. You just worry about taking care of your own part. You're drinking too much, you know."

"Been takin' care of my own part pretty good so far, ain't I? Scare the bitch and get her arrested. Torch the old lady's house to scare her some more. Everything. The bitch's ex-boyfriend. Then gettin' her out here today in her own goddamn car? Yes sir, I'd say I been takin' care of—"

"The boyfriend was your own idea."

"Yeah, well, he knew enough to be trouble for me, which would've meant trouble for you."

"Anyway, you're being well compensated for everything."

"Shit. Maybe not well enough? First you just wanna stop the Ragsdale bitch from fighting the mall. All the sudden you want her dead. And your own brother, too, so what's—"

"If you want the other half for these two, just do your job when he gets here. That'll be the end of it. You'll have made a bundle, and we'll go our separate ways."

"I should do her now. Then it's just him to—"

"No! I told you, you're to make it look like they killed each other. What if he doesn't come? Then I'd have to think of something else."

"Doesn't come? What about the 'Tommy'll be here' bullshit you were just giving me?"

"It's not bullshit," the man said. "But don't you understand? It's conceivable he could have an accident, or . . . whatever. He'll be here, don't worry. We just have to think of every contingency, that's all. If you weren't drunk, you'd see what—"

"So we wait. I don't give a shit." There was a pause, then a belch. "And I ain't drunk, either."

Make it look like Tommy Hurley and Eudora killed each other? Kirsten didn't get it.

The radio came on again, and with Galboa starting to sing along with whoever was on the air, it appeared the conversation was over.

She hurried around the front of the trailer and glanced into the Escort. No phone in sight, but she really hadn't expected one in Eudora's car. She'd try the Acura and—

Headlights swept across the entire area, and she dropped to the ground between the two cars. A third car was coming across the field, obviously too fast for the terrain, bouncing wildly up and down. Damn, what about Coral? But as the car came closer she realized that if Coral just stayed where she was, up close to the rear end of the trailer, she wouldn't be visible to whoever was coming.

The car came to a stop on the other side of the Acura from where Kirsten lay on the ground. The door of the trailer opened and a man stepped out. "Tommy?" It wasn't Galboa, but the man he'd been talking to. "Is that you?"

"Goddamn right it is!" It *was* Tommy Hurley, so the other man had to be John Michael, Jr. Tommy slammed his car door shut. From where she lay, on the ground between the Escort and the Acura, hidden in the shadows, she could see both men once Tommy got close to the porch. "You picked a helluva spot, Jack," he said. "Lucky I didn't get fucking lost."

"Don't call me Jack, huh? The old man's the only one calls me Jack, and I hate that name almost as much as I hate him."

"Grow up, will ya? Christ." Tommy went up the porch steps and his brother backed inside. "Is the broad here? What's her name? Eldora? Damn niggers all got funny— Hey!" Tommy stood in the doorway. "Who's this guy? I thought it was gonna be just you and—"

266

"C'mon in, Tommy boy." That was Galboa. "I'm just here to lend a hand."

"Who *is* this asshole?"

Tommy was inside now, but he'd left the door open. Kirsten was up and running toward the porch, the Colt in her hand.

"What's the fucking piece for?" Tommy was asking, as she reached the steps. "Jesus, Jack, what's going on?" She paused, wanting to hear the answer.

"Too bad, little brother," John Michael, Jr., said. "You should've put those shares in trust when you went away, not try to keep control by giving 'em to—"

"Turn around, Tommy," Galboa said, "and face me so I—"

By then she was up the steps and through the door and Tommy, to her right, heard her and spun around to face her. Galboa was beyond him. She kept going and drove her left shoulder into Tommy. He slammed backward into Galboa, and a gunshot exploded like a howitzer inside the cramped space. Tommy's momentum carried him and Galboa crashing into the table of a breakfast nook built against the wall at the front end of the trailer.

Her ears were ringing from the gunshot, and for some reason she was thinking that there wasn't another bedroom at the front end, after all. And then there was an arm around her neck from behind, and someone was squeezing hard, choking her. She struggled at first, but she couldn't breathe. It seemed like a long, long time that he kept on squeezing, until finally the gun dropped out of her hand—as though it were somebody else's hand—and she heard it hit the floor.

He let go of her then, but her throat hurt terribly, and all she could do was drop down to one knee and gasp and hack and fight to get her breath back. She wondered if he'd broken her windpipe or something, but finally she was able to take in air again. She looked around for her gun, but of course it wasn't on the floor any more.

Carpeting—threadbare and worn through to the plywood floor in spots—ran the length of the narrow interior. Directly opposite the door she'd just charged through was a kitchen sink, beyond that a stove with burners—probably propane—and then an empty space where a refrigerator must once have stood against the wall. Maybe that's where the vent to the outside was. The place smelled moldy and old, but the strongest smells were beer and bacon grease, and there were crushed cans everywhere, and an old-fashioned black iron frying pan sitting on the stove.

Tommy Hurley was on the floor about eight feet in front of her, sitting with his back against the oven door. His arms were crossed in front of him, his hands up and clutching his shoulders. He was moaning softly.

Galboa stood with his rear end backed up against the dining nook table. He had a small, cheap-looking revolver in his hand and was staring straight at her. She started to stand up, but he waved the gun. "Stay put!"

She did, but she turned her head to look at John Michael, Jr. He had her Colt .380 in his hand and was standing in the narrow corridor between her and the closed door to the bedroom where Eudora was. She deliberately kept from looking at the door and hoped to God Coral had run when she'd heard the gunshot.

"Hey!" Galboa yelled. "Turn around and look at me." She did, and he asked, "What are you doing here?"

"I'm just the point guard," she said, not sure how that expression popped into her head. "The rest of the team is on its way."

"What?"

"I mean the cops are coming. They'll be here any minute. So if I were you," she waved her hand around, "any of you, I'd get my ass out of here and not do any more damage than I'd already done."

Tommy tried to say something, but it came out as mindless syllables.

"Jesus," Galboa said, looking past Kirsten at John Michael, Jr., "your brother's sure a pussy, ain't he? Fucking little hole in his shoulder and you'd think—"

"We have to get out of here," Hurley said.

"Fuck that. The bitch is lying. There's no cops coming. If they were, they'd have come in with her. Besides, I *am* the cops." He looked at Hurley and grinned. "So, hey, drop the gun."

"Don't be silly. Just do what we said. Set it up the way we said, and let's get out of here."

"But there's another player here now, buddy boy. The fucking 'point guard.' What about her?"

"You'll have to take care of her, too. You'll get extra for that, don't worry. But we have to move fast."

"I don't know," Galboa said. "It's gettin' pretty complicated. I think we need a new plan. Let's see . . . say me and the Ragsdale bitch had come here for a quiet fuck. Then your brother and this private eye lady show up. But why? They gettin' it on together, too?" He grabbed a Dos Equis off the counter with his left hand, drained it, and set it down again. "I don't think that'll fly, do you, Jack?"

"Just do it. We'll work on the story later."

"Too many loose ends," Galboa said. "I better go with the 'I *am* the cops' version. So, asshole, drop the gun."

"What are—"

"Drop it!"

Hurley obeyed, and the Colt dropped onto the floor.

"What really happened is," Galboa continued, obviously making it up as he went along, "I been working undercover all the time, pretending to be a hit man. I did that once before, y'know, in Chicago. Anyway, you wanted to hire me to kill the Ragsdale bitch, and your brother, too." As he spoke, Galboa switched the revolver he'd been holding to his left hand. He reached behind his waist with his right hand and came out with a .357 Magnum.

269

"Since I'm a cop, undercover or not, I guess I oughta use my own firearm. Right, Jack?"

"You're not thinking straight," the man answered. "You're drunk."

"I didn't know if you were serious, but I strung you along and you brought me out here. The Ragsdale bitch and your brother were both here. Turns out you *were* serious, after all. So I told you you're under arrest for . . . whatchacallit . . . conspiracy to commit murder."

"Fine," Kirsten said. "Just arrest him and—"

"And make it his word against mine? No way." He looked past her, at Hurley. "What happened is, Jack, you pulled a gun on me. *This* gun." He waved the smaller weapon he had in his left hand, then put it on top of a cabinet high above the stove. "When you wouldn't put it down, I had to shoot you."

Kirsten shrank lower to the floor, pressing her hands against her ears, and at the same time looking around for her Colt. Galboa held his own gun with two hands now, pointed past her.

Hurley had his hands up in front of him, as though they might stop a slug from a .357. "Please!" he begged. "Please! You can't—"

Galboa shot him. Even with her ears ringing from the explosion, Kirsten heard the man behind her slam backward into the bedroom door, but she didn't turn to watch him go down. She'd be next. Her Colt was somewhere on the floor. Grab, turn, hit the safety, aim, and fire—all at once.

Fat chance.

Apparently the man wasn't dying fast enough, so Galboa shot him again. That deafened her completely, and she was frantic. Where was her own damn gun?

There!

In a single movement she grabbed, turned, hit the safety, aimed. It took forever. By now she should have been dead. But she wasn't.

Galboa's back was to her. He and Tommy were both on their feet facing each other down by the dining nook, screaming obscenities that she heard as if from a great distance. They'd have been circling each other, looking for an opening, but in that cramped space there was no room for that.

Why Galboa didn't simply shoot Tommy puzzled her—until she saw his right hand hanging empty down by his side. He was flexing his fingers, as though they weren't working right. The .357 Magnum lay on the floor several feet behind him, right by the door—the still open door.

Tommy had the frying pan from the stove in his left hand, brandishing it as a weapon. He had that same wild look on his face she'd seen behind the carnival booth at Mother of Mercy. He must have slammed the frying pan into Galboa's gun hand and now, frying pan or not, he was strong enough, and crazy enough, to kill Galboa with his bare hands. But then the pain showing on his face, and his heaving, labored breaths, reminded her that Tommy was wounded, too. A bullet in the shoulder, Galboa had said, and it must have been the right shoulder.

Their standoff wouldn't last forever. She was the only one with a gun now, and she wanted to keep it that way. So she stepped forward and reached down for the .357 on the floor.

Whether Galboa heard her, or saw something in Tommy's eyes, she didn't know, but he whirled around. She raised the Colt in front of her. "Hold it!" she screamed.

Galboa instinctively backed up toward Tommy, as she swept her foot across the floor and sent the .357 sliding on the carpet and out the door. She heard it hit the metal porch and then clatter down the steps. She glanced out the door and . . . saw someone.

"Run, Coral! Run!" she screamed, and then turned back to see Tommy bring the frying pan down on Galboa's head. It was a clumsy, left-handed blow, but it still stunned him, and he shook his head as though to clear his mind. Tommy hollered and hit

271

him again, and Galboa, although screaming back, must have decided that running was good advice for him as well.

He went out the door, still bellowing. But then he just stood there on the little porch, didn't go down the stairs. There were more gunshots, three or four of them, and Galboa stepped backward into the trailer. Tommy raised the frying pan again . . . but there was no need. Galboa sank back against the sink behind him, clutching his chest with both hands, and crumpled to the floor.

Kirsten waved Tommy back away from the door, and he obeyed and slumped against the table behind him. She saw for the first time the blood seeping through his sport coat at his right shoulder.

She stepped to the side of the open door. "Coral?" she called. "Are you still out there?"

No one answered.

"Coral?" she repeated. "It's me. Kirsten. I'm coming out."

No response.

Crouching low, she eased the gun around the edge of the door first, then her head. And then she stood up and stepped out onto the porch and down the steps, shoving the Colt into the holster at her back and snapping it in place. She knelt on the ground and wrapped her arms around the figure crouching in the weeds with her face buried in her hands. Galboa's .357 lay on the ground beside her.

"It's okay, Eudora," she said, and rocked the woman in her arms. "Everything's okay."

FORTY-EIGHT

inally, Dugan couldn't stand it any longer, and he'd told Cuffs he was going out to look for Kirsten. Cuffs said he couldn't make Dugan stay, any more than he could have kept Eudora there earlier that day.

He'd taken Mama Dee's car and driven around town. He went past the village hall, and Kirsten's car wasn't there. He'd have gone downstairs to the police station anyway, to ask about her, but if Frawley was there, he might threaten to lock him up, or run him out of town. He could think of only one other place to look—Mama Dee's—and the closer he got the more something inside him told him he was right.

But he got there, and he was wrong. No cars, no people.

The night sky was overcast, and it was very dark. He had no flashlight, so he drove the car out behind the ruins of the house and left the headlights on. He looked in the little barn-shaped shed, anyway, and then in the real barn, hoping the roof didn't fall in on his head. He even went into the silo. The only door was open a crack, and he pulled it some more and squeezed inside. He didn't even want to think about what he was walking on. It smelled like rat shit and something rotten—maybe corn, maybe animal flesh. But the silo was just a tall empty tube. The roof was gone, and he could see a circle of cloudy sky, a slightly lighter shade of black than the wall rising up around him.

While he was inside there he heard several explosions in the distance. No telling from which direction. Farm kids with firecrackers. God, he hoped it was farm kids with firecrackers.

He was back on Till's Creek Road, heading away from Mama Dee's, just on the bridge over the creek, when the call came.

He couldn't quite get what it was Kirsten was telling him. She was using Tommy Hurley's cell phone, she said. She told him to put Cuffs on the phone, and he said he'd left Cuffs with Mama Dee and the twins and was out looking for her.

"My God," she yelled, "where are you?"

He told her, and she said to keep going and stop by the second house trailer from Mama Dee's. He said he'd already driven by there, on his way out here, and hadn't seen anything.

"Just go there and wait for us, please," she said, and then she hung up. He called back, and her phone just rang and rang and he remembered she said she was using Tommy's phone.

Half an hour later Dugan pulled into Eudora's driveway. Kirsten still had Tommy's cell phone and, once they'd gotten off Till's Creek Road, she'd called 911 and reported the shooting. Then she'd given Dugan a quick rundown of what happened. She and Eudora and Coral were all in the backseat, and no one was talking. The Blazer wasn't there, and Kirsten said she'd told Cuffs on the phone to take Mama Dee and the twins away somewhere.

"I'm calling Lieutenant Terrapin's direct number," she said, when they were inside. "He won't be there, but they'll find him. This is his case. I'll get the name of a hospital in Kankakee and we'll go straight there. Terrapin, or someone he sends, can meet us."

"I'll call a lawyer," Dugan said, "one I can get out to Kankakee right away, tonight. And I'll get a photographer to take pictures of her at the hospital."

Kirsten sent Coral and Eudora to pack a bag for Eudora. "But don't put on any clothes. I want you walking into the hospital in just that torn up robe, looking like you do now, and I want some cops there when you do. I especially want them to see those long gashes on your sides and hips."

After the calls were made and the bag packed, the four of them piled back into Mama Dee's car, this time with Coral in the front seat with Dugan. Neither she nor Eudora had said a word since he'd picked them all up, and Dugan wondered if Coral was in shock or something. "You all right, Coral?"

"Uh-huh," she said. "I'm glad I had my jackknife, though."

"What?"

" 'Cause that's how I cut Miz Eudora loose, y'know? I got through that window pretty easy. But I sure didn't think Miz Eudora'd squeeze through, gettin' out . . . 'specially when she got stuck on them metal things. But she did."

It was quiet for a long time, until finally Kirsten said, "I hope the cops are out at that trailer already, and have found Tommy. He wasn't in any shape to drive."

"Yeah? Well, if we're lucky," he said, "he'll bleed to death."

"No," she said. "I need Tommy Hurley. I need him alive."

FORTY-NINE

"There's one thing I just can't figure out," Dugan said. "It's about Brownley."

He and Kirsten were drinking coffee with Mama Dee at Eudora's house. The lawyer he'd gotten for Eudora last night had insisted the hospital keep her at least overnight. Cuffs had taken the twins to Kankakee for a Saturday morning photo shoot. He claimed they were a nuisance. "A goddamn pain in the ass," is what he said, "but they gotta get there somehow, for chrissake."

Now it was almost noon, and Dugan's saying there was "*one* thing" was a world-class understatement. There was almost nothing he *had* figured out. He didn't know why John Michael, Jr., would hire Galboa to discredit Eudora when he'd been opposed to the mall and everything else his father did; or why he'd pay Galboa to kill his own brother and Eudora. But apart from motive and logic and what the hell this whole business was about, what bothered him now was he couldn't figure out who could possibly have killed Brownley.

Neither woman responded to his remark, though. Mama Dee got up from the table and went to the stove, while Kirsten seemed focused on her mug, as though she'd never seen white ceramic before.

"There's one thing," he repeated, "I just can't fig—"

"I know," Kirsten said, and then added, "I wonder when Cuffs will be back."

"I got a taste for pancakes," Mama Dee said, and opened the refrigerator door.

"Why don't we wait for the others to get here?" Kirsten said. "Maybe they—"

"Oh, they love my pancakes," Mama Dee said. "I'll make the batter now, and we'll have them for lunch." She set a carton of milk on the counter.

Kirsten stood up and put her hand on the older woman's shoulder. "Sit down," she said. "Everything's gonna be okay, really."

Mama Dee sat down then and laid her hands side by side, palms down, on the table in front of her. Dugan noticed for the first time that the backs of her hands were crisscrossed with old thin scars. Maybe she'd chopped cotton in her youth. He'd read somewhere that—

"Ask your question." That was Kirsten. She was sitting again, too, and was looking right at him.

"It's probably not important."

"I think I know what it is," Kirsten said.

"Really?"

She nodded. "And if I'm right, I'd like to get it over with now."

"Right about the question?" he asked. "Or right about the answer?"

"Both." She looked at Mama Dee, who didn't raise her head to look back, and didn't say anything. "And the answer might lead to a hint as to what these killings have been all about."

"Okay," he said. "It's Brownley. I can't figure out who could have killed him. I thought it was John Michael, Junior, to keep Brownley from talking later, or from blackmailing him or something. But he couldn't have done it—not personally, anyway. I've checked, and he was in Champaign last Saturday afternoon, at a faculty reception." He spread his hands in front of him. "Everybody's time is accounted for, at least everybody we *know* about. So then I decided he must have hired someone else to do it."

"But why?" Kirsten asked.

"That's the problem. If it was to keep Brownley from talking later, he'd have wanted to kill Clyborn, too. But you said Galboa admitted he did that on his own. Besides, if you hire one person to get rid of someone you hired before, then you have to hire someone to get rid of the new guy, too. And then . . . well, that could go on forever. Not very economical."

"Well then, go back a step," Kirsten said. "Maybe not everyone's as well accounted for as you think."

"But they are! However Brownley got that blow on the head, he sure didn't put it there himself, then drag himself to the cellar doors."

"That's right," Kirsten said, "which is why the cops are calling it a homicide."

Dugan counted off on his fingers. "Hurley was at his reception. Clyborn was at work at the scrap yard all afternoon. Frawley and Galboa were both on duty all day. They handled a car accident with injuries about noon and a fight in a bar after that, and they were both seen by too many people throughout the day, until about six o'clock. So, Galboa was around after that to torch Mama Dee's house, but he couldn't have killed Brownley." He shook his head and drank some coffee. "So who's left? I mean, *you* didn't do it; no one thinks Coral really did it; and even Eudora and Mama Dee are accounted—" He stopped, because Kirsten stood up abruptly and put the milk back in the refrigerator.

She turned around and looked at him. "You were saying?"

"I was saying . . ." He stared at her. "Oh, come *on*."

Mama Dee seemed about to say something, but then didn't. She looked too tired even to speak.

"Mama Dee?" he said. "Are you all right?"

"I don't know." She hesitated, then said, "Maybe I should just—"

"No." It was Kirsten, and she moved closer to the table and stood over them. "Don't say anything. Let me give you a . . . well . . . a hypothetical situation."

Dugan sat and watched Mama Dee rub her hands together, as though putting lotion on them. But they were dry, and in the silence they scraped across each other like dead leaves.

"Let's assume," Kirsten said, "a person was scheduled to drive a few friends somewhere Friday night, and then they were to join up with a larger group for Saturday and Sunday. Let's say there were groups from lots of churches, and it was a religious retreat, to be spent in silence, everyone staying to themselves. Assume even the Saturday supper was cafeteria style, and no one was to talk."

"I bet most people'd be talking, at least by evening," Dugan said. "I would've been."

"You wouldn't have been there in the first place. Anyway, assume the idea was 'no talking,' not till after mass Sunday morning. And people who took it real seriously might even be trying *not* to catch anyone's eye, especially a friend's."

"I suppose, if they're real serious about it and there are lots of people, it's possible they might not notice someone had left for a while," Dugan said. "But this is crazy. Why did *our* particular person leave?"

"You mean why *might* she have left. It's hypothetical."

"Wait," Mama Dee said. "Let me—"

"Stop, please." Kirsten held a palm up in front of the seated woman. "Just listen. It's all hypothetical, okay? I mean, I'm making it *up*."

"Okay," Mama Dee whispered.

"Let's assume our person was a woman, and that another person—a man—called her on Friday morning and insisted on seeing her. Wouldn't wait, had to be the next day, Saturday. He'd be at her house, he said, and she'd better be there . . . alone. He might have told her some of what he wanted to talk about, and what he said made her afraid *not* to be there. She couldn't even suggest a different time or meeting place before he hung up."

"Jesus," Dugan said. "Are you sure?"

"Please," she said, "it's all hypothetical. Let's say she gets home in time and he drives up in his convertible. She meets him at the top of the front porch steps. She doesn't want him inside her house. They talk, and what he says frightens her again. But it makes her mad, too. She gets so angry she just . . . well, she loses it. Maybe a short fuse runs in her family. She's furious, starts hitting at him, pushing him. He stumbles on the steps, falls backward. He twists and tries to get his balance but falls and smacks his head—hard—on the concrete at the bottom of the steps. She goes down after him, still angry."

"Kirsten," Dugan said, seeing the tears that were streaming down Mama Dee's cheeks, "why not—"

"Let me go on. The man doesn't move. He's not breathing. Now she's hysterical, terrified, not able to think straight. How can she explain what happened? Will anyone believe it was an accident? All her life she's never had reason to trust the police, and that creep Frawley sure isn't gonna be sympathetic. Worse yet, who *else* knows the man came there? Maybe he told her he worked for the . . . the Mafia, maybe. Besides, if she did call the cops, she couldn't tell them how the man threatened her because she doesn't want anyone to know what he said."

"This is an intelligent woman, though. She could have thought of something."

"Sure," Kirsten said. "If it was me, I'd have said he peeked in on me when I was undressed or assaulted me or something. She's smart, but right now this woman's hysterical, can't come up with any ideas. She needs time to think, so she drags his body around to the back of the house and hides it under the cellar doors."

"Stupid."

"Of course, and she probably even *knows* it's stupid, right while she's doing it, but she's crazy with fear. And then, while she's out behind the house, trying to think . . . she hears a car coming up Till's Creek Road. She runs to her own car, parked beside the house, but she can't just drive away. She'll be seen, so she pulls her car—I don't know—maybe there's, like, a path through the field, or—"

"Behind the barn," Mama Dee said, her voice very soft.

"You mean '*maybe* behind the barn.' We're talking 'maybes' here, right?" Mama Dee nodded, and Kirsten went on. "So she hides her car and starts to run back toward the house, maybe to lock the cellar door or something. But by then the other car has turned in and is coming up her drive, and she's afraid she'll be seen." Kirsten walked to the window. "She has to hide."

"She could have hidden in that shed," Dugan said. "Of course, the cats would know she was in there."

"A storm's on the way and the wind's blowing, but she hears someone—a woman—outside the shed, yelling at the cats. She's afraid the woman's a friend of the dead man. The shed door opens. She crouches behind the ride-on lawn mower and doesn't move, and then the door closes again. She's safe for now. Still, she knows she's going to be caught if she doesn't do *something*, even if it's risky."

"And she does."

"Yes. She peeks out and sees the other woman open the cellar door, then go down to look at the dead man. She runs over and slams the cellar door and then slides something—a bolt or something—through the hasp to lock the woman down there."

"And then . . . just drives away?" Dugan asked.

"She's panicked. She even forgets to relock her front door. She goes back to where her friends were, maybe in time for supper; maybe not. By the next morning, though, she realizes no one has missed her." Kirsten sat down at the table, finally, and sipped coffee from her mug. "Plus, of course, her friends would give her the benefit of the doubt if they talked to the police . . . maybe without even realizing they were doing so." She paused. "It's all hypothetical, of course."

No one said anything for a while.

Dugan thought hard and finally said, "I have to ask Mama Dee something . . . something that's *not* hypothetical."

"Why?" Kirsten said. "Why do you have to?"

"I just do, for my own sake. But I think I know the answer already," he said. "I sure hope I do."

"Fine. Ask her."

"Mama Dee," he said, "have you ever—"

"Wait. That's much too broad," Kirsten said, and he realized she was right with him. Hell, not *with* him . . . ahead of him!

"Look at me, Mama Dee." When she did, he went on. "Have you, at any time since that money was taken from Eudora's freezer, deliberately caused the death of any man?"

"No," she said. "I swear I never did mean to do nothin' like that."

"Or even deliberately tried to seriously hurt any man?"

"No."

"I believe her," Kirsten said.

"Me, too. And we don't have any real evidence she did anything at all, intentional or not." He breathed once, in and out. "But," he said, "now there's another thing I can't figure out."

"What's that?" Kirsten said.

"What did the man say that frightened our hypothetical woman so much and made her so mad?"

"I suppose," Kirsten said, "he threatened her."

"No, not me," Mama Dee said, and Dugan saw fire—anger or something—back in her eyes. "Worse than me. He said . . . he said he gonna get Eudora's babies taken away from her."

FIFTY

"M ama Dee," Dugan said, "that doesn't make sense. How could Brownley take away the twins?"

"He said he gonna *get* them taken away. He said—" She looked at Kirsten. "Do I have to tell you in that 'maybe this, maybe that' way?"

"Forget the hypothetical stuff," she answered. "What did he say?"

"He knew Clyborn Settles, and he said Clyborn had found out he couldn't have been the twins' daddy. He said him and Clyborn had figured out who it really was."

Dugan couldn't believe his ears. "How could they—"

"Wait," Kirsten said. "Let her talk."

"He said he wanted to buy my house," Mama Dee went on, "and what was left of my land, 'cause they was gonna be worth a lot when the mall went in. He said if I didn't sell, he'd tell the father that them babies was his . . . and then the father and his family would take them babies away from Eudora, 'cause people knew she couldn't give 'em nothin', bein' poor like she is—and now her bein' arrested as a thief and goin' to jail and all, he said. And I said what are you talkin' about and—"

"Wait a minute." Dugan couldn't keep quiet any longer. "Even if it was true, how could he and Clyborn know who the real father was?"

"It was partly guessin'," Mama Dee said. "I could tell that. But I knew they had got it right, 'cause I knew it already myself. Eudora had told me, when the twins was a few months old, that it wasn't Clyborn who had got her pregnant."

"If Eudora knew that," Dugan asked, "why the hell did—"

"Later for that," Kirsten said. "Did she say who it was?"

"She didn't tell me the father's name back then, or if she did I forgot it. She said she never told him the twins was his. It was just a mistake she made—she and *him* made. 'Just one time,' she said. Said it was her fault, that she had went after him for a long time, tryin' to make him love her. And I believe she did. She was just a girl and he was, you know, different than anyone she knew. Older and havin' so much education and all. Then come to find out she was pregnant. She knew she had made a big mistake, so she lied to the father. I could tell she loved him—I mean much as a nineteen-year-old child *can* love, you know— but even so she knew it was crazy. She couldn't marry him or nothin', and she didn't want him to get in trouble on her account. She wasn't gonna have no abortion, either. No way. So she covered up by having . . . having relations with Clyborn, which he'd been after her to do. She told the father she couldn't see him no more because she'd already got pregnant by Clyborn, before her and the father had did it. She even told him she loved Clyborn. The father was real sad, she said, but he believed her."

"He ever contact her again?" Dugan asked. "Call or anything?"

"Uh-uh. 'Cept after the twins was born he sent her a letter. She showed me the letter. She always been—"

"What did it say?"

"It said he had heard she had twins and he knew she didn't have no money. It was two hundred dollars in the envelope, cash money. He said it was to help with her and Clyborn's twin babies. He mailed it to her at my house, probably 'cause he knew she be there a lot, and he didn't wanna mail no cash money to her in the projects. I didn't open the envelope. I gave it to her the next time she brought the babies out for a visit. She showed it to me. That's when she first told me what had really happened. She was . . . she was cryin' like a baby herself."

"God," Kirsten said, "I'd have been crying, too. Do you . . . do you think he suspected the babies might really be his?"

"That's what I asked, but Eudora said no, and she's very smart about knowin' what people think. She said for sure he thought it was Clyborn. He was real sad to hear she been goin' with Clyborn—which she really wasn't, not till after she got pregnant."

"Did the letter say anything else?" she asked.

"It said he wished he could help more, but he didn't wanna interfere with her and Clyborn. And besides, he wasn't allowed to have much money, even though his family was rich. We sure didn't know he meant, like, millionaires. But he said ain't nobody in his family that needs money, and he had no one else to give nothin' to, so he had made a will. If he ever did have anything when he died, he said, he wanted her to have it, 'cause she the only one he close to who needed it." Mama Dee smiled, as though remembering. "I mean, that man was in love, you know? He thirty-some years old, and he in love with the same kinda love as Eudora . . . nineteen-year-old love. But it was real at the time he—"

"The will," Kirsten said. "Was there a will?"

"Uh-huh. He sent it in the letter. Just a copy. It said he leavin' some money to this and that charity and then all the rest, or some word like the 'rest,' to—"

"Residue?" Dugan asked.

"I guess. Somethin' like that. Anyway, everything else went to Eudora, if she still livin' when he dies."

"Jesus," he said.

"What if . . ." Kirsten hesitated, then went on. "What if she was dead?"

"Then it all go to his brothers. It said two brothers, I think."

"Who was it, Mama Dee?" Dugan asked. "Do you know his name now?"

"God, Dugan," Kirsten said, "haven't you figured that out?"

"I thought I said that already," Mama Dee said. "It was the *father*."

"I know, dammit," he said, "but who *was* the father?"

"I mean the *Catholic* father. You know, the priest. The one from the community center who put on them plays Eudora and Clyborn was in. He was, like . . . he belonged to an *order*, Eudora said, and that's why he wasn't s'posed to have no money of his own. Like a Franciscan or somethin'."

"The priest?" He couldn't believe it. "Father Hurley? The son of the guy who wants to build the mall?"

"Uh-huh, sure was." Mama Dee shook her head. "But back then we didn't know about his family or nothin'. Last year, when we first heard some rich folks was gonna cut down Emerald Woods, there was a meeting, and Eudora heard the name and then found out it was the father's daddy who was behind it. She was about outta her mind when she told me. I told her to call that father right up, see would he help us. She didn't want to. But later she did, or tried to. The community center gave her message to the family. One of his brothers called her back and said the father too sick to talk to her, in a coma or something." She shrugged. "So we just thought that was the end of that."

"Oh my God," Kirsten said. "I think I understand the rest of it, finally."

"Hey!" Dugan was lost. "I may never understand. But try me."

"I'll have to verify it all with . . . well . . . through Parker Gillson, I guess, and—"

"Come on, Kirsten," he said. "Give it up."

"John Michael Hurley... Senior... mentioned casinos to me, so I did a little research. He lost a bundle on one riverboat. But he—or a company of his called JMH, Incorporated—owns a huge chunk of a new one out in Stoneburg, eighty percent of it. It opens this fall, and you wouldn't believe the millions of dollars it's expected to generate every year. One of the articles I read said he'd given a small part of JMH, four percent of the shares, to one of his sons, Tommy, and made him an employee of the corporation."

"But Tommy can't have an interest in a casino," Dugan said. "Not legally. He's a convicted felon."

"I found that out, too," she said. "So that's what John Michael, Junior, must have meant by his comment to Tommy at the trailer."

"What comment?"

"He told Tommy he should have put his shares of casino ownership in some sort of trust—probably one that would satisfy the casino law. He said Tommy made a mistake when he tried to keep control of his shares by giving them to someone. If he said *who*, I didn't hear it."

"And now you think you know who," he said.

"Y'all losin' me here," Mama Dee said.

"Well," Dugan said, "the law says gambling casinos can't be owned by crooks, or at least not by crooks who've been caught. So Tommy Hurley had to get rid of his shares."

"He must have given them to his brother, the priest," Kirsten said, "the one the older Mr. Hurley told me loved everyone in the family. And the one Park said left the city for some monastery farm down near St. Louis, around the time Eudora got pregnant. Maybe to repent or something."

"Jesus," Dugan said. "Maybe he wanted to avoid something similar happening in the future."

"Like you said, Mama Dee," Kirsten continued, "the rules of Father Kieran's order probably say he's not supposed to own anything. But to help Tommy, he may have accepted the shares, anyway, thinking they weren't *really* his but Tommy's, and he'd give all the income to Tommy and then give the shares back sometime, too."

"Lord Jesus!" Mama Dee traced a cross on herself. "Now he's gonna die. I had forgot all about that will!"

"It's possible," Dugan said, "that he's made a new will since that one."

"It doesn't sound that way, though, does it?" Kirsten stood up and walked to the window. "I think somehow his brothers found out about the will. Maybe the head of Father Kieran's order—"

"He's probably the executor of the will."

"Right. So maybe he looked at Kieran's papers when he went into a coma and found the will and called the family."

"Why didn't he call Eudora?"

"Maybe he didn't know who she was or where she was," Kirsten said. "Maybe he even asked whether the family knew who she was. Anyway, Tommy arrived at the trailer thinking he'd find only John Michael, Junior, and Eudora. I think as far as Tommy knew, he and his brother were going to kill Eudora."

"My Lord!" Mama Dee crossed herself again.

"But his brother had a different idea. He'd hired Galboa to kill Tommy and Eudora both."

"But then," Dugan said, "why did Junior himself have to be there?"

"Maybe to make sure Tommy got there. He wanted Galboa to make it look like Tommy and Eudora killed each other. And who knows? Maybe he planned to kill Galboa himself. That'd finish off everyone who'd been involved, since Galboa had already killed Clyborn."

"These must all be *crazy* folks," Mama Dee said.

"Exactly," Kirsten said. "However, everything fell apart, and—"

"Wait," Dugan said. "If the plan was to kill Eudora, why the phone calls about not fighting the mall and the attempt to discredit her?"

"My guess is Junior wanted it known that she was being threatened because of her opposition to the mall. Once she's murdered, and the cops find out about the will, he's an obvious suspect. But he could point to the previous harassment, claim there are others with motive."

"Others," he said, "such as his father."

"Yes. Crazy, maybe, but when there's a lot of money involved . . . well . . ."

"But is it *enough* money?" he said. "You said JMH, Incorporated, owns eighty percent of the casino, and Tommy owned four percent of JMH. What's that worth?"

"I'll have Park check it out, but the paper quoted a casino expert who said the eighty percent, conservatively, would generate twenty million dollars every year."

"What?"

"And that's *after* taxes."

"And four percent of that is what?" He counted zeroes on his fingers. "Damn! That's eight hundred thousand dollars a year!"

"After taxes," she repeated. "Every year for the foreseeable future."

"Jesus." Dugan looked at Mama Dee. "You might end up with a rather wealthy granddaughter."

Mama Dee didn't look happy. "She ain't gonna want that money."

"What?"

"Because it would probably come out, somehow, that the father was her little girls' daddy, and she told me she'd never let no one know that."

"Why?"

"Because people would think bad of him, and she said that wouldn't be right when it was her who had made her mind up to get him to love her and ... and ... anyway, if that's gonna come out, she won't take the money."

"Even for her children's sake?"

Mama Dee shook her head, as though amazed at his ignorance. "How much you think havin' a rich daddy helped them three Hurley boys? The one had no money's the only one ain't crazy."

FIFTY-ONE

Cuffs finally got home with the twins and, when he saw they were going to have pancakes for lunch, went out again and came back with a couple dozen sausage patties—which he grudgingly shared with the others.

Dugan called Eudora's new lawyer. Her name was Renata Carroway, and he'd chosen her partly because she was a woman and partly because she was the best criminal defense attorney he knew of. So far she'd refused to make Eudora available to the state cops and had convinced her doctor to keep her in the hospital until at least Sunday morning. She had some broken ribs and was covered with bruises and lacerations. Emotionally, she was a mess, but the social worker on the rape intervention team was confident she'd be fine. Wankel, the state's attorney, was dropping the theft charge Dugan had been handling, but Renata thought that was so he could concentrate on a possible homicide.

"But even Wankel's not dumb enough to do that," she said, "although I almost wish he would. It'd turn into one of the most notorious cases Kankakee County's ever seen, and he'd go down so bad he'd never get elected again."

After that call, he and Kirsten left for home. They rode in

silence for half an hour or so, Kirsten driving, and he figured she was as grateful for a little quiet time as he was.

Finally, though, he had to say something. "I suppose that priest, Kieran, has the same dark complexion as Tommy and John Michael, Junior."

"Probably."

"Not African American–looking, I guess, but skin tone as dark as Clyborn's was."

"Uh-huh." She didn't seem very interested.

He decided to try another topic. "Even if they believe you about what happened out at that house trailer, do you think the rest of it can be proven?"

"The rest of what?"

"Everything. All this stuff about shares of casino ownership, the priest's will, Tommy thinking he's conspiring with Junior to kill Eudora so the shares will go to them, Junior actually conspiring with Galboa to kill Tommy along with Eudora, Galboa being the one who torched Mama Dee's house and killed Clyborn. All of it. How much of it can be proven?"

"More important," she said, "how much of it do we *want* proven? It might depend on Eudora's willingness to let her secret be revealed, or on whether it might make someone think harder about who could have killed Brownley, which might get Mama Dee a manslaughter charge—or worse." She paused. "Anyway, we can think about that some other time. My mind's elsewhere right now."

"Really? Are you thinking about getting me back to my office one of these days so I can work my ass off to help support our carefree urban lifestyle?"

"No."

"Then what? If it's not all this murder and mayhem, and not my career, what are you thinking about?"

"I've been thinking about the John Michael Hurley who's still

293

alive." He saw her look over at him—and then she winked, for God's sake. "We have an important job to do, darling."

There was that word again—*darling*—which meant he better keep his eyes open and his back covered. "We do?"

"Yes, we do." She reached over and patted his knee, maybe to comfort him. "We still have to save Emerald Woods."

FIFTY-TWO

Kirsten spent the next few days thinking about John Michael Hurley and about Emerald Woods.

On Sunday, Eudora went home to the twins and Mama Dee. Cuffs stayed on the job, mostly to harass and threaten the press whenever they dared show up. Dugan spent Sunday afternoon at his office, and all day on Monday, as well. Then on Tuesday he went with her to Kankakee, and at Lieutenant Terrapin's request, she gave another statement—basically a rehash of what she'd said before.

Terrapin was running the investigation of the Emerald Woods shootings, and she was glad about that. He was competent and, more important, he seemed to find her credible. By Tuesday, he had statements from Coral and Eudora, and though he wouldn't say, it was clear to Kirsten that all the statements corroborated each other.

Terrapin did reveal that Tommy had undergone surgery for his gunshot wound and hadn't yet been interviewed. She was the only one who'd heard what the two Hurleys and Galboa said, and she hadn't omitted any of that—or anything else—but nothing she said actually implicated Tommy in any crime.

A few days later, Renata Carroway called to say that one of

the items found at the trailer home was Eudora's answering machine. It didn't have a removable tape, so Galboa took the whole thing. "That should put an end to any thought of charging Eudora," she said.

Still, Kirsten worried some about how it would all shake out. Mostly, though, she thought about John Michael Hurley and what she could do to knock him and his mall on their rear ends and save Emerald Woods.

She figured the world didn't need another megamall, and she wouldn't mind saving a few of the rapidly disappearing trees on the planet from an asphalt shroud. She was city born and city bred, but she knew that forests and rivers and marshland, and the nonhuman creatures that inhabited them, all had their places in the grand scheme. Even the water moccasins, who'd left her alone, belonged. Maybe not those damn ticks, though, which she'd collected following Coral through the woods and which Dugan had found Saturday night, burrowed into her skin in various intriguing places. Intriguing to Dugan, anyway.

There were lots of environmentally focused reasons to fight the mall, but her reason was a little less . . . universal. Basically, she wanted to whip Hurley and save the woods because the guy had first patronized her and then advised her, with an arrogance so ingrained he wasn't even aware of it, that little girls should stay away from big boys' games.

I'm going to build my mall, you see. She could hear his voice in her head. *And no bunch of small-time, know-nothing environmentalists and radicals—with or without your help, my dear little lady—will stop me.*

An idea was brewing, though. It meant having to wait for an event that was another week away and relying on someone who—unfortunately, perhaps—seemed to enjoy hanging out with the big boys.

It was black tie required, so Dugan had to squeeze into his tux. She was in basic black, and feeling pretty good about the figure they cut as a couple, thank you. For five hundred dollars a plate you got a five-star meal, catered and perfectly presented by the chef of the area's oldest, most expensive French restaurant. So, even if you had to sit on a folding chair at a round table for eight and had to shout to be heard because the floor was hardwood, the walls were brick, and the ceiling was a couple of stories up there and made of concrete, who was complaining?

Another benefit for Mother of Mercy Village, and holding it in the gym on their grounds kept the overhead down and the attendees feeling virtuous. It came pretty close on the heels of the carnival, she thought, but this was a different group. The people at the carnival looked pretty upscale, and money'd been flowing like light beer at a wedding; but here there was no visible cash, and most of these people seemed off the top of the scale. Parker Gillson still had lots of contacts, of course, and wrangled invitations out of someone.

There was a long VIP table up on the stage, about a mile from their table, and Hurley was up there right next to Father Rooney. Everyone in the gym, except she and Dugan, seemed to know everyone else—or pretended they did—and lots of them spent more time wandering from table to table, laughing and yelling in each other's ears, than they did eating.

After the meal there was to be a performance by a pair of magicians from Las Vegas, and then a few celebrity benefactors would be given awards—called "Gifts from MOM" and in the form of realistic-looking pieces of apple pie, gold-plated and fixed to black marble "dessert plates." After that, Hurley was to anounce the kickoff of a new endowment being set up for Mother of Mercy. Finally, and to try to keep everyone there until after the boring parts, a panel of superstar sports figures would take the stage and field questions from the audience. The program mentioned Michael Jordan and Phil Jackson, but so far neither had arrived.

While the servers were bringing out dessert, *real* pieces of apple pie à la mode with some sort of brandy sauce, Kirsten turned to Dugan. "Let's go out for a cigarette, darling!" she yelled.

"We don't smoke!" he hollered back, but he got up and followed her out the door.

They didn't go outside the building, but down a deserted hallway and around a corner, then another hallway and another corner. She'd been here a few days earlier and told a janitor she was a security consultant, so he'd given her a quick look around.

When she came to a door that she knew led to the stage, she stopped and turned to Dugan, her hands on her hips. " 'We don't smoke'? That wasn't the way we rehearsed it."

"I know, but you didn't say 'darling' when we practiced, either. Besides, who the hell could have heard me? You could fire a .357 Magnun in there and no one—"

"Here." She handed him two of her business cards. "The notes on the back are both the same. March right up on the stage and give one to each of them. I can't do it because Hurley would recognize me and might have me stopped before I—"

"Kirsten?"

"What?"

"We went through all this."

"Okay. Anyway, the office is at the end of this hall." She pointed.

"And it says 'Father Rooney' on a plastic sign," he said, "a brown-and-white plastic sign."

"Oh, get going."

"I hope he has the office key with him," he said.

"The janitor says he always has the key. Hurry up!"

FIFTY-THREE

ive minutes later they were all in the priest's office: Kirsten in an uncomfortable wooden chair in front of the desk, Father Rooney behind the desk in an identical chair, Hurley standing a little to one side of him, and Dugan leaning back against the only door. It wasn't much of an office, about twelve feet square and no window. The phone on the desk must have been thirty years old.

"Remember me?" She gave Hurley her most dazzling smile, to irritate him.

"What do you want?" he said. "This note says—"

"It says to meet me here if you want to keep Tommy out of jail. And here you are, which means you want to keep Tommy out of jail."

"What it means is that I want to know what you're talking about."

"I was at that trailer when your oldest son was killed."

"Jack was killed by a rogue police officer who'd savagely beaten and raped a woman. My sons intervened, and he tried to kill *both* of them."

"Keep working on that story and maybe you can get it to make some sense," she said. "But meanwhile, did Tommy tell you I saved his life?"

"You're wasting our time," Hurley said. "What do you want?"

"Oh no," she said. "It's what *you* want that's important, and what you want is to keep your son—soon to be your *only* son—out of prison. I can put him there. And I will, unless you give me what I want."

"Excuse me." Father Rooney stood up. "I think it would be better if I left—"

"Sit down!" Dugan's voice was way too loud for the size of the room, and the priest dropped back into his chair. "That is," Dugan said, more gently, "we'd prefer that you stay here, Father."

"We won't be here long, Father," Hurley said, then looked at Kirsten. "You made that threat about sending Tommy back to prison before. It was a bluff then, and it's a bluff now."

"And because it's a bluff," she said, "you left the banquet and came here? I don't think so."

"If you have something to say," he answered, "say it."

"I know why your two sons were at that trailer. If I reveal that, Tommy'd be back in custody before—"

"Tommy's lawyers have seen your statements to the police, as have I. Nothing in either of them implicates Tommy in a crime."

"Gosh," she said, "*my* lawyer hasn't been able to get the cops to turn over any statements."

"*Your* lawyer," Dugan said, "has been busy making a living."

"Not being critical, darling," she said. "Anyway, I don't even need the trailer incident. Tommy attacked me and committed a battery on me, right here on these grounds, in front of witnesses. The state's attorney who prosecuted him when he almost killed his girlfriend thinks he's an animal. She'll charge him with a probation violation. Your son, Mr. Hurley, will be back in the slammer."

"You have no proof," he said. "Who's going to back up your—"

"I'm not counting on the truth from you, or from those two cops. But I was there, and Father Rooney was there." She saw a look come over the priest's face—a look that wasn't easy to read, but one she didn't like. "Besides," she said, holding up her little black handbag, "there's the tape, too."

"If that videotape actually existed," Hurley said, "I'd have heard from you long before this."

"Well, I admit it. I lied . . . a little. There is no videotape. But," she added, pulling a small cassette player from her handbag, "there's an audiotape."

"What sort of drivel is this?" Hurley took a step toward her. "You—"

"Hold it!" Dugan was right beside her chair. "Go back behind that desk, pal, or I'll put you there."

Hurley huffed a bit and then did as he was told. But it was his not picking up the phone that gave Kirsten's wavering confidence a big boost. "The mike was on me," she said, "and picked up everything everyone said back behind that booth."

"An audiotape can't possibly prove who moved first or whether physical contact was—" A roar of applause came through the wall from the gymnasium. "The magicians have been introduced," Hurley said. But he didn't try to leave.

"Listen to this," she said. She put the player on the edge of the desk and hit the play button.

Among the snatches of spoken phrases there were lots of spaces filled with distant crowd sounds, close-up breathing, scraping and thuds, the rustle of clothing. Ambient noise, mostly unidentifiable. The voices themselves, though, were clear.

Excuse me. That was Kirsten. *Mr. Hurley?*

Yeah? Tommy's voice. *What is it you want, lady?*

Excuse me . . . No one said anything to you, Bozo.

A long pause.

Tommy! Wait! John Michael Hurley. *She didn't mean any—*

Shut the fuck up! You heard what she said!

301

A still longer pause, this one filled with rustling noises and harsh breathing, and then a slap. Then grunts and groans, a sharp crack and a yelp of pain, and more sounds of moving around.

Please, miss, we should go. Father Rooney. *We should all get out of here.*

But I don't—

Listen.

Sam-MEE! Sam-MEE! A distant crowd, chanting.

There's been some terrible mistake. The priest again. *I've never seen him . . . We should all just forget about it.*

Not a chance . . . Give this to Hurley. Tell him I want to meet with him. Tomorrow. Wherever he wants. But tell him to keep that slug of a bodyguard he seems so worried about under a rock.

Bodyguard?

Yeah, the animal, the goon. You saw what he did.

Yes, I saw everything. I saw what he did. But that's not a bodyguard. That's Tommy. That's John Michael's son.

"That's it," she said, and hit the stop button.

"Play that tape a thousand times," Hurley said, obviously relieved, "and it doesn't prove Tommy came at you . . . or hit you. It doesn't prove one thing that'll get any judge to find a violation of Tommy's probation. It's still your word against ours."

"Maybe," she said. "But you heard Father Rooney say on the tape that he saw what Tommy did. He said he saw everything. Right, Father?"

"Yes," the priest said, but he didn't look up from the desk. "That's what it says."

"And when they put you on the stand and ask you what 'everything' was? When they ask you what you saw Tommy do? You'll tell them, right?"

The priest looked up at her. "Well, I . . . I suppose—"

"Forget that *suppose* stuff," Hurley said. "You told me you weren't sure you saw exactly what happened. It happened so fast you just couldn't be certain, right? Isn't that what you told me?"

302

"Yes, that's what I told you." He shook his head from side to side. "But, you know, if it comes to testifying in court . . ." He looked over at Kirsten.

Hurley leaned toward him. "Look up at me, dammit!" The priest did, and Hurley stared at him. "I'm on the fucking board of directors of this fucking place. I know it's on the edge. Everyone thinks you must have a huge bundle invested. But I know, and the whole goddamn board knows, it's not as much as you need, even in boom times. Because the money goes out so fucking fast. The federal government, the state, they've all cut back their funding. You have too many kids here already and you can't bear to turn any away. You got great new plans, new programs. That's fine. But where's the fucking money gonna come from?"

"John Michael," the priest said, "I'm very appreciative of all your help. But—"

"This new foundation, the Kieran Hurley Foundation. I'm putting in five million dollars, for God's sake. And when I do I've got others lined up who'll kick in big, too. We're gonna get you to where in a few years maybe you could tell the feds and the state to shove their money up their—" Hurley raised his palms in the air. "I mean . . . I'm sorry, I don't mean to use language like that. But do you understand? If you don't get some help, big time, this place won't survive five more years. And you know that."

"I understand, but . . . but hearing that tape . . . that is, I'd have to flat out lie under oath, perjure myself. Surely you wouldn't ask me to—"

"I'm not asking. I'm telling. You want that money, you see to it that nothing you say sends my Tommy back to that hellhole. Because he won't survive there again. Do you get it? He's my last son and he won't survive." Hurley straightened up and backed away a step. "Now, I'm going out there in a minute and announce that I'm kicking this thing off with five million bucks."

The priest sighed. "Thank you, John Michael."

"I wouldn't be too quick with my gratitude," Kirsten said, "not until—"

"You stay out of it!" Hurley turned back to the priest. "But she's right. Whatever I say tonight, if you send Tommy back to jail, you'll never see that money. Period."

"But how can we—"

"And," Hurley said, smiling as if he'd just thought of something, "if you testify the way you told me before, that you're not sure just what happened, it'll be six million."

Father Rooney stood up and turned away from all of them. "These are *my* kids, and they *need* that money." He turned back again. "And that's why I don't want to think long about this." He pointed at Kirsten. "Tommy attacked this woman. She was backing up. He slapped her, very hard, and kept coming after her. He'd have seriously hurt her if she hadn't hit him with that gun." He shrugged. "That's what I saw. I won't tell anybody if I don't have to. But if I'm called as a witness, that's what I'll testify to." He sat down. "And Mother of Mercy will keep on going. And if it doesn't? Well, let God figure it out."

"Christ almighty," Hurley said, and his whole body sagged. "I was afraid you'd say that." He took a deep breath and turned to Kirsten. "What is it you want? And if you say fifty fucking million dollars again, you can kiss—"

"I'll tell you right now what I want," she said. "If you agree, we got a deal. We'll work out the details tomorrow."

FIFTY-FOUR

Hurley agreed, but it took more than one meeting to work out the details. In about a month, though, the deal was pretty much done, with only a few housekeeping issues remaining.

Dugan decided Hurley may have figured he got away cheap. Surely he could find lots of other natural woodlands to bury in concrete, and since he probably paid his real estate lawyers every month what most people would take as an early retirement incentive and move to Arizona, the legal aspects couldn't have been much of a headache.

The entire tract of land she'd given to Miracle City was repurchased by Mama Dee and deeded to the state of Illinois as a wildlife refuge, "in perpetuity." The repurchase happened far more quickly than he'd have thought possible, but Kirsten reminded him it was voted through by the same village trustees who voted to breach the deal with Mama Dee and deliver the property to Hurley in the first place.

"Maybe he provided similar motivation to do what he wanted this time, too," she said.

All the old house trailers were hauled away, and the clearings around them cleaned up and the fences removed. On a steamy Saturday morning in July, there was a dedication ceremony in one of the clearings. Someone from the Illinois Department of Natural Resources showed up, gave a speech to the TV cameras and the other twenty people there—not mentioning any recent assaults or homicides nearby—and cut a ribbon. Then the official had her picture taken with John Michael Hurley, Mama Dee, the mayor, the police chief who'd replaced Frawley when the village board fired him, and some people from CREW, which got the credit for saving the woods. Eudora was there—with the twins and Coral, of course—but they stayed away from the cameras.

Dugan was there with Kirsten, and Larry Candle came, too. He'd wanted to ride along with him and Kirsten, but she said she couldn't take that long a dose of Larry, so he drove himself. During the speech he leaned close to Dugan. "I oughta get some credit for this, too," he said. "If it wasn't for me, you guys wouldn't even have gotten involved with—"

"Where's my two thousand bucks, Larry?" Dugan whispered, and Larry shut up.

Afterward, Mama Dee had them for lunch at her new home. It was a prebuilt, modular home, what she called a "double wide," set up right next to where her old house had been. "All on one floor," she said, "and easy to take care of." The remains of her burned-down house had been demolished and hauled away, and the basement filled in and graded over. The demolition people wanted to pull down the barn and the silo, too, but she said she was used to them creaking and banging and falling apart piece by piece in the wind and wouldn't feel comfortable without them.

Eudora brought the twins and Coral in her car, Dugan and Mama Dee rode with Kirsten, and Larry followed them. When they got to Mama Dee's, Cuffs was waiting there in the Blazer. He'd skipped the ceremony. "I wouldn't waste one goddamn minute of my life," he told Dugan, "listening to more bullshit from some asshole politician—especially a female. Besides, I might've gotten into it with that fucker Hurley. I might have killed the son of a bitch."

"He's not the one who threatened Eudora. He wasn't behind any of it."

"Bullshit. Him and his greed are to blame for everything. Besides, I hate real estate developers, and casino owners, too."

"Anyway, he had a driver there," Dugan said. "Obviously a bodyguard."

"Then I *know* I'd have gotten into it, just to whip the bodyguard's ass."

Mama Dee had everything ready ahead of time, and they all enjoyed a great picnic lunch. Late in the afternoon they were eating cake and ice cream on the deck when Dugan saw Eudora nudging Coral to stand up. Finally she did, but she just stood there looking at her feet.

"Go on, Coral," Eudora said, "you said you wanted to tell."

"Okay," Coral said. She took a deep breath. "Well, um, I just wanted y'all to know that . . . that Miz Eudora gonna be my mama."

"What?" Dugan dropped a spoonful of chocolate ice cream on his new yellow Tiger Woods golf shirt.

"I mean . . . not my *real* mama. My adopted mama. But I still gonna call her Miz Eudora, y'know? But maybe I'll call her mama . . . after a while. I'm thinkin' about it and . . . and, anyway, I have to go to the bathroom." She ran into the house, and the twins ran after her.

"We wanted it a secret until we knew it was going through," Eudora said. "Coral's cousin's cooperating. The judge says it'll be finalized next month."

"Really," Dugan said. "Is a lawyer helping you?"

"Sure," she said. "Mr. Candle. He's an expert in adoption proceedings."

"Oh?" Dugan pointed his spoon at Larry. "How many adoptions have you—"

"I have to go to the bathroom," Larry said, and he ran away, too.

"You do have a mean streak, darling, don't you?" Kirsten said, then turned to Eudora. "So, what about the estate?"

Father Kieran had died in June, with just the one will. His order claimed whatever he had was actually the order's property, based on its contract to provide for him forever in exchange for him turning all his property over to the order. So Dugan had gotten a probate lawyer for Eudora, this one a *real* expert. The lawyer learned that Father Kieran had requested the assignment in southern Illinois shortly after Eudora got pregnant. He'd been doing great work in the city, but the order sent him there partly because he insisted and partly because the place was considered "exile" and no one else wanted to go there.

"Yeah," Dugan said, "the estate. Is it gonna drag on forever?"

"Uh-uh," Eudora said. "It's pretty much over. Just some paperwork and stuff, I guess. I don't want any casino shares. I'm not fighting the case."

"Jesus Christ," Cuffs said, "are you—"

"Why am I not surprised?" Dugan interrupted. "You know, that order probably doesn't want to own a casino, either. But they'll sell those shares for present value, which'll be a fortune. You could do that, too."

"Uh-huh." She started gathering empty dishes and stacking them on the picnic table. "Those priests and brothers, they need that money for their schools and stuff. I don't want it. Plus, I'd have to answer questions." She'd lowered her voice, although they could hear the twins and Coral yelling from somewhere on the other side of the house. "You know . . . about me and Father Kieran, and . . ." She didn't go on.

"Hey, it's late," Cuffs said. "I gotta go, anyway."

"No," Eudora said, "you can stay."

He stayed, and Dugan was stunned at Cuffs having shown sensitivity—about somebody else's feelings, for God's sake!

"I don't want to get him in trouble . . . even now that he's dead. The girls don't know. Some day I suppose I'll have to . . . Oh, I don't know." She'd already stacked every dish in sight, so she sat back down.

"Well," Dugan said, "are they giving you anything at all?"

"They said they'd make me take something, whether I wanted it or not. So I'm getting enough to pay all of you for . . ." She spread her arms. "For everything. And then two small trust funds for Jessica and Jeralyn for college, and then something for college for me. I'd like to study environmental policy. You know, like—"

"We know," Dugan said.

An hour later, he and Kirsten were back in the Camry, headed home. Kirsten was driving, and they hadn't said anything for quite a while. Finally she said, "You know what I think I'll remember most about this whole business?"

"What?"

"When we were all in that little office behind the stage. Remember?"

"I remember." There was something about the tone of her voice, something he didn't like. "What about it?"

"That line of yours. You know, where you lowered . . . your . . . voice." She was dropping her own voice as deep as she could. "And then you said: 'Go back behind that desk, pal, or I'll put you there.' I mean . . . really! Talk about melodramatic." She reached over and patted him on the head. "But it was sweet, you know, protecting your woman."

"What? You think I was worried about *you*?" He shook his head. "I was afraid if he got close enough, you'd pull out a gun and whack him one, and he'd sue our asses off."

"Very funny."

"What I'll remember most is this morning."

"You mean when they announced they're changing the name

309

from Emerald Woods to Kieran's Woods? I thought that was touching, too. The end of Emerald Woods and the—"

"Not that," he said. "I mean all that tramping through the underbrush to get to the clearing, then standing around in those tall weeds for the dedication ceremony."

"Really?"

"Yeah. Drive a little faster, will you? I have this growing desire to get home—and examine your body for ticks."